The Widow of Slane

And Six More of the Best Crime and Mystery Novellas of the Year

The Widow of Slane

**And Six More of the Best Crime
and Mystery Novellas of the Year**

EDITED BY
Ed Gorman
AND **Martin H. Greenberg**

CARROLL & GRAF PUBLISHERS
NEW YORK

THE WIDOW OF SLANE
And Six More of the Best Crime and Mystery Novellas of the Year

Carroll & Graf Publishers
An Imprint of Avalon Publishing Group, Inc.
245 West 17th Street, 11th Floor
New York, NY 10011

AVALON
publishing group incorporated

Library of Congress Cataloging-in-Publication Data is available.

ISBN-10: 0-78671-791-2
ISBN-13: 978-0-78671-791-0

9 8 7 6 5 4 3 2 1

Book design by Maria E. Torres
Printed in the United States of America
Distributed by Publishers Group West

Contents

The Gin Mill
Doug Allyn   1

Wreck Rights
Dana Stabenow   59

Deep Lock
Clark Howard   95

Scrogged: A Cyber-Christmas Carol
Carole Nelson Douglas   147

The Widow of Slane
Terence Faherty   191

Tricks
Steve Hockensmith   227

A Tale of One City
Anne Perry   281

Permissions   323

The Gin Mill

Doug Allyn

Author of several novels and more than one hundred short stories, Doug Allyn's background includes Chinese language studies at Indiana University and extended duty in Southeast Asia during the Vietnam War. Later, he studied creative writing and criminal psychology at the University of Michigan while moonlighting as a songwriter/guitarist in the rock band Devil's Triangle. He currently reviews books for the *Flint Journal* while maintaining a full-time writing schedule. His short stories have garnered both critical and commercial acclaim and have been awarded numerous prizes, including the Robert L. Fish Award for best first story, the Edgar Allan Poe Award, the American Mystery Award, the Derringer Award twice, and the Ellery Queen Readers Award six times. Doug counts among his career highlights drinking champagne with Mickey Spillane and waltzing with Mary Higgins Clark.

Sunday morning in Malverne, a quaint little resort town dreaming on the shores of Lake Michigan. Autumn in the air, maples and elm trees streaked with auburn and burnished gold, the sweet scent of burning leaves perfuming the breeze. Lawns trimmed, sidewalks swept. Older homes faithfully maintained. The kind of town where people walk to church on a Sunday morning.

Not me. I was here strictly for the money. Scrounging for work on my day off.

Driving slowly, I threaded my pickup through the downtown business district. What there was of it. Like many western Michigan towns, Malverne was on hard times. I knew the feeling.

My computer map was perfect. Took us straight to the Belknap Building.

The old red-brick five-and-dime store towered above its neighbors, five stories tall, filling half a block. At street level, its display windows were soaped over, filled with crudely lettered signs. *FINAL DAYS! GOING OUT OF BUSINESS! EVERYTHING MUST GO!* From the shabby look of things, everything had gone. A long time ago.

A few windows in the second story still had glass in them. The upper stories were completely closed up, rows of gabled windows blinded with weather-stained plywood panels, eyeless and forlorn.

"Dynamite," Puck said grimly.

I glanced at him.

"Four sticks. We plant one at each corner, blow this baby into a big-ass brick pile, truck her to a landfill, and start over."

"C'mon, it's not that bad." A major difference between us.

Eyeing that relic of a building, Puck saw nothing but headaches. I saw a big-budget remodeling job that would keep my construction crew working indoors through the winter. Assuming the old brick monstrosity didn't come crashing down on our heads the first time somebody sneezed.

A new SUV pulled to the curb behind my pickup truck. A woman climbed out. Big woman. I'm six foot and she looked almost as tall. Dressed in denim, matching jeans and jacket, fashionably faded. So was she. Late thirties, easing into forty. Raven hair showing a few flecks of gray, careworn eyes. But still a very handsome package.

Puck and I joined her on the sidewalk.

"Mr. Shea? I'm Olympia Belknap. Pia, for short. Thanks for coming." We shook hands, looking each other over. I was wearing a sport coat over a flannel shirt, jeans. Work boots. Hadn't shaved for a day or two. North-country business chic.

"Sunday's a down day for us anyway, Mrs. Belknap. This is my foreman, Dolph Paquette. Puck, to his friends. And everybody else."

"Ma'am." Puck nodded. A long speech, for him.

"Have you looked over the floor plans?" she asked.

"I checked them, but Puck hasn't. Why don't you run the project past us?"

"All right. Simply put, Central Michigan University plans to build a satellite campus on the far side of the river. Six thousand students. I want to convert this white elephant of a building into off-campus housing. The ground floor will be subdivided into four units of commercial space. I already have options for two of them, a Borders bookstore and a Radio Shack. They'll supply their own requirements once the building is up to code. The other two units are to be prepped for rental: cleaned, carpeted, wiring and lighting brought up to commercial standards. Are you with me so far?"

"You haven't scared us off yet. Go on."

"I want the four upper floors converted to condominium-sized apartments, eight per floor. Each unit will consist of three bedrooms, two baths, full kitchen facilities. In addition, each floor will have its own laundry room, fitness center, tanning salon, and a communal game room with large-screen televisions and state-of-the-art Internet hookups. How does that strike you?"

"Like a place I'd like to live but couldn't afford."

"I meant as a project, Mr. Shea," she said impatiently. "Is it something you're interested in doing or not?"

"I don't know yet. It depends on the condition of the structure. If the building's solid, then the project should be feasible. Can we do a walk-through?"

"Certainly. This way." She set off at a pace so brisk I had to trot to catch up. Puck didn't bother, taking his time, looking things over. Pia Belknap unlocked the dime store's front doors first. Rundown counters, grimy linoleum-tiled floors, fluorescent tubes hanging on rusty chains from the high ceiling. About what I expected. A mess. But fixable.

"Do you have a timetable in mind?" I asked doubtfully.

"It's mid-October now. Ideally, I'd like the first floor finished by Christmas, the apartments above prepped and ready by next July. Is that possible?"

I glanced the question at Puck.

He nodded. "Structure looks sound. The guys who did

the original brickwork were craftsmen. Building must be a hundred years old, should last another hundred easy. Some of the bearing walls have been knocked out but the jack posts are still in place. Rebuild the partitions, level the floor, rewire everything from the ground up. Having the first floor ready by Christmas shouldn't be a problem."

"Okay," I said. Puck Paquette is a rangy, windburned Canuck who moves slow and talks slower. Impatient people assume he's lazy or even stupid. He's neither. He's a deliberate man.

Like me, he learned this trade from the business end of a hammer. He's good with machinery and men, not so hot with figures. Puck couldn't price out a job like this if his life depended on it. But he definitely knows whether a project is doable and what it'll take to make it happen.

"Shall we continue?" Pia Belknap asked. The second floor was a rabbit warren of small rooms, dusty, dimly lit. Apparently they'd been used for storage during the dime store's heyday. The wallpaper was faded, but the partitions looked solid, even the doors still hung true.

Puck and I were more interested in the outer walls. No staining or bowing; they looked as solid as the day they were put up. Our eyes met; Puck nodded.

I glanced down the long corridor, frowning. "What was this place? Originally, I mean?"

"It was a combination lumberman's hotel and mercantile building, built by my late husband's great-grandfather. There were shops and a general store on the ground floor, hotel rooms above. In a sense, we'll be restoring it to what it once was."

"Only better, I hope," I said. "Let's see the rest of it."

"Actually, this is as far as we can go. The building hasn't been occupied for more than twenty years and the stairways to the upper floors were sealed off even then. I haven't been able to find a way up, but according to the original plans, the floors above are more of the same."

"We'll need to see the roof," Puck said.

"There's a fire escape out back. Will that do?"

It did. The rear of the building faced a parking lot, with a loading dock probably used by wagons when it was built. Still, the fire escape seemed as sound as the rest of it, heavy wrought iron that barely vibrated as Puck and I made our way up to the roof, leaving Mrs. Belknap pacing impatiently below.

A long climb, but worth it. One hell of a view. Across the parking lot, an old factory as vacant as the Belknap Building. Beyond it to the west, Lake Michigan rolled away into the glittering distance. Ashore, the town spread out around us, quaint as an Amish quilt draped over the foothills. Higher up, multistory mansions stood like sentries overlooking the village.

"What do you think?" I asked.

"Definitely a fine-lookin' woman. And a rich widow to boot? Wish to hell I was twenty years younger."

"So do I, Puck. What about the job?"

"I'd say it's doable, Danny. Roof's sound, no sign of termites or water damage below, which is the big worry in a box this old. Walls look solid, almost perfect, in fact. Five stories of brickwork, not a crack or a bulge. They don't build 'em like this no more."

"It's outdated, though. The wiring will have to be completely replaced."

"That won't be so tough. Electricity was still new at the turn of the century when this sucker went up, so they ran the wiring in exposed conduits alongside the plumbing. It'll be easy to get at."

"How do you know it was built at the turn of the century?"

"See that big water tank at the corner of the roof? Before nineteen ten, water pressure in small towns couldn't climb above two stories. Taller buildings like this one had to have their own tanks. I'd guess this one went up in, say . . . eighteen ninety-six."

"Wow, you're exactly right," I said, surprised. "The date was on the plans she sent me. I'm impressed. How could you guess that from a water tank?"

"Because the date's stamped on the side, you young punk." Puck grinned. "We gonna take this job or not?"

"Looks workable to me and the lady can afford it. The Belknaps own half of this town and then some. Old money."

"New, old, just so it spends. We'll have to add some crew, a couple gofers, and at least one finish carpenter for the interior work."

"We're only forty miles north of Grand Rapids here. Should be able to pick 'em up locally. Let's nail this deal down before the lady changes her mind."

Ten days later, we invaded. Rolled into Malverne after dark, a caravan of work vans and pickup trucks. A gypsy construction crew, eight men plus Puck and me. North-country boys from up around Valhalla. Wild and woolly and rough around the edges. Hard workers who knew their trades.

We ripped into the Belknap Building like a wrecking crew, gutting the old storefront, tearing out counters, ripping up the tile floor. Filled three dumpsters with debris the first day, another three on the second. By then we were working in the glare of generator lights as the electricians ran new power lines in from the street to the basement.

Pia Belknap checked in every day to see how we were doing, but she didn't kibitz and didn't hang around long. Which was good. Pretty women and construction sites are a risky mix. They can break your heart. Or make you saw off your hand.

Work on the first floor went quicker than expected. But as we began moving up to the second floor, we hit major problems.

Puck guessed right, the building's original wiring was neatly boxed in with the plumbing. But nothing else was where it was supposed to be.

Walls didn't line up. Stairways were missing, apparently torn out or walled over. Crazy as it sounds, we couldn't find access to the upper floors anywhere in the building. Even the power lines ended at the second floor.

"I don't understand," Pia Belknap said, frowning over the blueprints I had spread out on a table in an empty second-floor office. "These are the plans registered with the zoning board."

"My guess is the building was remodeled at some point, and for some reason they didn't register those changes. Maybe they were trying to avoid zoning or building codes. Is there anyone who might be able to tell us what was done?"

"My husband's grandfather worked here many years

ago," she said doubtfully. "I can ask, but he may not remember. Some days he's a little hazy about who I am."

"I have days like that myself." I sighed. "Look, this isn't a deal breaker, Mrs. Belknap. I can redraw the plans as we go, but meanwhile we're working blind. An updated set of blueprints would be a huge help."

After she left, I scanned the plans again, trying to make sense of the measurements. Couldn't. They simply didn't line up. Hell, even the office I was in was the wrong size. According to the drawings, this room was supposed to be twelve foot by eighteen, but it was obviously smaller I quickly paced it off. Twelve by twelve, period. Not an inch more.

So what happened to the missing six feet? Frustrated, I grabbed a hammer and pounded a fist-sized hole through the wallboard. And saw the inside of the wallboard to the next room. An ordinary partition, six inches thick, tops.

Crossing to the opposite wall, I repeated the process. Or tried to. The hammer chipped the wallboard but rebounded. This wall was solid. And it shouldn't have been. According to the drawings, the building's outer walls were plaster laid over lath. I should have punched through it easily.

Frowning, I examined the wall more carefully. And found a seam in the corner almost perfectly concealed by the vertical molding strip. A false wall.

I pressed it, trying to gauge its strength, and it moved. Slid slightly to the left. Easing the hammer claw into the gap, I moved it a little further . . . and it just kept on going. Disappeared neatly into the adjoining wall. A sliding panel. That concealed a freight elevator.

I'll be damned. What was this about? I stepped into the cage, felt it shudder a little under my feet, giving me pause. How old was this contraption?

No roof on it, only a yoke supported by heavy steel cables that snaked up into the yawning darkness overhead.

Couldn't see a thing up there. The building's power was off and the generator-powered work lights in the office only cast shadows in the elevator. Grabbing a flashlight off my worktable, I played it around overhead.

An empty shaft, three stories, straight up. Couldn't see a landing on the next floor up. Or even the one above that. Apparently this elevator went from the basement to the top floor. Which made no sense at all. Why go to all this trouble to conceal it?

No floor numbers on the controls, just three buttons: up, down, stop. I glanced around, wondering how many years ago this relic had been boxed in, and why. I absently tapped one of the buttons—and the elevator lurched upward!

Stumbling back, I banged off the wall and went down. The elevator cage was still climbing upward, bucking beneath me like a ship in a hurricane. Somewhere in the dark a lift motor was howling like a mad thing, straining to shift rusty cables as stiff as steel beams. Naked light bulbs flared to life in the shaft overhead, revealing quivering wire ropes, then exploding, raining down fiery sparks and broken glass.

The cage was shaking so fiercely I couldn't get to my feet. So I crawled across the bucking floor on hands and knees, groping for the off switch—

With a deafening bang, something snapped. The cage

floor dropped out from under me, plunging six or eight feet before jerking to a halt, slamming me into the floor face-first, knocking my wind out.

And then I was scrambling desperately to get out of the way as the elevator cable came whistling down out of the dark, crashing into the cage, whirling around like a crazed snake, gouging the walls and floor as it coiled and recoiled on itself.

Its jagged head tore into my jeans, slashing my leg open—and then, suddenly, everything stopped. I sat up slowly, my head ringing like an alarm bell, shin on fire, blood oozing through my torn Levi's.

Puck's face appeared in the opening above, ashen, wide-eyed.

"Danny? You okay?"

"I don't know."

"What the hell happened?"

"Don't know that, either." Swallowing, I took a deep breath, then got slowly to my feet, taking inventory. Both arms and legs worked all right, no bones broken. Left shoulder was sore as hell where I landed on it.

Checked my leg. The ragged end of the broken cable had sliced a five-inch gash across my shin. Bleeding pretty good, but it didn't look too deep. Shin cuts always bleed a lot.

Okay. Working construction, hard knocks come with the territory. I was banged up, but not seriously. No thanks to the Belknap Building. That broken steel cable could just as easily have taken off my head.

"Danny?"

"I'm okay, Puck. The freakin' building just tried to kill me, is all."

"What happened?"

"Damned if I know. I hit the switch and the elevator kicked on but the cables were too rusty to take the strain. One snapped. Cage dropped half a story before the automatic brakes grabbed it."

"What do you mean, it kicked on? There's no juice in here. The mains are disconnected, all the power to the building is completely off."

"All I know is this cage jumped the second I hit the switch. Motor sounded like it was above me, so there must be juice up there somewhere and we'd better find it before somebody gets fried. I've had enough surprises out of this place. Slide a ladder down here before this damned cage drops me into the basement!"

No need to see a doctor. Mafe Rochon patched me up. Mafe is Ojibwa, full-blood. Hard drinker, serious bar-fighter, a major attitude case. We've tangled more than once. I put up with him because he's, swear to God, a genius with a torch. Mafe can cut metal or join it together so seamlessly you can scarcely see the line. But when you hire Mafe for his talent, his craziness comes with the deal.

As a bonus, I got an on-the-job medic, a skill Mafe picked up in the army before they booted him out. He's a fair hand at patching people back together. He's even better at busting them up.

Mafe was taping up my leg when Olympia Belknap showed up for her daily update.

"My God," she said, paling at my ragged, bloodstained jeans. "What happened?"

"Nothing heavy. Broken cable. On the upside, I solved our bogus floor-plan problem. There's a false wall at the east end of the building that conceals a freight elevator. Looks like there's another false wall at the opposite end, too. Puck's up on the roof, trying to find a way down. . . ."

I broke off, listening to a strange shuffling sound. Footsteps, coming closer. From somewhere inside the walls.

Easing down off the table, I walked down the corridor, listening, as the footsteps drew closer. Mafe and Pia followed.

The sound stopped. So did I. Facing a blank wall.

"Danny?" Puck's voice was muffled. "You out there?"

"Yeah. Where are you?"

"Back away from the wall, this thing's nailed shut." A couple of resounding kicks, and suddenly the wall burst outward. Swung open, actually. A concealed door, blended perfectly to match the paneling. Just inside, Puck was standing on a stairway, dusting himself off.

"Come on up," he said quietly. "You've gotta see this."

"The third and fourth floors are old hotel rooms," he explained as we followed him up the stairway. "Once they sealed the doors off on the second floor, there was no other way up."

"I don't get it," I said. "They aren't just closed off, they're hidden."

"You'll see why in a minute."

The stairway ended on the fifth-floor landing, facing a magnificent double door. Oaken, with leaded-glass panels. I pushed through it, and stopped. Stunned. It was a nightclub. A long, low-ceilinged room, filled with tables. A massive oaken bar at one end, bandstand at the other, facing a large dance floor with a mirrored ball turning slowly overhead, filling the room with swirling lights. Only a few lamps along the walls were still functional, but even in their wan glow, you could see how strange it all was.

The tables were still draped with dusty linen; some had plates, glasses, and silverware still in place, as though the revelers had just stepped out for a moment. Music stands still filled the stage, and there was a microphone up front. The bar still appeared to be stocked with liquor. . . .

A long sigh filled the room. As though the building were taking a deep breath. It sounded so . . . human, we all took an involuntary step closer to each other. Puck glanced the question at me, eyes wide. "Probably the wind." I shrugged. "Or maybe an air vent opening. The place has been closed up a long time."

"It doesn't look like it," Olympia said, wandering slowly among the tables. "Except for the dust, it could have closed ten minutes ago. Look, some of the plates still have food on them, or what's left of it. What happened here? Where did the people go?"

"It's your building," I said. "Don't you know?"

"I'm not from Malverne; I never heard of this town before I married Bob. When I asked his grandfather about the problems with the floor plans, he just said to stay away from this building. That it's a terrible place."

"What did he mean by that?"

"I have no idea. I told you he's a little drifty sometimes. That was all he'd say and it was the longest conversation I've had with him in months."

"I see," I said, nodding though I really didn't see. "In that case, do you know anyone else we can ask?"

"It was called the Gin Mill," Artie Cohen said, looking around the room, grinning like a schoolboy. He even looked like one, a gawky, fifty-year-old schoolboy with an unruly salt-and-pepper mop, sweater vest, and bow tie. Editor of the *Malverne Banner;* amateur historian. "My father told me about this place when I was a kid. I assumed it had all been torn out years ago."

"Obviously not," Pia Belknap said impatiently. "What can yon tell us about it?"

"Quite a bit, I think. This building was originally a hotel, built for the lumber trade around the turn of the century. By the twenties, the lumber was gone, so when Prohibition came in, the Belknaps converted the top floor of the hotel to a blind pig."

"A blind—?" Pia echoed.

"Blind pig, speakeasy. An illegal drinking establishment. A gin mill. A very classy one, I might add. Wow. Being in here is like stepping back in time. Look at that bar."

"It's great," I agreed. "So what happened to the place?"

"When Prohibition ended, they tried going legit, but things were tough in Malverne during the Depression. A lot of businesses closed, including the hotel. Then World War Two came along and saved everybody."

"How so?"

"The town boomed. Literally. Guncotton, a component in artillery shells, can be made from tag alder, a trash tree that grows wild around here. The Belknaps built a plant to process the stuff, and landed a big government contract. Which is where the trouble started. Malverne's a small town. So many men had already enlisted, there was almost no local labor available."

"What did they do?"

"They brought in blacks," Cohen said simply. "There's a village nearby called Idlewild, a black enclave in those days. Cyrus hired nearly two hundred colored folks to work in the plant. And when locals refused to rent rooms to them, he put them up in this hotel. And reopened the nightclub. As a black and tan—a place where blacks and whites could mix. Remember, in those days most of the country still had Jim Crow laws. Segregation was the rule, even in little backwaters like this one."

"So this was a black nightclub?" Olympia said, glancing around the room, taking it all in.

"More or less," Artie agreed. "And the place was a gold mine. Had a built-in crowd from the hotel. Cy hired a colored band from Detroit, Coley Barnes and the . . . Barnstormers, I think they were called. A big band. People flocked here from all over—Grand Rapids, Detroit, even Chicago. The place rebuilt the Belknap family fortune . . ." He trailed off, reading the surprise in Olympia's face. "I'm sorry, I meant no offense."

"None taken. I knew Bob's family was wealthy, I just assumed . . . you know. Business or real estate, that sort of thing."

"They did all of those things later, but their original bundle came from bootlegging, guncotton, and this gin mill."

"What happened to the place?" I asked. "Why was it abandoned like this?"

"There was a holdup," Artie said. "The summer of forty-five. The war was ending, so the government canceled the munitions contract. The Belknaps had to lay off the workers and close the factory, which pretty much emptied the hotel. Old Cy tried to keep the club operating, but there was no business. He was getting ready to close it down when Coley Barnes did it for him."

"The bandleader?" Olympia said.

"Yep. Held the place up at gunpoint, roughed some people up, and took off with the money and another man's wife. The Gin Mill closed down that night, never reopened."

"Until now," Pia Belknap said quietly. I glanced at her.

"Look at this place," she continued, walking slowly around the dance floor. "The bar, the bandstand, all these authentic fixtures? This place has an incredible retro atmosphere you couldn't replicate for a million dollars. And it's already here, free and clear. Could you bring the Gin Mill up to code, Mr. Shea?"

"I suppose so," I said, chewing my lip. "It'll need to be rewired, but we planned to do that anyway. The plumbing and light fixtures will have to be updated, but beyond that . . ." I shrugged. "Hell, the place looks like it closed a few weeks ago. How much trouble can it be?"

A lot.

I had Puck scope out the saloon while I rode herd on the crew remodeling the first-floor storefronts. At street level, we were well ahead of schedule. Which was a good thing. Because the upper floors were another story.

"Thing is, the Gin Mill may have *closed* in forty-five, but it was built back during Prohibition," Puck explained. We were at the Lakefront Diner, a little mom-and-pop joint just up the street from the Belknap. Our unofficial lunch-break spot. Cheap grub, draft beer in Mason jars. My kind of place.

The crew was at a large table, scarfing down enough chow for a small army. Puck and I were sharing a booth in the corner.

"The biggest problem is the wiring. They ran it in from

the factory across the parking lot, snaked it up phony drains so it wouldn't show on the hotel's electric bill."

"So? We'll have to replace it anyway."

"Hell, Danny, we can't even turn it off without getting access to the old guncotton factory and it's locked down tight as a drum."

"No kidding? So what's it like inside?"

"About what you'd expect." Puck grinned. "I got in through the skylight. The place folded the same time as the Gin Mill. Looks like they just turned off the lights and locked the doors. All the machinery's still in place and some of the storage rooms even have guncotton in them."

"Is it dangerous?"

"Nah. It'll burn but that's all. They only made the raw material here. The explosives were added to it somewhere else. I found the electric power lines against the back wall. I shut them down, but they'll have to be disconnected."

"Good. What else?"

"That water reservoir tank on the roof? It holds a couple thousand gallons, and it's nearly full. Must weigh seven, eight tons."

"Dangerous?"

"Nah. Tank's in good shape and the building could support one twice that size. Still, it's a lot of weight, and we should drain it, only the pipes were cut off years ago. We'll need a permit to pump it into the storm drains."

"I'll get one and—"

"Dan Shea?"

I glanced up. Three men, one in a suit, two in work clothes like my guys. All big.

"I'm Jack Romanik," the guy in the suit said. "Carpenters

and Laborers Union, Local Four Eighty-six. You called my office a few days ago looking for some men." He eased his bulk into the booth without asking. Puck slid over to give him room. Romanik needed it. Lard ass, roll of flab around the middle, pasty face, double chins. Razor-cut hair worn collar-length. Manicured nails buffed to a soft shine. Not exactly a working stiff. He didn't offer to shake hands. Neither did I.

"Actually, I called last week, Mr. Romanik, but who's counting? I need two journeymen and a finish carpenter. Hard workers. Can you help me out?"

"Three men? You're sure there's nothing else I can do for you, Shea? Give you a back rub, maybe?"

"I don't follow you."

"Then I'll spell it out." He leaned across the table, his face inches from mine. "You come into my town with your raggedy-ass backwoods crew, steal a big job away from my people, then you want us to help you out?"

"Hey, I didn't *steal* this job, Mr. Romanik, I bid for it like everybody else. We won it fair and square, and all my guys are in the union, so what's your problem?"

"I don't have a problem, Shea, you do. You stole a job that's too big for you. You need at least six more men."

"Three will do fine."

"And three's what you'll get. But you'll carry six on your payroll."

"Ah. I get three workers, but pay for six? And the three no-shows, they'd be you and your two pals here, right?"

"Who they are is none of your business, Shea. Consider it a tax for poaching."

"Poaching?" Puck echoed. "Sonny, I was in the union when you were still—"

"Put a cork in it, Pops, nobody's talking to you." Romanik didn't even look at Puck. Too busy trying to stare me down. Big mistake. Puck glanced the question at me. I gave him a "Why not?" shrug. And Puck popped him. Clipped Romanik with his elbow, just above the ear. The blow only traveled about five inches. And fifty-odd years. But it hit Romanik so hard his eyes rolled back. He was out cold before his face bounced off the table.

"Damn it, Puck!" I griped, sliding out of the booth. "Look what you did! The guy's gonna bleed all over my hash browns." By now I was up, facing Romanik's thugs, who were still staring in stunned surprise. "Just chill out, fellas," I whispered. "Don't buy into this."

The goons looked past me. Mafe Rochon and my crew were already up and grinning, eyes alight at the prospect of kicking some ass for dessert.

The biggest thug shook his head. Smarter than he looked. A pity.

"Good man." I nodded. "Now get your boss out of here before anybody else has an . . . accident. Okay?"

"You won't get away with this," the goon muttered as he and his pal helped Romanik up, heading toward the door. "We'll file a complaint with the union. We'll get you all canned."

"I wouldn't do that," I said. "If we're unemployed, we'll have plenty of spare time to hunt you up. We'll make messing with you a full-time job. Tell your boss that. When he wakes up. And tell him anybody he sends nosing around my job site had best have his major medical paid up. Clear? Now take a hike."

They hiked. We finished our lunch. But our problems were just starting. Later that day, Mafe found the booze.

"I'm workin' in the basement," he explained, grinning like a kid in a candy store as we toured the miniature brewery. "I'm tracin' down power lines when all of a sudden I smell it. Whiskey. Swear to God."

"I believe you." I sighed. The four stills were in a concealed room, in the back of the basement. Invisible to the eye. But not to an educated nose.

There were even a few bottles on a shelf. "Belknap's Best," Mafe read, blowing the dust off one of them. "Best what, I wonder?"

"Put it back," I said. "We'll have to turn it over to the law."

"Are you nuts? This stuff's gotta be fifty years old! Lemme have one taste, anyway." He took a deep draught, came up sputtering. "Whoa! Tastes like turpentine. But, man, what a helluva kick." He started to raise the bottle again. I snatched it out of his hands.

"One more jolt and you're fired, Mafe."

"You gotta be kiddin', Danny."

"Do I sound like I'm kiddin'? You know the rules."

"Yeah, yeah," Mafe said, wiping his mouth with the back of a greasy hand. "You're no fun anymore, Shea."

"He never was," Puck snorted. "Boy was born forty years old. Hey, check out the setup, boys, a Michigan twist. Car radiators instead of copper line to distill the hooch. Model T Fords, looks like, from the twenties. Must have set all this up during Prohibition, used it right on through the war. No booze shortages at the ole Gin Mill. Who do we report this to, Danny? Eliot Ness?"

"We'll let Mrs. Belknap worry about that. Meantime, nail the door shut, Puck."

"What the hell, Danny," Mafe protested. "Don't you trust me?"

"No," I said.

"Don't take it personal, Mafe," Puck added. "He don't trust nobody else, neither."

Mafe laughed. But Puck wasn't kidding.

I'd been staying at an el cheapo motel outside Malverne, but after the hassle with Romanik and his goons, I moved a sleeping bag into the Belknap Building. Just in case.

There were plenty of bedrooms, two floors' full. But I felt most comfortable sleeping in my office on the floor. Very lightly.

Which is why I heard the truck.

Early the next morning, six A.M. or so, a vehicle pulled up out front. Snapping awake in a heartbeat, I crossed to a window with a view of the street. A pickup truck was parked at the curb, engine idling, driver eyeing the building. Checking the place out before he made a move.

I made mine first. Grabbing a chunk of two-by-four, I trotted out to the truck. Black guy at the wheel. I rapped on the side window and he rolled it down.

Café-au-lait complexion, work clothes. Calm brown eyes. "Yeah?"

"It's awful early, pal. What are you doing out here?"

"It's a public street, isn't it?"

"Sure it is, but we've had some trouble. So I'm asking. Politely. Is there something you want?"

"I'm looking for Dan Shea."

"Why?"

"That's my business."

"Mine, too. I'm Shea."

"Really? You don't look much like a boss."

"I'm still Dan Shea. Want to check my driver's license?"

He smiled. A good one. Warmed his whole face. "I'm Guyton Crowell," he said, offering his hand. "I'm looking for a job. I'm a finish carpenter. Got a notebook here with some of my work in it."

He passed me the ring binder and I nipped through the photographs. Kitchen cabinets, entertainment centers, even a spiral staircase, all expertly crafted.

"You do good work," I said. "Or you fake good pictures. Did the union send you down here?"

"Nah, I heard you were fixing up this building, thought I'd come down, see if I could help out."

"Why?"

"My granddad worked here years ago. A waiter in the old Gin Mill. Had an accident. Fell down some stairs. Lost his sight."

"Tough break."

"Could have been worse. Old Cyrus Belknap took care of him. Paid his hospital bills, put him through a trade school. Did the same for my dad, later on. Back in the day, the Belknaps hired black people when nobody else would. I figure maybe I owe them something for that. Anything else you want to know?"

"Yeah. When can you start?"

Guyton Crowell was a treasure. A master craftsman, easy to get along with. He even hit it off with Mafe Rochon. Had Mafe laughing till the tears came two minutes after they met. A rare talent. One I envied.

Crowell also found me the journeymen I needed. Two young guys fresh out of trade school. Hard workers. I told Guyton about our trouble with the union but he shrugged it off.

"This local's no help to Aframericans. But folks around Idlewild still remember what the Belknaps did for 'em during the War. You just let me know if you need any more people."

Actually, I was getting more people than I needed. Artie Cohen, the gawky *Banner* editor, came by my second-floor war room of an office a few days later, with an older black gentleman in tow. A slender man, maybe seventy, a halo of silver hair around a bald pate, granny glasses, expensive gray suit, and a Moroccan leather briefcase.

"Mr. Shea, this is Reverend James Jackson, of the First Bethel Baptist Church. We were wondering if we could see the old Gin Mill."

"It's not exactly prepped for tourists—"

"I don't mind a little dust," Jackson said quickly. "It would mean a lot to me, Mr. Shea. My mother used to work there. And Artie said you had some questions about the old days . . . ?"

I had plenty of them, but I saved them until we were actually in that strange, silent room with the moving lights from its revolving mirrored ball dappling the dance floor and the tables.

Jackson looked it over, then walked slowly to the stage, staring up at the microphone for a long time. Then he nodded. When he turned to me, his eyes were misty.

"I was here a few times, as a boy. Twelve or thirteen in those days. Rehearsal days. My mama sang with the band, Coley Barnes and his Barnstormers. Lula Mae Jackson. Went by the name Misirlou. Wonderful singer. My daddy was high church, didn't approve of Mama singing here, but she loved it so. And truth was, the family needed the money. I brought some pictures with me."

Opening his briefcase, he took out several old black-and-white 8x10 photographs, publicity shots for the band. "That's the Barnstormers. A big band: five reeds, four brass, piano, bass, and drums. That's Mama at the microphone." A tall, slim woman in a dated dress, old-timey hairdo.

"She was beautiful," I said.

"I thought so." Jackson smiled. "The tall, thin fella next to her is Mr. Coley Barnes. Wonderful trumpet player. Sounded like a cross between Harry James and Louis Armstrong, only better. Played so fine that some folks said he'd been down to the crossroads."

"The crossroads?" I asked.

"You know the old legend. Swapped his soul to the devil in trade for his talent. Superstitious nonsense, of course, but that man surely could play a trumpet. And the way things turned out, he maybe knew the devil by his first name."

"What did happen, exactly?" I asked. "Artie said there was a robbery."

Jackson nodded. "On the Gin Mill's last Saturday night. The Barnstormers finished at two A.M. and the club emptied out. Afterward, a few folks hung around, drinkin'. Coley Barnes, my mama, some fellas from the band, old Cy Belknap. 'Course Cy wasn't old then, wasn't much more than a kid himself. Twenty, maybe. That's Cy in this picture here."

Jackson handed me a photo of the Gin Mill staff. Waiters, waitresses, black and white, all young, looking very proper in aprons, white shirts, bow ties. A lanky kid in a zoot suit stood at the rear. Glaring at the camera, hard-eyed. Trying to look older. Trying to look tough. I knew that feeling well. I passed the photo on to Artie.

"The way I heard it, Coley Barnes pulled a gun, made Cy empty the till. Pistol-whipped him, hurt him bad. Then Coley and the others took off. Took my mama with him. Nate Crowell, Guyton's grandfather, was there that night. Just a kid, but he'd been drinkin', too. When the trouble started, he ran, fell down the stairs. Lost his sight. It was a terrible thing, all of it."

"And your mother? Did she come back?"

"No, she never did. Or the others, either. They stayed gone, long gone."

"Didn't the police ever—?"

"Police weren't called into it. Cy Belknap was pretty bitter about what happened. Maybe he had a right to be. Wouldn't talk about it after, not to police or anybody else. With the A-bomb dropping on Japan and the war ending, nobody worried much about a gin-mill stickup. But there were rumors . . ."

"What kind of rumors?"

"You have to understand what those times were like. A lot of local rednecks resented blacks getting wartime factory jobs. Both the KKK and Black Legion had chapters here. There was talk maybe Coley and the others were caught by the Klan, lynched, and buried in the piney woods. Maybe that's why they never came back."

"Do you think that's possible?" Artie asked.

"I don't know, and it's a terrible thing not knowing the truth." Reverend Jackson sighed. "Which is worse, Mr. Shea? Thinking your mama might have been killed all those years ago? Or that she stayed gone because she cared more for her trumpet-playin' man than her own children?"

I had no answer for him. But I often thought of Reverend

Jackson in the following weeks. The pain of loss in his eyes, even after all the time that had passed. It's not fair. Good memories fade away while bad ones sting forever, painful as ripping a bandage off an open wound.

But I was too busy to worry about Jackson for long. The remodeling was going well. I was sure we could meet the Christmas deadline for phase one. If we didn't get fired.

Olympia Belknap and I were checking over the condominium plans when the doorway darkened. Huge guy standing there, ancient as an oak and nearly as tall. Black suit, white shirt, a cane clutched in one gnarled fist.

"Grandfather?" Pia said, surprised. "What are you doing here? Mr. Shea, this is my husband's grandfather—"

"Cyrus Belknap," I finished for her, offering the old gentleman my hand. "I saw your picture the other day."

"Who the hell are you?" the old man asked, ignoring my hand. "Pia's new boyfriend?"

"No, sir," I said, taken aback by his hostility. "I'm—"

"Mr. Shea is the contractor I hired to renovate the building, Grandfather. I told you about him."

"And I told you to stay the hell away from this place! It's a bad place, no decent woman should be here. I want these men gone, right now! All of them!"

"Grandfather, be reasonable. I explained my plans—"

"*Your* plans? You have no right to make plans. This is *my* building, and—" He broke off suddenly, listening. "What's that noise?"

With all the construction clatter outside, I wasn't certain which one he meant.

"It's just men working, sir. We're planing down the doors to—"

He waved me to silence, cocking his head to hear the

hallway racket better, his eyes flicking back and forth, anger and fear battling in them.

Fear won. He turned and stalked away without another word.

I glanced the question at Olympia.

"Bob's grandfather," she said ruefully. "He's a handful sometimes." Pia had shrugged off the old man's ravings, so I did, too. I shouldn't have.

A few days later I was on the phone arguing with a supplier when I got a call on my other line. Olympia Belknap.

"Something has come up, Mr. Shea," she said brusquely. "We need to talk. Can you come to my home, please?"

"Um, sure. When?"

"Now," she snapped.

Oh.

I hate those calls. Every contractor gets them, and it's never good news. Usually it means your guys have screwed something up, or your client wants to make big changes or rehaggle your price.

Sometimes it's even worse. Financing has fallen through, somebody's filed a lawsuit, your client's got cancer and wants to die in Tahiti. Bad stuff.

So far, Pia Belknap had been an ideal client. She stayed in touch, visiting the job site often, but never for long. She knew exactly what she wanted and wasn't shy about saying so. The only change she'd asked for was restoring the Gin Mill instead of converting it, which actually made our job easier.

Which was too bad. Because that meant any problem requiring an emergency meeting had to be dead serious.

I'd never been there before, but the Belknap home was familiar. It was one of the hillside beauties I'd admired from the roof of the Gin Mill—a three-story Georgian Colonial manor high on a bluff overlooking the lakeshore. Square and imposing, it had a magnificent view of the lake and town. Very handsome. Very pricey.

A maid answered my ring. Directed me to the library. I trotted up the broad staircase, taking it all in. A two-story foyer, Tiffany chandeliers, classic mix-and-match furniture, mostly leather. Elegant but homey. Old money.

Pia wasn't alone in the library. A guy in a suit was seated at a writing desk, looking over some paperwork. Mid-sixties, sleek, with silver hair; his jacket probably cost more than my truck. He didn't even look up when I came in.

Cy Belknap was there, too, standing off near the fireplace, gazing out the French doors that opened onto an observation deck with a panoramic view of Malverne and the lake. His frame was shrunken, his slacks and flannel shirt hung on him like death-camp pajamas, but when the old man looked me over it wasn't a comfortable experience. His face was puckered and drawn, but his stare was hawk fierce.

"I remember you," he muttered.

"It's all right, Dad, I'll handle this," the man at the desk said, closing the file with a flourish. "Mr. Shea, I'm R. J. Belknap, Olympia's father-in-law. I'm sorry to call you in on such short notice, but I've been away. I spend most of my time in Washington these days, serving on the President's Council of Economic Advisors."

He paused, waiting for applause, I guess. I nodded.

"I'm afraid you've stumbled into an unfortunate situation here," R. J. continued. "As an advisor, I was required to put my assets into a blind trust. I also deeded several family properties, including the Belknap Building, to my son Robert, which passed to his wife after his untimely death. This was not my intention. The Belknap Building bears our name, so naturally I want to keep it in the family."

"You've lost me," I said. "Isn't Pia a member of your family?"

"Of course, and always will be," he said smoothly. "But she's young. She may well marry again. In any case, I intend to purchase her interest in the hotel. Ergo, we won't have any further need of your services."

"Ergo?" I echoed.

"It means—"

"I know what it means, Mr. Belknap. It's Latin for 'You're getting screwed.'"

"No need to get testy, Mr. Shea. I'm willing to compensate you for your labor and expenses to date. Within reason, of course."

"No offense, Mr. Belknap, but I don't know you from Adam. My contracts are with Mrs. Olympia Belknap. Are you saying she didn't have a legal right to sign them?"

"No, of course not. She had a *legal* right, but—"

"Then hold on," I said, cutting him off and turning to Pia. "Have you changed your mind about going ahead with this?"

"No," she said firmly. "I wasn't even aware there was a problem until R. J. flew in this morning. The building isn't part of the family trust; I own it free and clear. Or I thought I did."

"The point is, Mr. Shea, the project is the focal point of a family misunderstanding," R. J. interjected, "that Pia and I need to work out within the family, and there's no need for you to be caught in the middle. As I said, I'm willing to compensate you—"

"I heard what you said, Mr. Belknap. You apparently didn't hear what I said. I don't have a contract with you. Only with Pia."

"Then let me clarify things for you, Mr. Shea. I'm a presidential advisor, and as such, I have considerable political influence, especially in this part of the state. I can be a generous friend, but you don't want me as an enemy. Are we clear?"

"Yeah, I followed that."

"Good. Then let's settle this like gentlemen. I'll pay off the balance of your contract. Today. Every dime, plus a ten-percent bonus. You can have the check in your hand when you leave this room. Your services are no longer required."

"Whoa. You're willing to pay me off in full? Just to walk away?"

"Plus ten percent. It's a very generous offer."

"It sure is. But I don't understand. Why do you want to buy me out?"

"That needn't concern you, Mr. Shea—"

"But it does. I've got a contract with Mrs. Belknap. Since you're asking me to break it, I'd like to know why."

R. J. flushed, visibly trying to control his temper. "Very well. Since you've been working on the building, I'm sure you've heard some ugly rumors, of . . . illicit liquor sales and—"

"I've heard some stories. We've also found the stills. So?"

"They say behind every great fortune is a great crime,"
R. J. continued uncomfortably. "The family bootlegging
business is not a story I care to have revived at this point
in my career. Pia's a wealthy woman, Mr. Shea, I don't think
she realizes what having real money means yet. There's certainly no need for her to become a saloonkeeper—"

"I'm not opening the Gin Mill, R. J.," Pia snapped, "I'm
reopening it! It's already there, in perfect shape, and I'd be
a fool not to make use of it. Maybe I'll even put a few bottles of Belknap's Best on the bar—"

"You snotty little bitch!" Cy spat. "You got no right—"

"Dad, stay out of this, please! Pia, you can see how
upsetting this is to my father. You must understand—"

"I only understand that when Bob died, I nearly did, too.
I started this project just to keep busy, but rebuilding the
Gin Mill is important to me now, R. J. If having a saloon-
keeper in the family embarrasses you and Cyrus, I'm sorry.
At least I'll be a legal one. As for buying me out, the
Belknap Building isn't for sale. Period."

"Very well, if you intend to ignore my wishes, I guess the
matter rests with Mr. Shea. My offer is still on the table,
sir, full price plus ten percent. What do you say?"

"Damn," I said, shaking my head. "Your offer's
tempting, Mr. Belknap. The problem is, I've got a contract,
and more importantly, I gave my word. The only escape
clause is an act of God and since you're not Him, I guess
I'm stuck."

"You'll regret this, Shea."

"Mr. Belknap, I regret it already. Now if you folks will
excuse me, I have to get back to work."

* * *

"Thanks!" Pia Belknap shouted. We were in my rat-hole second-floor office later that day. I could barely hear her over the hammering and Skilsaw whine from down the hall.

"For what?"

"Don't be coy, Shea. For standing up for me."

"Yeah, well, I'd like to play the hero but I can't, I didn't do it for you. Will your father-in-law cause trouble?"

"Probably. He's obsessed with protecting his career and reputation. Claims reopening the Gin Mill could damage his prospects in Washington."

"Maybe he's right. I don't know much about politics."

"I gathered that from the way you roughed up the union rep," she said drily. "But R. J. can bring more pressure than Romanik. Licensing boards, inspectors. He wasn't kidding when he said he's a bad man to cross."

"Then why cross him? Why are you doing this? I take it you don't need the money, right?"

"This isn't about money. My husband was a good man, too good in some ways. He handled all our financial affairs, every dime. But now I'm alone and this project is the first thing I've tried since Bob's death. If I don't see it through to the finish, I'll end up like Cyrus, just another ghost drifting around that mausoleum on the hill."

"Then we won't let that happen."

"No," she said, gathering herself, "we damned well won't. I want you to pick up the pace, Mr. Shea. Hire more men, do whatever you have to, but I want this project finished before my father-in-law finds a way to stop it."

"Yes, ma'am," I said. "Whatever you say."

But it was a lot easier said than done.

For openers, I stretched our shifts from nine hours to

twelve. Nobody griped. Most of the men were bored with motel living anyway. Longer days for overtime pay? Where do we sign up?

Adding more crew was a tougher nut to crack.

Swallowing my pride, I called the union rep, Jack Romanik, and asked for his help. He told me to screw myself. Big surprise.

I found Guyton Crowell in the basement, leveling the jack posts. Told him the situation and asked if he knew any local men who might be willing to sign on.

"I can find a few. They aren't in the union, but they're good workers. All from Idlewild. Black. Any problem with that?"

"Not as long as they can swing a hammer."

"Good. I'll see to it, then. Need a favor, though."

"Name it."

"It's my grandfather. He's a cabinetmaker, did some of the finish work in that portfolio I showed you. He worked in the Gin Mill as a boy and he really wants to be a part of reopening the place. I could use his help on the kitchen remodels once we hit the second floor."

"Didn't you tell me he lost his sight?"

"He won't be any trouble. He's worked construction his whole life, Mr. Shea. He's not a civilian. I'll look out for him."

"You'd better. Okay, we'll try it, but if there are any problems . . ."

"There won't be."

Actually, there were lots of problems, but Guyton's granddad wasn't one of them. With the extended shifts, we finished off the carpentry on the first floor a week later. It still needed carpeting and whatever customizing the tenants required, but phase one was finished, and the crews moved completely up to the second floor.

Which made my temporary office almost unworkable. Between the dust and din of construction, I couldn't hear myself think in there. Amid all this chaos, Guyton introduced his grandfather.

Nate Crowell was half of a before-and-after photo of his grandson. The "after" half. Long after. Tall, spare, stooped, and bald as a billiard, the old man had to be in his mid to late seventies. But he carried his years and his blindness well.

He shook my hand with an iron grip that could have been painful if he'd wanted it so.

"Pleased to meet you, Mr. Shea. My grandson tells me you're the man gonna turn back the clock on the old Mill. Hope I can be of help."

"Guyton says you're a master cabinetmaker, Mr. Crowell. Are you as good as he is?"

"Even better." The old man smiled. "The boy still gets impatient sometimes. I never do."

"What?" I yelled, as a Sawzall's chatter drowned him out.

"If you wouldn't mind," Nate continued, "I'd like to do my work upstairs in the Gin Mill. I used to wait tables in the ballroom so I know my way around pretty good up there."

"No problem, we aren't working there yet."

"Maybe you should be. Noisy as hell down here. Why ain't you usin' the main office?"

"What office?"

"In the Gin Mill. C'mon, I'll show you."

It was odd being led by a blind man, but Nate Crowell had no trouble navigating the hallway or the stairs. Using a cane to probe ahead, the old man moved only a step slower than normal and seemed to have an unerring sense about obstacles, circling around men and machinery without a misstep.

He paused on the fourth-floor landing. I thought he needed a breather. He didn't.

"This is where I ended up that last night," he said, aiming his cane at a corner. "Sixteen years old. Got a snoot full of joy juice, fell down these stairs, busted an arm and a leg, lost my sight. Damn."

"Sixteen was a little young to be drinking, wasn't it?"

"It was closing night for the place, everybody was doin' their best to drink up the last of the stock, even me. Only I didn't have no belly for it, had a bad fall. God's punishment for a drunkard, I guess. Ain't had a taste since. C'mon."

He trotted up the final flight, stepped into the ballroom, and stopped, his face wreathed with a wide smile.

"Man, it's like comin' home," he breathed. "Even after all these years. That was my section over there, from the dance floor to the far wall. Runnin' my ass off every night from six until midnight. Mr. Cy always closed at twelve sharp, didn't want nobody to be too hung over to work in the mill the next day. His office is over there by the bandstand. See that big mirror with the table beside it?" He aimed at it with his cane. "That's Mr. Cy's table. Sit there every night, tryin' to look hard. Wasn't much more than a boy hisself in them days."

"How do you . . . remember all this? Where everything is, I mean?"

"The Gin Mill was my first job." Nate shrugged. "And except for them stairs I fell down, this ballroom was the last place I ever saw."

He showed me Cy's old office, concealed behind another nearly invisible sliding door. A perfect setup, insulated from the noise below, a desk big enough for blueprints, even a cot in the corner for catnaps. I moved my gear into it the same day.

Nate set up shop beside the dance floor, pushed four tables together to make a workbench, and began trimming out the cabinetry for the apartments below. His work was impeccable. The problem was, he kept scaring the hell out of me.

I'd find him up there working with no lights. Darkness didn't bother Nate, of course, but it startled me to step into the ink-black ballroom, switch on the lights, and—whoops! Hello, there.

Mafe Rochon was more trouble than Guyton's grandad. He's always had a problem with booze, but as long as he doesn't drink on the job, I ignore his morning-after surlies. But with the longer working hours, he didn't have time to sober up entirely before work. A risky situation.

Puck warned me Mafe was sliding out of control, but I was too busy with our new schedule to worry about it. Mafe was still carrying his weight, so I let it pass.

And that was a mistake.

Romanik and his two goons showed up at the site one morning, taking pictures of the crew as they arrived for work, jotting down the license-plate numbers of their vehicles. Intimidation, pure and simple.

And I wasn't in the mood.

I went storming out. Romanik saw me coming, waved his two buddies away, but stood his ground.

"Mr. Daniel Shea, just the man I want to see."

"You've seen me. Now take a hike."

"Don't push it, Shea, it's a public sidewalk. And I'm just here to deliver a message."

"Messenger boy is about your speed. Say it."

"You're a backwoods rube, Shea. You don't understand who's got the juice in this town. You're backing the wrong Belknap. Mr. R. J.'s offer is still on the table but the clock's running on it. You'd better take it."

"What's that to you?"

"I know construction sites, Shea. How dangerous they can be. And I'm telling you to quit now before somebody gets hurt."

"You're threatening me? You two-bit—" I was half a second from clocking him when Puck grabbed my arm.

"Don't be stupid, Danny," he whispered. "Look up the street."

He was right. A patrol car was parked half a block away, two uniforms in it. One had a camera, getting the whole scene on video. Romanik *wanted* me to deck him. In front of witnesses. The local law would bust me and Mr. R. J. Belknap could use his political juice to keep me in the slammer until I was as old as Guyton's granddad.

I was so hot I nearly punched Romanik's lights out anyway.

Didn't, though. Instead, I dusted off his lapels, waved to the camera, and walked calmly back inside. Then punched my fist through a wall. Brand-new drywall, freshly painted. Which Puck made me patch all by myself as a penance for being a moron.

After I finished repairing the wall, I headed upstairs to my office to cool off. But I didn't make it that far. As I neared the fifth-floor landing, I kept hearing a strange sound. A steady thump. Not hammering. Heavier than that. I could feel it through the stairs, like a giant heart-beat. Coming from the ballroom.

Easing through the door, I froze as the full wall of sound hit me. The room was pitch black, but a big band was playing, hammering out a tune I'd never heard, drums and bass fiddle thumping in my chest like a pulse.

Couldn't see a damned thing. Fumbled for the light switch. Couldn't find it.

And somewhere in the dark a soft voice said, "Good evening, sir. Welcome to the Gin Mill. Table for one?"

My heart seized up, frozen solid as an ice block. "Nate?" I managed. "Is that you?"

"Of course, Mr. Shea. Just practicing. Maybe when the place reopens, I can get my old job back, waiting tables."

"Maybe you can. Where the hell is that music coming from?"

"The jukebox, there next to the bandstand . . . oh. Are the lights off?"

"Yeah, they are. And I can't seem to find the switch."

"Hang on a second." Nate threaded his way between the tables to the switch and the place came to life. "Sorry about that. I forget; you handicapped folks need lights to get around. You don't mind about the jukebox, do you?"

"No, I—to tell you the God's truth, Nate, you scared the hell out of me. Again."

"Why? Oh, hearing the music in the dark, you mean? What did you think? Ol' Coley Barnes came back from hell to play an encore?"

"Something like that," I admitted.

"Well, that's the Barnstormers all right. Great band. Misirlou Jackson singing, Coley wailing on that trumpet. Hearin' them makes me feel like I'm sixteen again. Like somehow them times are comin' back. Maybe we should call us up a couple foxy ladies, have ourselves a dancin' party up in here."

"The way my day's going, Mr. Crowell, I'd trip over my own feet and break a leg."

"That bad, huh? Then maybe you can help me out with somethin'. When I was makin' my way to the jukebox, I found this on the stage." He placed a small, finely tooled leather case on his worktable. "Know what it is?"

"Looks like an instrument case," I said, looking it over. "Maybe for a trumpet. It's got a brass nametag on it . . . Coleman Barnes."

"Thought so. The case was beside Coley's music stand. Funny, isn't it?"

"What is?"

"Look here," he said, flipping open the latches, reversing the case to face me. "It's empty."

"Well, considering he'd just robbed the place, I expect he left in a hurry."

"Maybe. Strange, though, that he took his trumpet but not the case."

And it was.

It seemed like there were a lot of strange things about this job. One Belknap wanted it built, another wanted it stopped. Stairways were hidden in the walls and a freight elevator almost killed me. The union rep should have been glad to supply me with men; instead, he was trying to shut us down. And after fifty years, men from Idlewild were working in the Gin Mill again. Maybe Nate was right: In a strange way, history was repeating itself.

Compared to all that, an empty trumpet case shouldn't have mattered much. But it did. Somehow that empty case seemed to symbolize everything that was wrong.

After my run-in with Romanik, I decided to keep a weather eye out for trouble, just in case. That night I set my alarm to go off every two hours. I'd wake and take a quick look around the building. Never saw anyone, but I had the definite sense of . . . a presence. Of movement. Odd noises.

Nothing I could put my finger on, just an uneasy feeling of evil lurking just around the corner. In another room. Or another time.

Dog-tired after making my rounds, I still couldn't fall back to sleep. My mind kept trying to make sense of it, to find some connection. Can bad times really come around again? All the elements were in place. Workers from Idlewild. Nate Crowell, blind now, waiting tables in the dark. *"Table for one, sir?"*

Coley Barnes and Misirlou playing in the ballroom again. With his empty trumpet case still on stage. As though he'd just stepped out. And he'd be right back.

I finally managed to nod off, but still couldn't rest. Tossing and turning, hearing Coley's big band playing on stage. Withered corpses in tattered tuxedos, playing rusty instruments, their rotting skin sloughing off. And then Misirlou stepped to the microphone . . . and *screamed!*

Sweet Jesus!

I snapped awake. My freaking alarm clock was buzzing. Time to get up, for real. Stumbling to my feet, I got dressed, feeling like I hadn't slept five consecutive minutes all night. Which wasn't far from the truth.

I made my morning rounds anyway, making sure everybody was where they were supposed to be. But they weren't. Mafe Rochon was missing.

"I don't like it," Puck said. "Maybe you'd better check on him."

"Check, hell, he's juicing again. You told me so yourself."

"Maybe, but it ain't like Mafe to miss work. And with our schedule, we need every man we got."

"Fine, I'll go check on him. But if he's tanked up, Puck, I'm gonna fire him. And then I'm gonna kick his ass around the block."

"Hell, in that case I'll come with ya." Puck grinned. "You been moody all week and Mafe's mean as a snake when he's hung over. The two of you havin' a go ought to be worth seeing."

"You don't think I can take him?"

"Damned if I know, Danny. Maybe. Maybe not."

"I don't know, either," I admitted. "But I'm in the mood to find out."

The Aztec Motel was on the low-rent end of Malverne, two dozen cheap rooms with a Burger King on one side, Slaney's Tavern on the other. Perfect spot for a gypsy construction crew. Most of the men shared rooms. Not Mafe. He preferred to drink alone, and nobody wanted to be in the same country with him when he woke up.

Except me. I hammered on his door. "Rochon! Wake up, dammit! Come on!" No answer. Tried again. Still nothing. Puck and I glanced at each other, worried now.

"What the hell?" Puck frowned. "If he's here, he's gotta be awake by—whoa. Somebody's moving in there. Mafe? Are you okay?"

". . . help me . . ."

It was barely a whisper but we both heard it. Rearing back, I kicked in the door. The stench of booze and vomit rolled over us like riot gas. Mafe was on his hands and knees by the bed, head down, drooling, panting like a dog.

"Danny?" he said, staring blankly toward us. "I can't see."

"Do you know what he drank?" the intern asked. We were at Malverne's tiny emergency hospital, a four-bed doc-in-the-box.

"This," I said, handing him the half-empty bottle of Belknap's Best I'd found on the nightstand.

"My God," he said, wincing as he sniffed the bottle. "Bad bootleg. Probably enough lead in it to poison a regiment."

"Lead?" Puck echoed.

"Sure. Good bootleggers use copper tubing, bad ones use automobile radiators. Faster, cheaper, and deadlier. Radiators are soldered together with lead. The longer they're in use, the worse the mix gets. Is your friend a heavy drinker?"

"Compared to what?"

"Oddly enough, that's in his favor. His body's built up some resistance, and he's got the constitution of a Kodiak bear. His system should purge the worst of it in thirty-six hours or so, but it was a near thing. I worked Detroit before I moved up here. I've seen men go blind and suffer permanent brain damage from bad hooch. Some even die. Your friend was lucky."

"Think so?" Puck shrugged, eyeing Mafe, still unconscious on the gurney. "He don't look so lucky to me."

"Where did he get it?" I asked. We were headed back to the
Belknap in my pickup.

"Hell, Danny, he found the still, remember? Probably
stashed a half-dozen bottles before he told us about it."

"This started out to be a simple job, Puck. Remodel the
storefronts, convert the upper floors to condos. Should
have been easy, a warm indoor gig for the winter. But since
we found that damned Gin Mill, everything's coming
unglued."

"Told you that first day we should dynamite it—What
the hell is all that?"

Ahead of us, the downtown district was a sea of flashing
lights, emergency vehicles, fire trucks, cops.

"It's the Belknap," I breathed. "It's on fire."

The streets were barricaded, so we ditched the pickup
and ran the last two blocks to the site. Fire trucks were
hosing the building down from the street side. My crew
was huddled in a group behind the fire lines.

"What happened?" Puck asked, grabbing Deke LaPlaunt
by the arm, leading him away from the others.

"Place blew up. Some kind of blast in the east side of the
basement. Fire took off from there, tore up the elevator
shaft. Hosin' it down from out here won't do nothin', Puck.
It's in the walls. We tried to tell 'em, but—"

"Okay, okay," I said, cutting him off. "Was anybody
hurt?"

"A couple. Guyton Crowell got coldcocked by the blast,
they hauled him off in an ambulance. Jimmy Fee got

burned, but not too bad. EMTs are tapin' him up. Everybody else is okay."

"Thank God for that," I said, taking a deep breath, scanning their faces. And coming up one short. "Where's Nate?"

"Who?"

"Old Nate Crowell, Guyton's grandfather. He's been
working up in the Mill."

"Jeez, I forgot all about—" But I was already running.

Vaulting the tape line, I sprinted past the firemen,
ignoring their shouts. Bursting through the front doors, I
charged up the stairway with Puck only a few steps
behind. Deke was right. There was a lot of smoke, no
flames. The fire was still contained within the elevator
shaft, but as soon as it burned its way out, the old building
would go up like a box of matches.

We found Nate Crowell in the Gin Mill, sitting calmly at
his worktable, hands folded in his lap.

"Nate, are you okay?"

"So far, Mr. Shea." He smiled. "I smelled the smoke,
wasn't quite sure what to do. Figured you or Guyton would
be along presently. I was just beginning to wonder."

"No sweat, everything's under control," I lied. "We'd best
use the fire escape, though. There's a lot of smoke below
and we don't want to be halfway down when the fire breaks
through. Let's go."

We hurried through the ballroom to the fire exit that
opened onto the roof. But at the last second, Nate stopped
and turned back toward the room. Not seeing it, of course,
but taking it in. One last time.

And then we were through the door, onto the roof. Five
stories below, a fire truck was hosing down the building.

Firemen shouted at us to come down. No problem, we were on our way.

Puck helped Nate onto the cast-iron fire escape. As soon as he got his bearings, the old man moved right along. At the bottom we passed him off to two young firemen, who headed off around the building, yelling at us to follow. I didn't. Couldn't. I was frozen, staring up at the roof.

"What are you waiting for?" Puck shouted. "Let's go."

"That old water tank," I said, pointing upward. "It's right over the elevator shaft. If I can punch through it, it'll drown the fire."

"Don't be crazy! If the fire breaks out while you're up there, you'll be trapped!"

"Dammit, Puck, we've worked too damned hard to lose this now." I didn't wait for his answer. Grabbing a fire ax off the truck, I was scrambling back up the fire escape before anyone could stop me.

Puck watched me go, cursing. Then started up after me. At the top, I halted, swallowing hard. The tarred roof around the water tank was already bubbling, puffs of smoke popping through, cooking in the flames roaring up the elevator shaft. The whole damned roof could collapse at any second.

No time to worry about that. Racing to the water tank, I was squaring off to swing as Puck clambered off the fire escape.

"Hold on, Danny," he gasped. Gray-faced, panting, he knelt, trying to catch his breath.

"Puck, I can't wait—"

"Dammit, listen to me! Don't hit it on a seam. If the rivets start popping, the tank could split open and blast us both down to the parking lot. Punch a hole in the middle of a panel, the lower down the better."

"Okay, I got it. Now get off the roof."

"Hell no! I'll croak of a heart attack if I try them stairs again. Bust it, Danny! Now! Before we burn!"

He was right, I could already feel the tar going spongy beneath my feet. Setting myself again, I took a savage swing. The ax head clanged off the tank, denting it but not breaking through. I swung again, and again, with the heat and smoke boiling up around me. But I couldn't do more than dent it.

The hell with this! Moving over a step, I squared off and swung with everything I had, slamming the axe squarely on a riveted seam.

And punched it through!

With a roar, the gout of water ripped the axe from my hands, sweeping my legs out from under me, blasting me across the roof like a cockroach headed for a drain. Tried to get up, got a mouthful of foul water instead. Then something grabbed my throat, dragging me under. Trying to twist free, I managed to get a hand on—Puck's arm.

He'd seized my collar as the flood swept me past. Clinging to the fire escape with one hand and me with the other, he was the only thing keeping me from being swept off the roof.

Rolling onto my hands and knees, I crawled across him, both of us clinging to the iron rail as the water roiled and swirled around us. With a shudder, a section of roof beneath the tank caved in, pulling the plug on the flood, sending thousands of gallons hurtling down the elevator shaft. Fire and flood collided in a swirling maelstrom, shaking the building like an earthquake, blasting a geyser of steam and superheated gas skyward before the crushing weight of the water prevailed, drowning the blaze in a matter of seconds.

A lifetime later, maybe a minute or two, Puck and I struggled to our feet, shaken, soaked, and damned lucky to be alive. Water was still gushing from the ten-inch gash I'd opened, but it was already losing pressure as the level of the tank dropped.

"Whoa," Puck said, taking a deep breath, "that was closer than I like 'em."

"Thanks for saving my neck."

"Hell, nobody'd miss you much. Buy me a beer sometime. C'mon, let's get below and find out what happened."

After checking the crew to make sure everybody was okay, Puck and I headed for the basement. The local chief of police, a concrete block of a cop named Brodie, was already sloshing around the elevator shaft. Most of the water had vanished down the storm drains, but the basement was still awash, knee deep in filthy water.

"Not much of a mystery," Brodie said, pointing at scorch marks seared into the concrete walls. "Fire started here with a bang, then howled up the shaft like a blowtorch."

"Arson?" I asked.

He nodded. "Definitely. Recognize this?" He opened his hand, revealing a dripping wad of greyish lint.

"Guncotton," Puck grunted. "There's a pile of it stored in the old factory across the back lot. Where did you find it?"

"All over the place. The initial blast scattered it around like dandelion fuzz. Looks like somebody stacked a couple of bales of guncotton in the elevator shaft and touched it off with a blasting cap. Raw guncotton's flammable but not explosive, burns like gasoline only a lot hotter. If you boys hadn't doused it when you did, the whole block might have gone up."

Leaving Puck to scout the basement for structural damage, I made my way upstairs, checking out each floor. Despite the intensity of the blaze, there was remarkably little damage. Both fire and water had been confined to the elevator shaft, limiting the harm to that end of the building. Nothing that couldn't be fixed. Even the Gin Mill was unmarked. Timeless as ever.

The roof was a different matter. The flood had ripped huge gouges in it. The whole thing would have to be retarred. The holding tank was only dripping now, drained to the level of the gash I'd opened. The support timbers directly beneath it were trashed: burned nearly through, then drowned. They'd all have to be replaced. A major repair job. And an expensive one. Damn.

I was taking a last look around when something caught my eye. An odd coil of metal was jammed in one of the water-tank braces. I tugged it loose. It was so twisted I didn't recognize it at first. And then I did.

It was a trumpet. Corroded by time and warped by water pressure. But a trumpet all the same.

I didn't have to ask who it belonged to. I even knew where its case was. But what the hell was a horn doing out here? Both Puck and I had examined this roof carefully before we ever took on this job. It definitely wasn't here then.

So where had it come from? I scanned the roof again, but it was only a roof, stark and barren. There were no secret doorways up here. Nowhere to hide anything.

Only one thing had changed. And I was getting a sick feeling in the pit of my stomach.

Ducking inside the Gin Mill, I grabbed a flashlight, then scrambled up the water tank to the inspection door. It was rusted shut, but I managed to yank it open, nearly tearing it off its hinges.

Inside, the tank was oddly pristine, its gleaming metal panels protected from the elements and ageing. Only a few rusting scratches near the top showed the passage of time. The bottom of the tank still held roughly three feet of water, roiled and stormy, reflecting my flashlight beam eerily on the dripping metal walls.

At first I couldn't make out anything, and when I finally saw the twisted form, I couldn't comprehend it.

Something monstrous was crouching at the bottom of the tank, the skeleton of some prehistoric beast . . . no.

It wasn't a skeleton.

It was five of them.

The bodies were tangled together in a macabre jumble, welded by silt and sixty years into a single grotesque body. One was probably Coley Barnes, one was Misirlou. The others? God only knew.

Straightening slowly on the ladder, I realized I was staring across the rooftops and the river to the mansions on the North Bank. And even at this distance I could see the rear deck of the Belknap house. And the tall man at the deck rail who was watching me through binoculars.

Old Cy. We stared at each other a long moment, across the miles and sixty years. And then I raised my arm, pointing my finger at him. It wasn't much of a gesture, but he damned well understood it.

Lowering his binoculars, he turned calmly and went into the house.

They didn't have to tell the truth. The crime was ancient and the bodies in the tank couldn't testify against anyone.

"No, I want to settle this," R. J. said quietly. "We've carried this weight long enough. It's time to put it down." We were in his library: myself, Pia, and Malverne's chief of police, Jonas Brodie, wearing a blue dress uniform and a respectful attitude.

Old Cyrus was sitting in an armchair beside his son's desk, watching us in silence, his eyes smoldering like a banked fire.

"You're entitled to have a lawyer present, Mr. Belknap," Brodie reminded R. J.

"I *am* a lawyer," R. J. said firmly. "I'm well aware of my rights, including the right to end this interview anytime I choose. Ask your questions."

"You knew about the bodies in the tank?" Brodie prompted.

"My father told me about them years ago. That's why we kept the building empty, never tried to do anything with it."

"What happened?" Pia asked. "How did they die?"

"An accident. It was the Gin Mill's last night. After they closed, a few diehards stayed on, drinking. My dad, Coley Barnes, Misirlou, a couple of boys from the band. Even the waiter had a few."

"Nate Crowell," I put in.

"Right." He nodded. "They hadn't been drinking long when it hit them. My dad got sick, said he felt like he'd been kicked in the belly. The others were even worse off.

Foaming at the mouth, vomiting, passing out. It was horrible. Dad tried to go for help but collapsed. He was unconscious for several hours. When he woke, they were dead. All of them."

"Why didn't he call the police? Or a doctor?" Brodie asked.

"To say what? That his bootleg whiskey killed five people? Go to jail for years? It was an accident."

"Prohibition was over," Brodie pointed out. "Why were they drinking bootleg whiskey?"

"That was Coley's idea," Cyrus put in quietly. "Got me a taste for bootleg, he said. Let's drink up the last of the Best, he said. Stupid black bastard."

"In any case, bootlegging was a minor offense then," R. J. continued hastily. "My father is only guilty of concealing the bodies. Granted, he used poor judgment, but he was quite sick himself at the time."

"Was he?" I asked. "Apparently he wasn't too sick to tote five bodies up that ladder."

"Stay out of this, Shea," R. J. snapped. "Chief, I admit this was an ugly business, but even if my father committed any . . . minor infractions, the statute of limitations expired on them years ago."

"You're probably right, Mr. Belknap," Brodie agreed. "Which brings us to the arson."

"My father will admit to hiring a man named Romanik to set the fire. But since no one was hurt—"

I scratched my fingernails across the end table beside my chair, startling R. J. and Brodie. They both glared at me but I ignored them.

My eyes were locked on Cy's face as I scratched the

tabletop again. He paled, swallowing hard, his hands gripping the head of his cane so tightly I thought he might snap it.

"You know that sound, don't you?" I said. "It's what frightened you so badly in my office that day."

"Look, Shea," R. J. said, "I've been patient with you, but—"

"You don't get it, do you, R. J.? Your father didn't put dead bodies in that tank. He put people in there."

"No!" Cy shouted, lurching to his feet. "They were dead! All twisted up, foaming at the mouth. Coley hanging on to that damned trumpet. But he was dead! They all were. I felt their necks!"

"So you dumped them in the tank like so much trash. They were only blacks, right? Who'd care? But at least one of them was still alive. The water must have revived him."

"That's a serious accusation, Shea," Brodie warned.

"The claw marks are still there in the tank, untouched all these years. And you heard it, didn't you, Cy? Heard someone trying to get out. Why didn't you help?"

Agony and rage battled in Cy's face, giving him a demonic look. Like a madman. For a moment I thought he was going to deny it. But R. J. was right—he'd been carrying the weight too long.

"I couldn't reach him!" Cy sobbed, his voice breaking. "It was Coley. The water woke him up but he was too far down. I ran to get a rope, but when I got back . . . he was gone. They were all gone."

"My God," Pia said softly. No one else spoke, all of us staring at the old man.

After a moment Cy looked up, meeting our eyes. "You've got to understand," he said, his voice quavering. "I'd been breaking my back for years, working days in the guncotton plant, nights in the Gin Mill, trying to get ahead. I couldn't throw it all away over a stupid mistake. I thought they were dead, dammit. It wasn't my fault. I found Nate on the stairs, took him to the hospital, made up the story about the robbery. Later on, I even helped out the families a few times. What more could I do?"

He looked at each of us in turn, as though he expected an answer. No one said a word. "God, I'm tired," he said, sagging back in his chair. "I thought telling about it would help, but . . . I just feel so tired."

"Go ahead, Mr. Belknap," Chief Brodie said. "We'll talk again later." Rising stiffly, Cy shuffled slowly out. I didn't think he'd make it to the door. He moved like a man carrying a world of guilt on his shoulders. Or perhaps the weight of five bodies.

When he'd gone, Pia crossed to R. J.'s desk, staring down at him like a stranger.

"You knew about this, didn't you? All this time?"

"Not all of it, but . . . yes. I knew. Believe me, Dad's paid dearly for what happened. I've had to sit up all night with him sometimes, ghosts all around him, taunting him, reducing him to a blubbering child."

"I imagine the families of those poor people had some bad nights, too."

"What could I do, Pia? Turn in my own father? I know you can't make a thing like this right, but we did what we could. Made sure the families were taken care of, paid tuition for—"

"Tuition? My God, he's a murderer! And you shielded him."

"For my family. For my son. Even for you."

"No, not for me, R. J. I never asked you for anything and I wouldn't take it now as a gift. I'm leaving. But there is one last reparation you can make. Pay off Mr. Shea and his men. I want nothing more to do with that . . . terrible place. Or with you. Ever!"

She stalked out, closing the door behind her with an icy click. The sound couldn't have been more final if she'd slammed it off its hinges.

Brodie rose as well. "I'll have to confer with the prosecutor about charges, Mr. Belknap. In the meantime, don't leave town. Keep yourself available. Clear?"

And then R. J. and I were alone. Neither of us spoke for what seemed like a very long time. Eventually R. J. pulled himself together. He asked how much it would take to settle our account and I gave him a figure. And he wrote me a check. Wages and expenses for my entire crew, including the men from Idlewild. Eight months' pay. Just like that.

R. J.'s a very wealthy man, with a magnificent home and political power.

But I wouldn't trade places with him for anything.

The bodies from the water tank—Coley Barnes, Misirlou, and their friends—were laid properly to rest in a hillside cemetery overlooking Lake Michigan, the Reverend James Jackson officiating. He delivered a moving graveside eulogy for his long-lost mom and the others. He even forgave old Cy for his part in their deaths.

Pia's gone home to Detroit to start her life over. The local prosecutor made some noise about charging Cy and R. J., but I doubt he'll push it. The evil is too old, and time is taking its own vengeance anyway.

What goes around, comes around.

Old Cy has disappeared into the past completely, talking only with the dead. Pleading for forgiveness. His victims are waiting for him on the dark side of forever, and before long he'll join them there.

If R. J. concealed his father's crime to protect his family, then seeing that family destroyed is probably punishment enough. His hopes for political office are gone, vanished in the smoke of the Gin Mill fire. He still owns most of Malverne, but the townspeople spit when they hear his name.

As for me, I came here looking for a job that would keep my crew working through the winter. And I found it. But not the one I wanted.

After R. J. paid me off for the unfinished remodeling job on the Gin Mill, he hired us again. For one final service.

We're going to do what Puck suggested that first day, dynamite the Belknap Building. Knock it down, load it into Dumpsters, and haul it away.

With the fire and water damage to the roof, saving it was an iffy proposition. And anyway, it's the Belknap Building, and R. J. wants it gone. And I can't say I blame him.

But despite all that's happened, it's not a job I'll enjoy.

In foreign countries, some buildings are a thousand years old and more. Here in America we trash our heritage like kids stomping sandcastles.

Don't get me wrong, I'm a builder. And proud of it. I like construction sites, the whine of power saws, the slam of nail guns. The fresh, clean scent of pine lumber. I love seeing new buildings rise straight and true, knowing I had a hand in creating them.

But I'll be sorry to see the old Gin Mill fall.

There was something special about that place. Everybody felt it. Maybe because so much happened there. Good times, bad times. Music and passion and violence. And death.

A building like the Gin Mill is more than cement blocks and drywall. Over time, the lives it shelters become as much a part of it as its very bricks. When we destroy it, we lose more than a structure. We lose our last contact with the ghosts and memories that linger there.

Scientists might laugh, but anybody with feelings knows what I'm talking about.

Some buildings have souls. Characters so strong you can actually feel them. Like the Gin Mill.

I sensed it when I first stepped into that empty, light-dappled ballroom.

And heard it sigh.

Sure, maybe it was just the wind. Or an air vent opening. But I don't think so. Not anymore.

I think the Gin Mill stood silent and empty all those years.

Waiting.

For me.

~~~~~~~~~~

Wreck Rights

Dana Stabenow

~~~~~~~~~~

Dana Stabenow was raised on a 75-foot fish tender in the waters of Alaska. No wonder her novels about the colorful and sometimes treacherous land of Alaska are so compellingly authentic. Stabenow's first Kate Shugak novel, *A Cold Day for Murder*, won the Edgar award for Best Original Paperback in 1993. And while the Shugak books continue to appear, she's also launched a series about Alaska state trooper Liam Campbell. Stabenow's work is both new-fashioned and old-fashioned—new in the sense that it strives for absolute reality; old in that it honors the verities of the best mysteries—careful plotting, believable characters and great, vivid storytelling. Her most recent novel is *A Taint in the Blood*.

A twenty-four-year-old woman in a 1991 Ford supercab pickup had been driving back from the liquor store that pretty much justified the existence of Crosswind Creek. She was there because she'd run out of whiskey, and not because she'd been serving it to guests.

Her drinking was no longer a problem. Sergeant Jim Chopin of the Alaska State Troopers wouldn't have minded so much, except that on her way out of the liquor store's parking lot, she'd T-boned a 1994 Dodge Stratus four-door sedan with a mother, two children, and a set of grandparents inside. The grandfather was DOA. The thirteen-year-old had a chance if the medivac chopper made it to the hospital in Ahtna in time.

The rest of the living were on their way to the hospital via ground transportation, and the dead were in body bags when the second call came in. Another accident, this one about halfway between Tok and the Ahtna turnoff to the Park. A forty-three-year-old man driving a 1995 Toyota 4Runner had collided with a nineteen-year-old man driving a 2001 Ski-Doo snowmachine. The snowmachine driver had been on his way to visit his girlfriend in Glenallen, and from the tracks at the scene had been operating his vehicle along the side of the road as he was supposed to, until he came to the Eagle Creek Bridge. Eagle Creek was narrow and deep and fast and never froze up enough in winter to take the weight of a snowmachine, so the driver had come up off the trail next to the road to use the bridge. Demonstrating a totally ungenerational care for his hearing, he'd been wearing earplugs, which was probably why he'd missed the sound of the oncoming pickup, which, again according to the tracks, had seen the snowmachine only at the last minute, when it had been too late to swerve and there wasn't any room to swerve anyway. The weather hadn't helped, a day of wet snow followed by a night of freezing rain, resulting in a road surface suitable only for hockey pucks.

The 4Runner driver was dead drunk, with three prior DWIs to his credit, not to mention a suspended license. The snowmachiner was just dead.

Jim had barely contained that scene when a third call came in, this one from just south of the Park turnoff. Kenny Hazen, Ahtna's police chief, was already there when Jim's Blazer slipped and slid to a stop. Hazen, a big, square man, hard of eye and deliberate of speech, met Jim halfway, ice crunching beneath the grippers pulled over his boots. "The Ford Escort was making a left on the Glenn when the asshole in the Chevy pickup T-boned her. Near as I can figure, he was doing about ninety-five. And you know that curve, there's that hill and you can't see a damn thing around it, especially on a winter night."

Jim knew the curve. "Alcohol involved?"

"Smells like it."

Jim sighed. "My night for drunks in pickups."

"Every night's a night for drunks in pickups," Hazen said. "The woman driving the Ford Escort is dead. So's the eleven-year-old riding in back of her. The teenager riding next to her has at least a broken arm. The baby was in a car seat in the back, for a miracle buckled in correctly; it seems okay. The pickup driver's stuck, can't get either door open. The fire truck and the ambulance are coming from Ahtna, I—"

The rest of what he had been about to say was drowned out by the sound of shrieking brakes and skidding chains coming at them fast from up the hill and around the curve.

Jim didn't wait, he dove for the ditch, and he'd barely hit snow when Hazen's massive figure hurtled over him and landed two feet west with a solid thud and a grunt. Jim had maybe a second to admire Hazen's 10.0 form before the semi currently screeching sideways down the hill slammed into the snow berm above their heads. For another very long second it seemed as if the berm would hold, but no. The double trailer, already jackknifing, broke apart. The rear trailer rolled right over the berm and the tops of their heads, the ditch providing the minimum required amount of shelter. It rolled downhill twice more until a grove of pines slammed it to a halt. Its sides tore like paper and pallets broke open and cases of canned goods went everywhere, a box of mandarin oranges nearly braining Jim when he stuck his head up to take a look.

The front trailer teetered on the edge of the road about fifty feet down the hill from where the rear one went over. Jim thought it might have had a chance if the snow berm had been higher. As it was, inertia and momentum took charge and over it went, rolling at least half a dozen times, the doors bursting open and more pallets breaking apart and more boxes flying everywhere to explode upon impact. Cans of soup and green beans and tomato paste, bags of pasta and popcorn and potato chips, sacks of rice and sugar and flour, six-packs of juice and pop, bottles of vanilla and soy sauce and red wine vinegar, boxes of Ziploc bags and Equal, packages of toilet paper and paper towels, it all tumbled down in a runaway landslide of commercial goods.

Jim, watching from the safety of the ditch, said in an awed voice, "I've never really appreciated the phrase 'bombs bursting in air' before."

"It is kinda like Da Nang," Hazen agreed.

When it appeared certain that the semi tractor was going to stay on the road, Jim and Hazen climbed out of the ditch and over the berm. The tractor was jammed against the side of the hill out of which the road had been cut. The motor was still running, the headlights still on.

Hazen climbed up and opened the passenger-side door. "Hey, you all right in there?"

A low moan was his reply. Hazen climbed inside the cab. "She smacked her head pretty good," he said, "but I think the rest of her's okay. Get on the horn, why don't you?"

On suddenly shaking legs, Jim walked to his vehicle and raised the Ahtna emergency response team, who didn't sound thrilled about a fourth callout in as many hours, especially one in which no bodies were involved.

At dawn, Jim was even less happy to be able to supply them with one.

As usual the news hadn't taken long to get around and by the time the sky lightened to a pale gray the hillside was swarming with Park rats picking over the detritus.

"They're like seagulls," Jim said.

Hazen yawned, resettling his cap against the steady drizzle. Traffic swished by on the damp pavement behind them, vehicles slowing down when they saw the police vehicles pulled to the side of the road. The semi was long gone, towed to Ahtna. Hazen had taken the driver to the hospital there, along with the victims of the previous accident, and returned to the scene before daylight.

Hazen grunted. "Except they don't shit all over everything. You talked to the shipper?"

Jim nodded. "Yeah, I called Anchorage. They called the store in Tok. I think they're trying to decide whose insurance company is liable for damages."

Hazen jerked his chin at the swarm on the hillside. "Think we should stop them?"

"Think we could?" Jim said.

"Probably not."

"Not wading around in hip-deep snow that's mostly ice by now anyway," Jim said. "They'd be gone before we got down there. Besides, the shipping guy said not to bother."

"Not like it hasn't happened before," Hazen said, nodding. "They're performing a public service. Cleaning up the mess so the shipper or the state don't have to."

"What about the trailers?"

Hazen snorted. "What about them? Couple of Budds, straight haul, look about thirty years old. You could pick up a couple more just like 'em off the Internet for seventeen, eighteen hundred dollars." He saw Jim's look. "I did some driving, back when. Anyway, the tires might be worth something, but like you were saying, you'd have to be willing to climb down and wade around to get them. Not to mention haul them back up. Easier just to buy 'em new and already on the trailer. Hitch up and go. No missed deadlines that way, and believe you me, truckers are all about deadlines."

"Yeah." Jim frowned. "Did you hear that?"

Hazen's brows drew together. "Yeah, sounded like a scream. Look." He pointed. "Somebody's waving at you. I think they want you down there."

Jim regarded the waving and screaming at the bottom of the hill with distinct disfavor. "Why me and not you?"

"This is a state highway," Hazen said virtuously, and grinned when he saw Jim's expression. "I wouldn't dream of overstepping my authority, which after all stops at the Ahtna city limits."

"My ass," Jim said.

He heard Hazen chuckle when he began the slippery descent of the hillside below the highway. It was one long wet slide punctuated by tree trunks that had an uncanny habit of leaping out in front of him just when he'd achieved too much momentum to stop. It didn't help that the spruces among them were beginning to ooze sap. He was covered with it by the time he reached the small knot of people clustered around a tiny hollow, all staring down at something, which accounted for the ill-humor in his voice when he said, "All right, what's the problem?"

They turned as one and stared at him out of white faces. Some he knew, a few were unfamiliar. Marty and Dickie Grayling were regulars at the Roadhouse. A girl had her face tucked into Marty's armpit; all Jim could see of her was a lot of black hair. Her shoulders were shaking. A heavyset man with a permanent scowl turned that scowl on Jim, like the girl crying was Jim's fault.

Jim didn't take it personally, having a lot of experience with shock in all its various forms. More gently this time, he said, "What's the problem?"

Another woman, this one older and thicker through the middle, her ruddy cheeks leeched of color, motioned with her hands. The circle parted, to reveal the body of a man, mostly white, maybe some Native if the straight black hair was an indication, the fleshy nose of the drinker beneath eyebrows so stingy they looked moth-eaten. A slack mouth sat over a receding chin with a faint down of ragged beard that looked more like neglect than fashion. He was probably in his late thirties, wearing jeans, blue plaid flannel shirt, thin nylon windbreaker, high-top tennis shoes over thick socks.

No hat, and no gloves, either, although Jim had to turn him over to tell because his hands had been tied behind his back with the same kind of rope that bound his ankles.

"So whaddya think, suicide?" Hazen said, after they'd put the victim in a body bag, tied it off to a length of polypro, and hauled it to the road.

"What was your first clue," Jim said, "the bullet hole in the back of his head?"

They stooped to examine the entry wound. "Twenty-two?" Jim said.

"Handgun," Hazen said, nodding. He turned the body face up. "And no entry wound. We got mob in Alaska?"

"Not so's you'd notice," Jim said. He looked back at the body. "Up till now."

Hazen jerked his head. "Took a look at the skid marks."

"Oh yeah? Anything left?"

"Enough. There was no reason for her to slam on the brakes the way she did. Some black ice, sure, here and there, but she had her chains on, moderate rate of speed, fair visibility. I checked her driving record. She's clean. Got a good rep with her outfit, I talked to her boss and he's ready to take her back on as soon as she gets out of the hospital."

"Let's go talk to her," Jim said.

The semi driver was lying in a bed in the Ahtna hospital,

brow bandaged, both eyes black and swollen. "When the fuck do I get outta this place?" she said when Jim entered the room.

"Beats me," he said, removing his cap. "I'm Sergeant Jim Chopin, with the Alaska state troopers."

"I know who you are," she said malevolently, "the so-called Father of the goddamn Park. I want my goddamn pants."

Hazen nudged him in the back and said in a stage whisper, "That's got to be the first time you've heard a woman say that."

Jim moved into the room. "If I find you your pants, will you answer some questions?"

She glowered at him. She was short-limbed and thickset with pale, freckled skin and fine orange hair cut like a Marine's. "Find me the pants first."

There were the usual objections from the hospital staff, but in the end the nurse wilted beneath one of Jim's lethal smiles and produced the clothes—black jeans and a navy-blue sweatshirt advertising Hulk Hogan and the WWF. Nobody had washed them, and the dried blood did not add to the semi driver's manifest charms. They turned their backs without being asked as she dressed. When they turned back, she said, "Got a smoke?" Hazen produced a pack of unfiltered Camels and she lit one and expelled with a voluptuous sigh.

Her name was Bertha, Bertha O'Shaughnessy. "Call me Bert," she said, the flame eating halfway down the cigarette on the next inhale.

"Okay, Bert," Jim said. "Why'd you hit the brakes?"

She narrowed her eyes against the smoke. "So I wouldn't hit her."

"Hit who?"

"Whaddya mean, who? A woman ran out in front of the tractor, I hit the brakes so I wouldn't hit her." She looked from Jim to Hazen. "What, you haven't talked to her?"

"This is the first we've heard of her, Bert," Jim said.

Bert stiffened. "She was like inches off the goddamn front bumper. I hit the brakes and jacked the wheel around. There's no shoulder on that sonofabitchin' hill or I might have saved the cargo." She saw their expressions and her voice rose. "There fucking was a fucking woman, goddammit!"

"What did she look like?" Jim said.

Bert shrugged. "Shit, who could tell at that speed?" She sucked in smoke. "Skinny, dark clothes, why I didn't see her until the last minute."

"You sure it was a woman?"

"Long hair flying out behind her like a goddamn kite. Don't know many men with hair that long." Bert shook her head. "She was a woman. She moved like one."

"Did you hit her?"

"No, goddammit, I didn't hit her, I put the cargo over the side of that fucking hill so I wouldn't hit her."

"Would you recognize her if you saw her again?"

She shook her head. "It was too dark and everything happened too fast." The cigarette burned down to the end. Bert tossed the butt on the floor and ground it out beneath her heel. She looked at Hazen and tapped two fingers against her mouth. Hazen tossed her the pack and the matches. "Keep them," he said.

"Thanks." Bert lit up again. The fingernails of her stubby hands were stained yellow. She walked to the door and they parted so she could get to it. Halfway through, she paused. "Funny thing."

"What?"

"She didn't look scared."

"You didn't see her long enough to recognize her again," Hazen said, "but you saw her long enough to see she didn't look scared?"

Bert frowned, not rising to the bait. "She didn't *move* scared, I guess is what I mean. Something sort of, I don't know. Deliberate? When she showed up in the headlights." She stuck the cigarette in her mouth and dropped her arms to her sides, bending her elbows into right angles and clenching her hands into fists. "Like she was in a god-damn race instead of getting the hell out of my way." She shook her head, ash dropping off the end of the cigarette clamped in a corner of her mouth. "Crazy fucking story. I don't believe it myself. Probably losing it. Thanks for the smokes."

He heard her footsteps long before she appeared and his mouth went dry. His breath shortened and his heart might even have skipped a beat. Was that any way for a grown trooper to act? Thank god Hazen was back in his office making some calls. It certainly wasn't any way for a grown trooper to be observed to be behaving by a fellow law-enforcement professional.

The door swung inward and there she was, all five feet nothing of her. A short, sleek cap of hair as black as night framed a face with tilted hazel eyes, high, flat cheekbones and a full, firm mouth. She wore a dark-green parka with a wolf ruff around the hood open over a white T-shirt and a navy blue fleece vest, and faded blue jeans tucked into Sorels.

She had to be the only woman alive capable of looking sexy in a morgue. Somehow the scar that bisected the otherwise smooth, golden skin of her throat, literally from ear to ear, faded from its original ugly red gash to today's thin white rope of skin, only added to the effect.

There was a scrabble of toenails on linoleum, and a gray furry torpedo launched itself at him. "Okay, Mutt," he said, fending off the attentions of the 140-pound half-husky half-wolf. A long pink tongue got in several swipes before she was satisfied and dropped back down to all fours. Her big yellow eyes were filled with love and her tail was wagging hard.

He looked up and swallowed, trying to work up some saliva. "Kate," he said, and hoped it didn't sound like the croak he was sure it did.

She gave a short nod. "Jim." Her voice was a low husk of sound, the effect of the scar. She nodded at the body beneath the sheet. "That him?"

He took a deep and he hoped unobtrusive breath. "That's him."

She walked to the table. He followed, coming to stand opposite to her. He raised his hand to lift the sheet, and paused. She met his eyes. "It's all right," she said. "Go ahead."

He raised the sheet. She didn't flinch. She did sigh, and shake her head. Mutt curled her lip and went to sit down next to the door, her back pointedly to them. "Put it back."

He did. "You know him?"

She nodded. "It's Paul Kameroff. Some kind of third

cousin's son to Auntie Vi." She sounded tired. "How did he die?"

"A bullet to the back of the head. No exit wound."

Her gaze sharpened. "Small caliber weapon?"

"A twenty-two, we think. Haven't recovered the bullet as yet."

She was silent for a moment. "Where'd you find him?"

"At the bottom of Hell Hill."

She frowned. "Someone shot him and then tossed him out of a car window?"

"Looks like. We'd never have found the body if it weren't for a semi jackknifing over the side on top of him."

"Another one? That's the fourth this winter."

"And the state says there's nothing wrong with the grade of that curve," he said. "So anyway, the seagulls were out, scavanging like mad, and some of them stumbled over Paul here. His hands and feet were tied, by the way."

"Tied, and then shot, and then tossed," she said.

"Yeah. What was he into?"

"Nothing." She saw his expression. "I mean it, Jim. Nothing. Paul was, well, to tell the truth he wasn't too bright. He was a couple of years behind me in school, and he never would have made it through if his sister hadn't carried him. Sonia," she added. "They were a year apart, I think."

"He live in the Park?"

"She stayed, he left when someone—probably Emma or Auntie Vi—finagled him a Teamsters' card. Last I heard, he was working roustabout for RPetCo up in Prudhoe Bay. Week on, week off, free food and board while he was working, good salary, pretty cushy deal all around. Paul might not have been very bright but he was smart enough not to screw that up." She looked down at the body. "Or so I would have thought."

"What does a roustabout do?"

She shrugged. "Whatever they ask him to. Oilfield cleanup, moving flow pipe around the Stores yard, on the emergency response team for fires, loading and unloading luggage for the charter, driving crew change buses, supervising the stick pickers."

"What kind of trouble could he get into on that job?"

"I told you—"

"Yeah, you told me." He jerked his chin at the body. "And yet here he lies with a bullet in his brain." He let the silence lie there like a wet, heavy blanket, and knew a fleeting gratitude that at least she didn't turn his knees to water when he was on the job.

"Let's go out there," she said.

"Out where? You mean where we found the body?"

"Yeah."

It was as gray and drizzly at the scene as when he and Hazen had left it. You wouldn't have known that a ragged ridge of tall mountains was holding up the edge of the eastern sky if you hadn't seen them on a clear day, or that a river draining twenty million acres of national park was winding its serpentine way through the valley below. No, this was just a barely two-lane road hacked out of the side of a steep hill, with one too many switchbacks in it for safety.

As witness the wrecks of the two trailers below. "You're not going to make me climb down there again, are you?" he said dismally, but she was already over the snow berm and scaling the snow-covered hillside. Mutt gave a short, joyous bark and leaped the berm in a single bound, vanishing into the underbrush in search of the elusive arctic hare. Sighing heavily, Jim followed less gracefully, grabbing for bushes and tree limbs to slow his descent. He reached the bottom of the ravine just as she was climbing inside the remains of one of the trailers. "Kate!" he said sharply. "Wait, don't go in there, the whole damn thing's probably ready to collapse!"

She went in anyway and cursing, he followed. "For crissake," he said, picking a gingerly path through twisted boards and splintered pallets, "what's left to look at in here? Everything got tossed outside when the trailers went over."

She'd brought the flashlight he carried with him in the Blazer, and she was quartering what was left of the floor of the trailer, not an easy task because the trailer had come to rest upside down. He crunched through a pile of chocolate chips, fuming. "What are you looking for?" he said. "What the hell's the wreck got to do with Paul Kameroff?"

She clicked off the flashlight and clambered back outside. He gritted his teeth and followed her through the trees still standing to the second trailer. This one was resting on its side, or what was left of it. Jim noticed that, like the other trailer, all the tires were missing. The Park rats hadn't wasted any time, but he did wonder what they thought they were going to use them on. It wasn't like you could mount the tire of an eighteen-wheeler on a Ford Ranger F150 pickup truck. Not and go unnoticed, at any rate.

He had time to think all this as he slogged through the knee-deep snow, and time to wish he'd never called Kate in, or better yet, never met her in the first place ever in his whole life. Trouble, that's what she was, nothing but trouble. And the proximate cause of his boots being wet through to his socks. He swore.

"Give me your hand."

He looked up and she was standing in the hole of the trailer, looking perfectly natural surrounded by twisted metal and torn wood. "Why?" he said. "Wasn't anything in the other one, everything the trailer was hauling is now piled up in some Park rat's cache, what the hell is there to see?"

"Come up and find out," she said.

It was a challenge, and he took her up on it, using her hand and the rickety side of the trailer to pull himself up. A can of cream of mushroom soup came rolling out from a dark corner and he stumbled over it to bump into Kate.

He froze.

She smiled up at him, not moving. "Gosh," she said, "you've picked up some snow, Jim." She leaned over to brush a clump that clung to his pants leg, and she took her time standing up again. There was the inevitable reaction, fight it though he would. He stood very still, his jaw working. She smiled again, and the pitiful thing was she wasn't even working him at full power.

"What," he said through his teeth, "was so all-fired important in here that you just had to see?"

"Over here," she said, leading the way.

The surface beneath his feet shuddered and shook. He wasn't sure if it was the wreck or him. *What's the difference?* he thought, and almost laughed.

She played the flashlight over an intact corner of the trailer. "Look. You see it?"

Jim tried to focus. "What? Wait." His voice sharpened. "What's that?"

"Blood, I think. On what used to be the floor."

Jim had a lowering feeling that he knew what she was getting at, but he said stubbornly, "So what? Maybe there was a side of beef strung up in that corner. Maybe it dripped a little."

"This isn't a reefer, Jim, it's straight storage. Nothing but dry or canned goods. I think you should take a sample and get the lab to run it through their magic machines."

"You're a witch, aren't you?" he said two days later. "Go ahead, you can say it, I won't tell. I may personally burn you at the stake, but I won't tell."

They were sitting at the River Street Café in Niniltna, where Laurel Meganack presided over grill and table and dispensed not-awful coffee out of a large stainless-steel urn. The village of Niniltna (year-round population, 403) wasn't large enough for a street sign, but the Niniltna Native Association board of directors, which had been persuaded to front the money for the café against their better judgment, didn't want to be publicly coupled to the business. The Kanuyaq River was about twenty feet from the front door, and there was a kind of a game trail that ran between the two, and that was enough for Laurel.

"Whose blood was it?" Kate said.

Mutt sat between them, pressed up against Jim's leg, looking back and forth between her two beloveds. Jim gave her ears an absentminded scratch. "It was Paul's," Jim replied. "But then, you knew that."

"I thought maybe," she said.

"Yeah. So his body wasn't on the ground when the trailer went over, it was in the trailer and got thrown out when the trailer hit bottom and broke open."

"Yeah."

"So Paul Kameroff wasn't killed in the Park. He was probably killed in Anchorage and loaded into the trailer there." Jim brooded over his coffee. "To what purpose?" he said. "To be unloaded with the rest of the groceries in Tok?"

"It doesn't seem likely."

"No." Jim sat back and looked at her, and there was no trace either of seduction or of a susceptibility to seduction in his steady gaze. "You want to tell me what the hell is going on?"

Laurel Meganack swished by with the coffee pot and a bright smile. "You sure you folks don't want something to eat? I make a mean asparagus omelet."

Jim had a hard time controlling his expression. "Thank you, no."

Kate didn't bother hiding her grin.

"What?" Laurel said.

"He hates asparagus," Kate said.

"Hmmm." Laurel topped off their mugs and said to Kate with a grin of her own, "And you would know this how?"

Jim noted with interest the faint color in Kate's cheeks, and kept watch as she became involved in doctoring her coffee with evaporated milk until the coffee was a nice tan in color. After that came the sugar, a lot of it. Jim averted his eyes and tried not to shudder. "Ballistics took a look at the bullet."

"And?"

"They ran it through every possible database going back to the Civil War. No matches."

"There wouldn't be," she said. "This was a hit, Jim. Whoever did this was a pro."

He thought of the neat knots on Kameroff's wrists and ankles, the equally neat placement of the bullet in the back of the head. It was all very, well, neat. "Yeah," he said. "That's pretty obvious. Tell me something."

"What?"

"We got mob in Alaska?"

She considered. "We got the Aleut mob," she offered. "You don't want to cross them, they'll sic Senator Stevens on you."

When he stopped laughing, she said, "I been asking around since I saw you last."

"Asking who? And asking what?"

"Paul's family. Sonia, mostly, although she's not saying much."

"Sonia's the sister."

"Yes."

Her expression was unreadable. He waited. When nothing else came, he said, "And you found out what from all this asking around? Anything that will help us find out who tied up Paul Kameroff and put a bullet in his brain?"

She glared at him. "I don't need to be reminded of the object of the exercise."

"Funny, I thought you did. I won't let the Park's tribal loyalty screw up my investigation, Kate."

"Neither will I."

"Good to know."

She drank coffee, a delaying tactic to regain control over her temper. "For one thing, I found out that my information on Paul was out of date. He wasn't working for RPetCo on the Slope anymore, he'd moved to town."

"Who was he working for?"

"Masterson Hauling and Storage."

He paused in the act of raising his mug. "Really."

"Really."

"That would be the same outfit that owns the tractor trailer that went over the side of Hell Hill a couple nights ago."

"It would."

"Well," Jim said, putting down his mug. "Isn't that interesting."

"You might even call it a clue," she said. "When do you leave?"

"Immediately." He reached for the cap with the trooper seal on the crown.

Mutt got to her feet, tail wagging. She was always ready for action. "Got room for two more?" Kate said.

He paused. "I meant what I said, Kate."

She replied without heat. "I did, too."

"I won't hide what I find, no matter who it involves."

"I know."

He put his cap on and tugged it down. "All right, then. Let's move like we got a purpose."

The Cessna was fueled and ready at Niniltna's 4800-foot dirt airstrip. Kate untied her while Jim did the preflight and they were in the air fifteen minutes later. He leveled them out at five thousand feet and set the GPS. It was only then that he realized he'd be spending an hour plus touching shoulders with the one woman in all the gin joints in all the world who like to drive him right out of his mind. He could hear her inhaling over the headphones, and clicked off the channel, but that didn't help because he could still see the rise and fall of her breast out of the corner of his eye. He knew she didn't wear perfume but he could smell her anyway, an alluring mixture of soap and woodsmoke that his renegade pheromones translated as all heat.

A cold nose against the back of his neck made him jump, and Kate laughed. It was a very seductive laugh, or so it seemed to him, and he found himself leaning forward into the seat belt as if he could push the plane along faster by doing so. He had never been so grateful in his life to hear Anchorage ATC come on the headset and he burned up the Old Seward Highway like he was driving for NASCAR, only at five hundred feet. The landing at Merrill Field was a runway paint job and he was out of the plane the instant it rolled to a stop.

It didn't make him feel any better to see the tiny smile tugging at the corner of her lips.

Masterson Hauling and Storage was headquartered in a massive warehouse in midtown off Old Seward near International. It was surrounded by a lot of other warehouses, car dealerships, a candy factory, a strip club, and the Arctic Roadrunner, home of the best cheeseburger in the state. "What time is it?" Kate said.

"Not lunchtime."

She gave him an exaggeratedly hopeful look. "After?"

Jim was partial to a good cheeseburger himself. "Works for me."

The reception area of Masterson Hauling and Storage was a small room behind a door with a window in it. There was a yellow-and-green striped love seat much the worse for wear next to a pressed board telephone stand laden with a phone and a phone book and a stack of *American Trucker* magazines. At a desk, a young woman with bleached blonde hair spiked into a Dalí sculpture was applying more liner to brown eyes that already looked strongly racoonish. "May I help you all?" she said. She saw Mutt and the burgeoning smile went away. "I'm so sorry, we can't have animals in here."

Jim smiled down at her. "Sure you can," he said in a suddenly slow and very deep drawl. He let an admiring gaze drift down to the tight white man's shirt that was straining at its buttons, and from there to the nameplate on the front of the desk. "Candi."

Candi forgot all about Mutt, and when she spoke again her voice was a little breathless. Candi was not long out of the very deep American South, and her *R*s had a tendency to defer to her *H*s. "You all are a trooper?"

"I am that." Jim didn't bother to introduce Kate, which was okay because Kate wasn't registering even on Candi's extreme peripheral vision. "Who's your boss, Candi?"

Her hands and eyelashes fluttered uncontrollably. "Why, that would be Mr. Masterson. Mr. Conway Masterson."

He let his smile widen. "I like the way you say his name, Candi."

More fluttering. "Why, I, why, thank you kindly, mister, officer—"

"It's Jim Chopin, Candi, Sergeant Chopin of the Alaska state troopers. I'd like to speak to your boss for a few minutes, if it's convenient for him."

"Why certainly, Sergeant," Candi said, and reached for

the phone. She missed it on the first try, and blushing again, had to disconnect from Jim's eyes.

Jim looked at Kate. To his surprise, she was grinning and not bothering to hide it. "The Father of the Park has his uses," she said.

"I told you I never did deserve that title," he said.

She fluttered her eyelashes. "Ah, but did you earn it, Sergeant Chopin, sir?"

He thought longingly, not for the first time, just how much he'd like to wring her neck. Well. After.

Candi hung up and twinkled up at Jim. "Mr. Masterson can see you now, Sergeant Chopin."

"Thank you, Candi."

"Just on up the stairs now, first door at the top. And don't forget to stop off to say bye."

"I don't think any man worthy of the name could forget to do that," Jim said gallantly. Mutt was waiting for him around the corner. "What are you grinning at?" he said to her, and escaped up the stairs behind a Kate whose shoulders were shaking slightly.

Conway Masterson's office was large and utilitarian, the desk piled with bills of lading and maintenance schedules and correspondence, more of the same stacked on top of a wall of filing cabinets. There was one window overlooking the interior of the warehouse, and one of the flourescent lights was flickering overhead. One wall was given over to a large dry board divided into grids indicating trucks out on runs to Homer, Seward, Valdez, Tok, Fairbanks, Coldfoot, and Deadhorse, including departure time, estimated arrival, and cargo. A radio was playing country-western music, which didn't add to the ambience, and Masterson himself was talking on the phone as they stood in the doorway. He waved them inside and kept talking. "Well, get to it, I've got four loads scheduled for the Fairbanks warehouse already this week and I'm down two trailers." He hung up. "You're the trooper," he said to Jim. To Kate, he said, "Who're you? And who the fuck said you could bring a dog up here?"

Mutt's ears went back, and a low growl rumbled up out of her throat.

Masterson bared his teeth and growled back.

Kate put a hand on Mutt's shoulder before things got out of hand. Mutt stopped growling, but she didn't sit down and she didn't take her eyes off Masterson.

"Kate Shugak," Jim said. "She's working the case with me."

"What case?"

"The murder of one of your employees," Jim said bluntly. "Paul Kameroff."

Conway Masterson was about fifty, with a bulbous, veiny nose barely separating small dark eyes, red fleshy lips, and a stubborn chin that looked days past its last shave. His comb-over extended from just above his left ear to being tucked behind his right ear. He wore a rumpled navy blue suit off the rack from JC Penney's, an unknotted red tie featuring a Vargas girl, and a white shirt with the third button down sewn on with brown thread. His eyes met Jim's without a trace of awareness, but he took a little too long to answer for Jim's taste. "Paul Kameroff? Who the hell's he?"

"He used to drive for you," Jim said. "His body was found in the wreckage of that semi your driver put over the side of the Glen Highway three, four days back."

Masterson's eyes narrowed. "Bert's rig?"

"Bertha O'Shaughnessy, yes."

"It's that fucking hill, what do my guys call it? Hell Hill, that's it. It's the worst stretch of that fucking road, we've put I don't know how many goddamn rigs over the side there. It's so fucking steep we can't recover any of our cargo, and half the time the tractors go over the side with the goddamn trailers. Bert was fucking lucky. It's getting so I can't afford insurance on that fucking run. What the hell am I suppose to do, run everything up the goddamn Parks through fucking Fairbanks?"

"What can you tell me about Paul Kameroff?" Jim said.

Again a slight hesitation, barely noticeable. "I run a lot of trucks and a lot of cargo out of this warehouse, I don't know the name of every last fucking employee." He reached for the phone. "Candi? We got an employee named Paul Kaminski?"

"Kameroff," Jim said.

"Whatever," Masterson said. "If he's got an employee file, make 'em a copy." He hung up. "That all?"

"No," Jim said. "I'll need to talk to anyone who worked with Paul Kameroff."

"What the fuck for? My delivery schedule's already down the shitter this month, I don't need you fucking around in the warehouse slowing things down even more!"

"Nevertheless," Jim said, imperturbable.

"That didn't take long," Kate said as they sat down with loaded trays.

"No, it didn't, did it?" Jim said, reaching for the mustard. "Amazing how in a crew of twenty Masterson couldn't remember Paul Kameroff."

"Amazing how any of a crew of twenty barely remembered that Paul existed," Kate said, and dug in. There was silence for a few bliss-filled minutes. Murder was a serious subject, but a good cheeseburger deserved attention and respect.

Jim grabbed a handful of napkins to clean the juice that had run down his hands. "Going to be hard to prove that anyone in that warehouse had anything to do with Kameroff's death."

"Next to impossible, I'd say," Kate said. She licked her fingers, one by one.

He managed to resist the urge to offer to do it for her. "There used to be rumors about the truckers in Alaska."

"There used to be facts about the truckers in Alaska," Kate said, sitting back in the booth. "They were a pretty rough crowd during the pipeline days. I was just a kid when they first had oil in the line, back in, oh, June. July of 1977, I guess, but I remember hearing about how they expected a body to come out the other end with the first of the oil."

"Did it?"

"No. If there were any bodies, there's almost six hundred thousand mostly uninhabited square miles out there to have dumped them in."

"Which naturally begs the question, why was Paul Kameroff's body dumped in the back of a trailer that was going to be unloaded in Tok the next day?"

Kate met his eyes. "Whoever killed him wanted his body to be found," they said at the same time.

Jim shoved his tray to one side. "It was a very formal little murder. He was bound first, hands and feet, no possibility of a struggle when the time came, and then shot. They wanted that bullet to go right where it did."

"An execution," Kate said, "part of the message."

"Hi, you all," a voice said.

They looked up to see Candi standing next to their table, tray in hand and a bright smile on her freshly made-up face.

It took Jim a second to remember her name. But only a second. "Candi," he said, and flashed out his broadest, most welcoming smile. He scooted over in the booth. "Have a seat."

Candi didn't even look at Kate, who stood up and said, "I'll just check on Mutt."

Jim didn't need to see her meaningful look to know what he was supposed to do. He put his arm along the back of the booth and smiled down at little Candi. "How nice to see you again."

Little Candi's blush was so powerful it caused her pancake makeup to glow like pale pink neon.

"Well?" Kate said. She was sitting in the crew cab she had borrowed from Jeannie, the clerk at Stoddard's Aircraft Parts, and since it was coming up on Jeannie's quitting time, she was getting a little restive.

"She didn't know anything, either," he said, slamming into the passenger seat. Mutt poked her nose into the front seat and rested a consoling chin on his shoulder.

"Did she know Paul, at least?"

"Yes, she knew Paul, enough to give him his paycheck every two weeks. Oh, and to forward his calls to the shop."

"What calls?"

He gave an irritable shrug. Mutt gave him a wounded look and withdrew her support. "Seems like his sister called a lot."

"Sonia?"

He nodded. "Yeah."

Kate, in the act of starting the engine, paused with her hand on the key. "Define 'a lot.' "

"Often enough for Candi to recognize her voice. Maybe once or twice a week."

Kate stared out the windshield at the unprepossessing city winterscape. There was a lot of slush on the road, a lot of snow on the sides of the road, and the hum of studded tires on pavement as vehicles so dirty you couldn't make out their color, never mind their make, splattered by. "Why at work, I wonder?"

"I don't know. Maybe when he was at work was the only time she could get to a phone. She lives in the Park, right?"

"Yes, outside Niniltna. And no, I don't think she has a phone, she'd have to go into town to make the call."

"Maybe he couldn't afford one."

"If he was a Teamster, he could afford a phone. But then why call so often? A couple of times a week, what's that about?" She started bouncing her knee, a sure sign of intense Shugak rumination. "Their parents are okay, last time I checked. There aren't any other brothers or sisters. Why's she calling him twice a week?" She looked at the clock on the dash and started the truck. "We've got to get this truck back before Jeannie thinks we've taken it and headed for California."

The three of them were back in the Cessna and halfway home, crossing the silver ribbon of the TransAlaska

Pipeline five thousand feet below when she spoke again. "Jim, do you have a list of dates of when semis have skidded off of Hell Hill?"

"No," he said in surprise. "Hazen probably does, since he's the one who responds to them most of the time."

"Let's go to Ahtna," she said.

He changed course without asking why. It was well after dark when they landed. He taxied up to the Frontier Air terminal, where the Ahtna police chief was waiting. "I hope you've got something to tell me more interesting than my dinner," the police chief said, "which I was about to sit down to."

Kate brightened. "We going to Tony's?"

Tony's was the Ahtna Lodge, a hotel on the edge of the river. What it lacked for in the way of rooms, which were converted Atco trailers, it more than made up for in its chef, Tony's partner in life and in the business.

Hazen sighed. "I guess we are."

Both men knew there was no point in asking Kate Shugak any questions until she was on the safe side of her exquisitely charred sixteen-ounce T-bone, not to mention the green salad with blue cheese on the side, a baked potato with all the trimmings, and pumpkin pie to follow. The Ahtna police chief, who was a big man with a bigger beer belly, said, "Where the hell does she put it all?"

"Maybe she diets," Jim said, who was thinking of the cheeseburger and wondering the same thing.

Kate surfaced for long enough to say "Diet?" like it was a bad word.

When the plates had been cleared, they all sat back with

similar satisfied expressions on their faces. A high pressure system had moved in from the northwest, and outside the window the river's icy surface began to glow, a reflection of the light of the rising moon. The snow-covered peaks of the Quilaks stood out in bold relief against a black starry sky. Mutt, recipient of her own steak, served rare, gave a satisfied sigh and lay down on Jim's feet.

Jim stirred. Admiring the view was all well and good, he had been known to pause in his duty on more than one occasion to do so, or why live in Alaska? But a man had been murdered. "You have that list?" he said to Hazen.

"Sure. Although I'm still waiting to find out why you want it." Hazen handed it across.

Jim put it on the table between him and Kate. He was aware with every breath that he took that she was mere inches away from him. It felt like the right side of his body was being cooked over a slow fire. He wondered if she knew.

She met his eyes and smiled at him, a rich, almost languid smile. Oh yeah, she knew.

"Why did you want this list?" Jim said.

Her smile widened at the brusque tone of his voice.

"Like me to get the two of you a room?" Hazen said, his voice heavy with sarcasm, and if you listened for it a trace of envy.

"Thanks for the offer," Kate said lazily, not taking her eyes from Jim, "but we can always get our own."

Jim could feel the color rising up into his neck and could do nothing to stop it. He tapped the printout on the table between them. "The list, Shugak."

She actually pouted. He hadn't known she could do

that. But she picked up the piece of paper and studied the columns. "Hell Hill's body count is up this year," she said.

"Yeah," Hazen said, "I noticed that, too, when I was putting the list together. We'll get one, at most two semis jackknifing on that curve in a year. This year there have been four."

"What accounts for four, do you think?" Kate said. "Weather, maybe?"

Hazen frowned and shook his head. "This winter's been no worse than normal."

"Maintenance?"

Hazen shook his head again. "Far as I know, it's been business as usual. The guys up at the state highway maintenance station are always griping about their equipment, always wanting the next new John Deere hundred-and-fifty-five-horsepower road grader, but they're all still employed. I imagine the governor knows well enough to leave Pete Heiman's district alone when it comes to budget cuts."

Kate handed the list to him. "Did you notice anything else on that list of yours?"

Jim had but he remained silent.

Hazen looked at the printout. "Okay," he said after a moment. "Three of the four semis were owned by Masterson Hauling and Storage."

"You don't have the cargo on the list."

Hazen stared at her. "Probably groceries for the AC store in Tok. Not a lot of construction supplies being hauled up the highway in the winter. Okay, Kate, what's going on?"

The waiter brought them coffee all around, with a small aluminum pitcher of half-and-half just for Kate. She rewarded him with a warm smile, and he turned away and ran into a customer sitting at the next table, who knocked over his wine glass.

When the resulting disturbance died down, Kate said, "Have you guys ever heard of wreckers?"

"Wreckers?" Jim looked at Hazen. They both shrugged. "Guess not. Who or what is a wrecker?"

"Wrecking, as it was defined in England, particularly on the coast of Cornwall, was the deliberate luring of a cargo-laden ship onto an offshore reef, usually by means of false signal lights, or by extinguishing the lights of lighthouses built to warn ships away from dangerous waters. The ship would run aground, break apart, and the cargo would float to shore, where the wreckers were standing by to pick it up."

Hazen looked at her. "Where the hell do you get this stuff?"

She shrugged. "I read a lot."

Jim, unheeding, was thinking back to that drizzly morning below the curve coming off of Hell Hill. "Are you saying—"

"One, Paul Kameroff went to work for Masterson Hauling and Storage last fall, leaving a perfectly good job on the North Slope for no good reason. Two, his sister Sonia called him at work once or twice a week from November on. Three, Bert O'Shaughnessy said she braked because she saw a woman run in front of her semi. Four, all the Masterson trucks were hauling groceries bound for AC in Tok."

"Jesus Christ," Hazen said.

"You're saying that the grocery loads Masterson Hauling was running to Tok were deliberately targeted?" Jim said.

"By this Sonia? Who's what, the sister of the dead man?" Hazen said.

"By Sonia and who's-ever in it with her," Kate said. "There were a lot of people on the hillside that day, you told me. She was just one of them." She drank coffee. "You should talk to the drivers of the other trucks that went over. See how many of them saw someone run in front of their semi."

"And Masterson found out," Jim said.

Kate nodded. "He'd lost at most one truck per year in previous years, and there are other trucking outfits that make that run. He must have wondered why he was being picked on."

"So," Hazen said, "Paul Kameroff was fingering loads for his sister, Sonia?"

"There was a big dry board in Masterson's office," Kate said. "It had all the trips on it, all the trucks, where they were going and what they were carrying, when they were leaving and when they were scheduled to arrive. I think Sonia called Paul a couple of times every week just to see what was heading our way."

"I don't get it," Jim said. "The trucking firms lose a semi of stuff a year, maybe, and they don't make a fuss about who picks it up after. The Park rats are onto a good thing here. Why get greedy, why ruin it? Is the Park having a rough year?"

"I don't think they were picking up stuff for subsistance purposes," Kate said.

"You think they were reselling it?" Jim said.

She nodded. "Otherwise, why so many? It was bound to attract notice. Which, of course, it did."

There was a brief silence. "You think—" Hazen said.

"I think Masterson figured it out, killed Kameroff, and

tossed the body in the back of Bart's trailer knowing it was going to be run off the road like the others had been," Kate said. "Knowing that the body would be a message to the people at the other end."

"Jesus Christ," Hazen said again. "The driver could have been killed."

"She sure could," Kate said. She looked at Jim. "I told you. That's a tough crowd."

Jim found a friendly judge and got a warrant to toss the premises of Masterson Hauling and Storage. He didn't find anything. The three drivers of the previous three wrecks had taken early retirement and had moved Outside long before he ever got there. Candi was genuinely distressed when she couldn't find their personnel files. The union local knew a different judge and Jim never did get a look at the union's membership files.

Sonia Kameroff cried a lot during her interrogation, and said very little. Jim talked to a few of the others he had seen at the wreck that day, only to be greeted with blank stares. "Trucks always go off that hill," one man told him. "Always will, it's a bad hill. Shit, Jim, we're doing a public service by cleaning up the mess. That trucking outfit sure ain't gonna do nothing. And no point in letting all that food go to waste."

"I can't prove a damn thing," Jim said to Kate.

"No," Kate said, face turned up to the sun. They were in back of her cabin, sitting on the boulder perched at the edge of the cliff overlooking the stream. March had come in like the proverbial lion and the snow cover was melting almost as they watched.

"They could have killed someone, Kate."

"Someone did get killed," she said.

Jim hated to let any case go, especially murder. "Got any thoughts about the gun?"

She opened her eyes and looked at him, not without sympathy. "Sure. They probably tossed it off Point Woronzof, let the tides take it out. That's what I would have done."

Nettled, he said, "You're taking this awfully calmly. You went to school with the guy. Don't you care?"

She was silent for a moment. "Those wreckers I told you about?"

"Yeah?"

"Sometimes they drowned. Sometimes they got caught, and sometimes they got hanged. Sometimes people off the ships drowned. But most of the wreckers were peasants living way below the poverty line, no jobs to speak of, no homes, no way of feeding their kids. They thought the risk was worth it."

He was silenced.

"Wreck rights," she said after a while. "We call it salvage rights now, but it was wreck rights then. If it washes up on shore and you find it, it's yours."

"And if it falls off the highway and you find it—"

"Then that's yours, too," she said.

Mutt came back with a ptarmigan and sat down to lunch. The three of them sat in the sun for a while longer, and then Kate went back to her cabin, and Jim went back to town.

Deep Lock

Clark Howard

Clark Howard has been a full-time professional writer for more than thirty years. His work ranges from twenty-one contemporary novels and true-crime books, to more than two-hundred short stories and articles in the mystery, western, and true-crime genres. He has won the Edgar Allan Poe Award and four Ellery Queen Readers Awards for short-story writing, and has a dozen nominations in the short-story and true-crime categories from the Mystery Writers of America, Western Writers of America, and Private Eye Writers of America. He has also written a boxing column for *The Ring* magazine, and has had his work adapted for both film and television.

Camille Minden, at the wheel of her ten-year-old Chevy, glanced over at her daughter in the passenger seat. Abby, who was eleven, was working on a temper fit.

"I don't see why I have to spend this weekend with Dad and his Barbie-doll wife! I spent last weekend with them! This is supposed to be my weekend with you!"

Camille had just picked Abby up from St. Catherine of Alexandria parochial school, where she was a headstrong C student in sixth grade. At the moment, they were driving away from San Francisco across the Golden Gate bridge toward Marin County and the upscale community of Delavane, where Brian, Camille's ex-husband, Abby's father, now lived in a half-million-dollar home with a pool and two little boys who looked exactly like their handsome stockbroker father.

"It isn't fair!" Abby seethed. "I never have any fun there! All I end up doing is having to play with those brats! Two weekends in a row! Just tell me why!"

"Honey, I already told you why," Camille said patiently. "We have a high-risk federal transit prisoner being brought in for the weekend and all Adjustment Center shift lieutenants are pulling duty. I'm sorry. There's nothing I can do about it."

"Well, why can't you have a regular job, like working in an office or a department store or something? Why do you have to be a San Quentin guard lieutenant, anyway?"

Camille sighed quietly. It was those exact words that had led to the beginning of the end of her marriage to Abby's father. And another relationship she'd had before him. And further back, another one before that. Thank God she'd only had a child with one of them.

"Sweetheart," Camille said quietly, "I'm a San Quentin corrections officer because that's how things turned out for me. It's a good job and I'm good *at* it. I'm sorry it upsets you."

"But why do you have to work *this* weekend? You worked *last* weekend!"

"I told you, honey. It's because of this high-risk federal prisoner."

"What's so high-risk about him?" Abby demanded to know.

"He's an escape artist. Escaped from federal custody three times. Very embarrassing to the government."

At that explanation, Abby merely rolled her eyes and fell silent.

When they arrived at the Delavane house, the new wife, Cindy, came out to meet them, her two toddlers right behind her. Camille got Abby's backpack out of the trunk.

"You must be roasting in that outfit," Cindy said, referring to Camille's olive drab and khaki uniform. "Hello, Abby."

"Hullo," Abby muttered, not making eye contact.

"The uniform's not so bad, really," Camille said. "It's cool inside the prison. Listen, I really appreciate this, Cindy. I hope it's not too much of an inconvenience."

"I have to tell you, Brian's a little upset about it. We're having a pool party tomorrow night and, well, Abby just kind of sulks around when she doesn't want to be here. Kind of puts a damper on things, you know."

"I've had a talk with her about her attitude," Camille said. "I think you'll find it a lot improved this weekend." She gave her daughter a hug. "Right, sugar?"

"Sure, right," Abby muttered, picking up her backpack and starting for the house, the two toddlers following right behind her.

"Incidentally," Cindy said, "I guess I should give you a heads-up that Brian's been talking about going back to court and asking for full custody of Abby. He seems to think he's got a pretty good chance of getting it, what with you living in a subsidized apartment in San Francisco, and the kind of people you come into contact with on your job, your erratic hours, Abby having to be with a sitter after school, that sort of thing. You know, compared with what we could give her here."

"But Brian doesn't even enjoy his *weekends* with her, Cindy, for God's sake. Why would he want her all the time?"

"He thinks living with you is what's giving her the poor attitude. He's convinced he could change that. I'm not taking sides, understand. I just thought you should know." Cindy tossed her blond hair and shrugged innocently.

She really did, Camille thought, look like a Barbie doll. Just as Brian looked like a Ken.

Driving back down Highway 101 toward the San Quentin turnoff, it was all Camille could do to keep from feeling sorry for herself. On top of tuition and school uniforms for Abby, rent, groceries, car repairs every month, it seemed, and some female problems she was beginning to experience, now she had to worry about the possibility that her ex might try to take her kid away from her.

Life really sucked sometimes, she thought.

Most of the time, actually.

At that moment, an unmarked sedan arrived at the main entry gate of San Quentin State Prison. The man in the front passenger seat identified himself to the gate guard.

"Special Agent Edward Revere, FBI. We have a high-risk federal prisoner to be housed here until Monday morning. Warden Dixon is expecting us."

The gate guard directed the driver, a United States marshal, where to proceed, and the car was passed through.

"Seems to me you're going to a hell of a lot of trouble, Eddie," said a voice from the rear seat. It belonged to Gerald Fane, who sat squeezed between two other U.S. marshals. Fane, in a federal-prisoner orange jumpsuit, was handcuffed, shackled, and belly-chained.

"No trouble at all, Gerry," Agent Revere replied, glancing over his shoulder at the prisoner.

"You could just as easily have kept me in the federal lockup back in San Francisco. Boarding me out at San Quentin is a waste of taxpayers' money."

"What the hell do you care, Fane?" one of the marshals asked. "You don't pay taxes."

"Shut up, cowboy," Fane replied. "I don't talk to federal marshals, only FBI agents."

"You'll be talking to San Quentin guards tonight, big shot," the other marshal said with a smirk. "You'll be in the A.C.—San Quentin's Adjustment Center—with the worst psychos in California."

"This is cruel and unusual punishment, Eddie," Fane said to the FBI agent. "I'm a federal bank robber and a federal prison escapee; I'm entitled to be incarcerated in a federal lockup."

"You brought it all on yourself, Gerry," the agent reminded him. "If you hadn't already escaped from three federal lockups, this wouldn't be happening."

The marshal driving the car glanced curiously at Agent Revere. "You two guys seem to be pretty friendly, first names and all. What's with that?"

"Gerry and I go back a long way," Revere said. "Went to

Calhoun Elementary back in Chicago. Then to Crane Tech High. Used to box in the Police Athletic League together. Later on, we joined the Marine Corps together and served in the same outfit in 'Nam."

"So how come one of you turned out okay and the other didn't?"

From the backseat, Gerry Fane said, "I've often wondered myself what made Eddie go wrong."

"I guess I just didn't get the breaks," Revere said drily.

The driver pulled into a visitor space in front of the Administration Building and a man in civilian clothes and three uniformed corrections officers carrying restraining chains came out to meet them.

"Deputy Warden Fred Shaner," the man in the suit introduced himself. "I'll take your prisoner from here."

"I understood I was to turn him over to Warden Dixon himself," Revere said.

"Warden Dixon was called to Sacramento for a meeting with the Director of Corrections," Shaner said. "But I have the authority to accept the prisoner. You have his transfer-of-custody order?"

Revere hesitated. This was a minor departure from procedure. No big thing, really—except that Gerry Fane had escaped federal custody three times. The least little deviation in procedure started Edward Revere's stomach churning.

"What time is the warden expected back?" Revere asked.

"Not until late, I'm afraid. It's a hundred miles to Sacramento, and sometimes these meetings run long." The deputy warden noticed Revere's uncertainty. "If you have a problem with my taking custody instead of the warden, you can bring him back tomorrow—"

"No, that's not an option," Revere decided quickly. It would mean a drive back into San Francisco, transferring him back into custody there, arranging to keep him under electronic surveillance all night, then starting all over again the next morning. The SAC—Special Agent in Charge—would raise hell. The chief U.S. marshal would throw a fit, the marshals assigned to the escort would piss and moan—and it wouldn't help matters at all that Gerry Fane would be enjoying every minute of it. "No, we'll turn him over to you, Deputy Warden," Revere said.

As Fane was being taken out of the car, the marshal he had told to shut up gave him a solid kick in the ankle for his insolence. "Sorry, Fane," he said, "my foot slipped."

Fane bit his lower lip in pain. Revere looked hard at the marshal. "Make sure it doesn't slip again," the agent warned.

The marshals removed their sets of chains from Fane and the San Quentin corrections officers replaced them with a set of their own. "Take him to the A.C.," the deputy warden instructed. "They know where to put him."

Agent Revere and Deputy Warden Shaner exchanged signatures and documents, and then Shaner watched as the federal officers drove back toward the gate.

When the car was out of sight, Shaner turned and threw a casual salute up to Warden Earl Dixon, who was watching from a window of his office.

The Adjustment Center was a prison within a prison. It was a separate high-security, three-story cellhouse that on one side housed a triple-tiered death row, and on the other had three tiers of isolation cells for the most volatile and dangerous noncondemned inmates from the prison's general population. At present, the top tier of isolation cells was unoccupied, and it was in the end cell of that tier, the farthest from the steel steps that connected the three levels, that Gerald Fane was put.

Still wearing the orange jumpsuit with FEDERAL PRIS-ONER stenciled on it, still cuffed, shackled, and belly-chained, he sat on a lumpy blue-tick mattress on the wall-mounted bunk and stared straight ahead at nothing. In the corridor outside his cell, a tall, muscular guard lieutenant, tanned and crew-cut, harangued him with an ongoing litany of insults.

"Not such a big shot now, are you, Fane?" he asked rhetorically. The nametag on his shirt read WOODBURY. Fane ignored him completely. "Big-time bank robber, huh? Big-time escape artist, huh? Well, the word we get in here is that when you go to federal court for sentencing on Monday, the judge is going to bury you with a three-hundred-year sentence so's you'll never take a free step again. And you know where they'll send you? To the new super-max federal joint in Florence, Colorado, where you'll be locked up twenty-three hours a day. You get a twelve-inch black-and-white TV set with two channels, no window so's you'll never see the daylight again, two meals a day at ten and four in your cell, no communication with any other cons, and your toilet flushes automatically every twenty minutes, day and night."

Fane heard the footsteps of several people coming down the corridor. Presently, four people walked up to his cell, two in civilian suits—one of them Deputy Warden Fred Shaner—and the other two, one a woman, wearing guard-lieutenant uniforms like the officer named Woodbury who was badgering Fane. The older of the two men in suits glanced at Fane, then spoke to Woodbury. "Why haven't this man's chains been removed, Lieutenant?" There was a hint of annoyance in his voice.

"Because of the risk level, Warden. I thought—"

Before Woodbury could finish, the warden turned to his deputy and said, "Get his chains off."

Fred Shaner spoke into a two-way palm radio he carried. "Deputy Warden Shaner to A.C. Control. Rack open Cell AC-Thirty."

When the cell door electronically slid open, the warden nodded brusquely to Woodbury, who immediately entered the cell and with a master shackle key removed the chrome-covered steel chains from Fane's wrists, ankles, and waist. When Woodbury came out of the cell, the warden went in. He stood just inside the open door. Fane did not bother to look up.

"Fane, my name is Earl Dixon. I'm the warden here."

"Congratulations," Fane said, unimpressed, still not looking up.

"My older brother is retired Captain Sam Dixon, of Leavenworth. My nephew is Sergeant Ray Dixon."

Now Fane looked up, his expression becoming keen with interest. He rose to his feet, causing the guards outside to tense. "How are they?" Fane asked.

"Pretty well, considering. My brother has migraines from the head trauma he suffered, but he draws a nice disability pension and does a little security consulting on the side. Mostly, though, he takes his two granddaughters fishing. Wife and daughter-in-law claim he's making tomboys out of them."

Fane smiled slightly. "What about Ray?"

"The knife wounds were superficial except for the one that nicked his lung, but he's fully recovered. Back on the job. Been promoted to sergeant, as I said."

Fane nodded. "I'm glad to hear that they're both okay."

Warden Dixon turned to his four subordinates outside the cell. "You may or may not have heard this yet, but in the Leavenworth riot six years ago, my brother and nephew were among the staff hostages the convicts took. My brother was beaten about the head and suffered a concussion; my nephew was stabbed twice with a homemade shank and one of his lungs collapsed. Both of them would likely have died had it not been for this man here. As you might imagine, because of his reputation he has a great deal of prestige and status on the inside. Even though he was not a participant in the riot, he personally took charge of my brother and nephew, took them into his cell and tended their wounds as best he could, and then successfully hid them by lying them on their sides under his bunk and letting his blanket hang down to conceal them. The doctors said later that without Fane's help, neither my brother or nephew would likely have survived."

As the warden was speaking, the woman in the guard-lieutenant's uniform was studying Gerald Fane curiously. Her nametag read MINDEN and when Fane looked at her perusing him, he saw a woman with a deeply severe face— long sculpted nose between flared cheekbones, and piercing green eyes. When she saw him returning her scrutiny, she quickly shifted her eyes away.

"Don't lay it on too thick, Warden," Fane said when Dixon finished speaking. "You'll ruin that reputation of mine you mentioned."

"Well, it was necessary for me to bring the matter up," Dixon said. "Apparently the federal officers didn't make a connection between us; if they had, I don't believe you'd be here. But—" he spread his hands in vexation—"you *are* here, and it has put me in a somewhat uneasy position."

"How so?" Fane asked.

"The story of what you did to help my brother and nephew started spreading throughout the inmate population early this morning when word first reached the prison that you were going to be locked down here over the weekend." The warden put his hands in his trousers pockets and casually leaned against the wall. "You know as well as I do, Fane, how the convict mentality works. When something is owed, it's owed. And when it's owed, it has to be paid. Right now, half the inmates in this facility are talking about how I owe you for what you did to help my brother and nephew. And they're already speculating about how I'll go about paying you."

Fane shook his head. "Forget it, Warden. What happened at Leavenworth didn't concern you at all. You don't owe me anything." He sat back down.

The warden shook his head. "You may not think so. And I may not think so. But I've got three thousand cons in this place who probably *do* think so."

"I get it," Fane said. "You need to figure out a way to pay me back so you can save face, right?"

"That's about it," Dixon admitted.

"I suppose letting me escape is out of the question."

The warden merely smiled.

"How about a bottle of Tanqueray gin and a bucket of ice?"

"Regulations don't even permit me to do that for the condemned men I execute."

Fane grinned and said, "I hear you've got four women on death row. How about letting me cell with them. We could have recreation together."

The warden shook his head and Camille Minden had to suppress a smile. "I'm required to keep you in deep lock," Dixon said. "Anyway, they're housed in a different facility."

Fane rested back against the cement wall his bunk was attached to and shrugged. "Why don't we just forget it, Warden? Spread the word around that I said we were even."

"Won't work, Fane. The cons wouldn't buy it. It's important that they *know* I actually did something for you."

"You're really serious about this, aren't you?"

"Totally serious. With your reputation, after what you did for my brother and nephew, the way you're treated while you're here could affect my inmate morale situation for months to come."

Lieutenant Minden stepped forward. "Excuse me, Warden. May I make a suggestion?"

"By all means."

"Since Mr. Fane isn't technically a state prisoner, I don't believe we're bound by Department of Corrections equality-of-treatment regulations. His treatment doesn't have to conform with the treatment of all the other inmates in our population."

"What are you getting at exactly, Lieutenant?"

"What I'm getting at, sir, is that we could make Mr. Fane's short stay here much more comfortable than it would ordinarily be in an A.C. cell. For instance, we could have his cell scrubbed down, a hospital mattress sent down from the infirmary, with clean sheets, a pillow and case, a clean blanket. We could get him a new set of denims, new underwear, new socks, a pair of death row house slippers, and let him get out of that grungy federal jumpsuit he's wearing. Let him have a nice hot shower and shampoo. Get him some decent shaving gear, magazines, newspapers. Have his meals sent over from the staff dining hall. Roll a TV set in front of his cell." She paused for effect, then added, "Set him up like that and the word would be all over the institution in three hours."

Warden Dixon tapped his chin with a forefinger. "What do you think, Fred?"

"Works for me," said the deputy warden. "Even the leaders of the Aryan Brotherhood, the Mexican Mafia, and the Black Guerrilla Family won't be able to put you down for that."

"Sir," the lieutenant named Woodbury interjected, "all that sounds very nice, but in my opinion every concession we make to this man decreases our security a notch. This felon has a serious escape record. Treating him like some kind of special guest will send a message to the entire staff that it's all right to relax safeguards on him."

"Woodbury has a point, sir," said the deputy warden. "It wouldn't look very good if *we* lost him."

"Warden," Gerry Fane countered, "I like Lieutenant Minden's idea. It may be the last time I get to enjoy any privileges at all. What if I agree that I won't try in any way to escape from your custody? If I give you my personal word—"

"Your *personal word!*" Lieutenant Woodbury scoffed. "You're a career criminal! What good's your personal word?"

"It's as good as yours, mister," Fane retorted, glaring coldly at Woodbury.

Dixon studied his temporary prisoner thoughtfully. Momentarily he then locked eyes with Lieutenant Minden. She was his only female lieutenant, but more than once she had come up with solutions to problems that his male officers had not known how to deal with. Her judgment had never let him down.

"Your personal word, Fane?" the warden asked.

Fane held out his hand. "My personal word, Warden."

The two men shook hands. Lieutenant Minden smiled very slightly. Woodbury looked as if he might become ill.

As the prison officials left, Lieutenant Minden glanced back at Gerald Fane to see if he was looking at her.

He was.

An hour later, two corrections officers removed Fane from his cell and escorted him to the opposite end of the tier to a secure shower cell. Fane worked his feet out of the laceless high-top black shoes and stripped off the orange jumpsuit the feds had kept him wearing for four days. Because they had not provided him with underwear or socks, his crotch was rashed and he had blisters on the heels and ankles of both feet. At forty-four, Fane's body was lean and trim; whether as a convict or fugitive, he religiously exercised and had given up cigarettes two decades earlier. Under extremely close-cropped gray hair, his face was on the cusp of being craggy, but when he was amused, when he smiled or laughed, women usually thought him attractive. On a ledge just outside the shower stall were a folded pair of new dark-blue denim trousers, a light-blue denim shirt, a set of white briefs, undershirt, sweat socks, and a pair of gray wool soft slippers that condemned men wore. On a shelf above the ledge, Fane found soap, shampoo, and a towel. *Now,* he thought, *if only the water in this joint is hot . . .*

It was. When he turned on the spray, got under it, and began to lather up, he felt as if he had died and gone to heaven. He even began to hum a jazzy version of "Memphis Blues." Outside the shower-cell door, his two escort guards looked at each other dumbfoundedly.

They let him stay in the shower as long as he wanted to. When he finally felt clean again, he got out, dried, and dressed. The clean, new clothes could not have felt better if they had come from Desmond's in Palm Springs. When he stepped back onto the tier, he was handcuffed and belly-chained, then told to sit on a metal folding chair near the cell from which they had taken him. The two officers stood guard on each side of him. Outside the open cell door was a cleaning cart on wheels with a soapy water tub, mops, brushes, and a large plastic dispenser of the chlorine-smelling yellow disinfectant that Fane had smelled in every lockup in which he had ever been. Inside the cell, two trusties were finishing up a thorough blitz cleaning of the cell floor, walls, bunk, sink, and toilet. When they came out and were getting their cleaning cart back in order, they worked slowly and stared in awe at Gerry Fane, a living legend in the criminal community. As Lieutenant Minden had predicted, they would shortly be spreading the word all over the prison about the special treatment Fane was getting.

"Never mind eyeballing this prisoner," one of the guards said. "Finish up and beat it."

As the cleaning men rolled their cart down the tier, another trusty came past them carrying a pillow, fresh bed linen, and two blankets. Behind him came two others carrying a hospital mattress three times as thick as the usual cell mattress. Immediately behind them came Lieutenant Minden, carrying a large paper bag. Fane could not help noticing how nicely her uniform pants fit her hips. She was, he thought, probably twelve or fifteen pounds heavier than she wanted to be, but that, in his mind, was just a female fallacy; most women, he knew, had no idea how good they looked with a few extra pounds.

Lieutenant Minden stood silently as the mattress was put in place and the bunk made up. Then she told the lead trusty, "Stop in the shower cell and pick up an orange jumpsuit and a pair of high-tops. Take the jumpsuit to the laundry to be washed and ironed, and the shoes to the shoe shop to be cleaned up and reconditioned."

"Yes, ma'am," the trusty replied with a half salute.

To the guards, Minden said, "Unchain him and put him in his cell."

When the chains were off and Fane was inside, she unsnapped a radio from her duty belt. "Lieutenant Minden to A.C. Control. Close Cell AC-Thirty." As the cell door slid shut, she told the two guards, "Okay, you guys can go back to the control room now. I'll be along shortly."

After the guards left, Fane held his arms out in a mock pose and smiled. "Here I am—all dressed up and no place to go." Then his expression became serious. "I appreciate this, Lieutenant. There's no way I can really thank you."

"Sure there is," she said. "Be a good boy. Keep your word. Don't screw up my boss." She handed the paper bag through the bars. "Toothpaste, toothbrush, shaving cream, disposable razor, deodorant, a few candy bars, box of crackers, cheese spread, couple of magazines." Fane emptied everything out on his bunk.

"With treatment like this, I might even be rehabilitated."

"Could you?" Camille asked quietly.

"Could I what?"

"Ever be rehabilitated."

Fane's expression became reflective. He stepped closer to the bars, where she stood. After a moment, he shook his head and replied, "I don't think so. Too much water under too many bridges. Plus, too much time hanging over me. I'd grow old and die behind the walls."

"That's true," Minden said. "I forgot about that aspect of it for a moment."

"But I do have a way out of the life I've led," he confided. "Want to hear about it? Off the record?"

"Sure. If you want to tell me."

"Word of honor that it'll be just between us?"

"Sure. Word of honor. The warden took your word, you can take mine."

Fane bobbed his chin at the metal chair on which he had sat while his cell was being cleaned. "Pull the chair over and sit down," he suggested. "Want a candy bar?"

Camille moved the chair over to face the bars and sat down. "No candy bar, thanks, I'm on a diet."

"Don't tell me you're one of those women who wants to be skinny?"

"Not skinny. Just *skinnier.* Now tell me about your way out."

Fane sat on the end of the bunk and lowered his voice. "Do you know how many bank robberies I've engineered?"

"A lot."

"Thirty-one. I selected them, scoped them out, planned

the job, and picked my crew. The banks we hit averaged us between three-eighty and four hundred thousand dollars. My cut was half, because the jobs were mine; the rest of the crew cut up the other half. Thirty-one successful bank robberies—"

"But they weren't all successful," Camille cut in. "You were caught and sent to federal prison twice."

"But," Fane emphasized, "my share of the money was not recovered either of those times. Some of my crew were nailed with some of the money still in their possession— but never me. So when I say *successful* robbery, from my point of view, it means I got away with my share." Pausing, he dropped his voice even lower. "And my share from the thirty-one jobs came to just over six *million*."

Camille pursed her lips in a silent whistle. Fane felt a little tickle at the base of his spine over the way her lips looked when they were pursed.

"Now here's the trump card: Two-thirds of my take— four million—was always FedExed out of the country to a trust account in my name in a Cayman Island branch bank in a small Central American country—that has no extradition treaty with the U.S."

Fane unwrapped a Snickers bar and took a bite, chewing it with a self-satisfied smile and studying the somewhat severe expression of the woman outside the bars. He wondered what that grave face would look like when she was being made love to. The right way.

"So with that money stashed, you were going to start a new life somewhere," Camille said.

"Already have started one," Fane confided. "I have a beachfront home with a dock, a boat, and boat shelter, a beautiful garden with a swimming pool, a custom-made SUV, an international satellite dish—and it's all in a new name with new identity papers. The only thing I don't have is furniture; I've never actually lived in the place, just stayed in a sleeping bag now and then for a few days."

"What'll happen to it now?" Camille asked.

"I'll live in it. Just like I planned."

"You mean you'll escape again?"

"Sure."

She frowned. "But not from here?"

"No. I won't break my word to you."

"You mean to the warden."

"Sure. You. The warden. Whoever. I keep my word."

"There's talk you'll be sent to the new super-max federal prison in Florence, Colorado. They say it's an escape-proof pen."

"There's never been an escape-proof pen *built*," Fane scoffed, "except maybe Alcatraz—and even that's open to debate. Anyway, they'll never get me to their new super-max joint. I'll be long gone before that happens."

Camille Minden's radio sounded and she answered. After listening for a moment, she said, "Okay, I'll be right down." To Fane she said, "I have to go down to our electronics shop and sign out a TV for you."

Fane stood and leaned both hands through the bars, putting his face close to them. He feigned a dramatic sigh. "What would I ever do without you?"

"Wiseass," she said, walking away.

As he watched her go, Fane decided that her uniform pants looked as good on her from the rear as they did from the front. Maybe better.

* * *

A little while after Camille Minden left, Lieutenant Woodbury came walking down the tier and stopped in front of
Fane's cell.

"Comfortable, big shot?" he asked snidely.

Fane looked up from a *Newsweek* he was reading. "Well,
it's not the Belaggio, but under the circumstances it'll do."

"You lucked out good, Fane. If it'd been left up to me,
you'd be sleeping on the floor in a strip cell."

Putting the magazine aside, Fane rose and faced the
bars—not close enough for Woodbury to be able to reach
in and grab him. That was an old corrections-officer trick:
grab a con and jerk him forward to slam his face against
the bars, then rip his own uniform shirt open and claim
the con grabbed him first.

"Yeah, well, it wasn't left up to you, screw," Fane said
flatly. "That pretty lady lieutenant saw to that."

Woodbury scowled. "Listen, scumbag, that pretty lady
lieutenant, as you call her, happens to be a close personal
friend of mine. You make any kind of a move on her, or say
anything out of line, and I'll see to it that between now and
Monday morning, something of yours gets broken. Toes,
fingers, nose, eardrums, something."

"I wish you'd spoken up earlier, Woodbury," Fane said
blandly. "Now you're too late. Lieutenant Minden and I just
got engaged—"

Woodbury's arms shot through the bars, but fell four
inches short of Fane's face. "You lowlife son of a bitch!"

"Don't get sore, Woodbury." Fane was smiling now. "I
was going to ask you to be my best man."

"What the hell's going on here?" a loud female voice said

from down the tier. Woodbury pulled his arms back through the bars. Camille Minden stalked up to the cell, her piercing green eyes flashing annoyance. "What are you doing here, Woody? This is my assignment."

"I just walked over to see if you needed any help—"

"How? By reaching into this prisoner's cell?"

Woodbury looked down at his shoes. "I guess I lost it for a second. He made a crack I didn't like—"

"Go back to your own assignment, Woody," she told him sharply. "Don't come around here while this is my watch."

Casting a threatening glance at Fane, the burly lieutenant walked away. As he did, a trusty came up pushing a table on wheels, which held an industrial-model 12-inch black-and-white TV. Dismissing the trusty, Camille attached an extension cord to the TV, plugged it in across the tier, and rolled it as close to the cell bars as she could.

"What was that all about?" she asked.

Fane waved off the question. "It was nothing. Forget it."

"I want to know." Firmly.

"Look, I don't want to start any trouble between people who have to work together."

"I said I want to know." Insistent now.

Fane shrugged resignedly. "He came over here to warn me about my conduct around you. He told me he'd take it very personally if I made any improper comments to you, or tried to touch you in any way. He said you and he were engaged to be married—"

"He said *what?*"

"That you two were engaged. Anyway, what happened was probably my fault. I got a little out of line."

"How?"

"Well, I was surprised, you know? And I said something like, 'Man, it seems to me that a woman like her could do a lot better than a slug like you.' That's when he grabbed for me." Fane paused, then asked, "He your boyfriend or something?"

"Was," she snapped. "For a short time. Very short."

Fane moved close to the bars. His voice became quiet and gentle. "How the hell did someone like you get into this line of work anyway?"

Camille drew the metal chair over and sat down. "Long story." She glanced down the tier. "Listen, do you smoke?"

"No."

"Well, I do. But I'm not allowed to smoke on my shift." Pulling up her pants leg a little, she removed a pack of cigarettes and a book of matches from the top of her sock. Lighting one, she said, "If I hear anybody coming onto the tier, I'll hand this in to you and you pretend you were smoking it." Her eyes narrowed slightly. "Deal?"

"Sure."

After a couple of drags, Camille said, "I was a file clerk for the warden over in Folsom. I married a correctional officer. He later fell for the warden's secretary. She was a really stacked redhead. Eventually they ran away together. The warden was a real nice guy. He and his wife felt sorry for me, so he suggested I let him sponsor me to take correction officer's training. I did and became a C.O. There are quite a few women in corrections today, more than most people realize. As a matter of fact, a woman is now the *warden* of Folsom.

"Anyway, I studied hard, worked hard, and became a good officer. Eventually, the old warden, before he retired, promoted me to sergeant. Later when a lieutenant's position opened up here at Q, I applied for it, made the top of the list on the exams, and was given the job."

"Is that when you started going out with Woodbury?"

"No, that came later. Before that, I married again. Some of the officers here were invited to attend a Rotary Club luncheon where Warden Dixon was the guest of honor. It was down in San Francisco and there were a lot of young guns present from local commerce, industry, banking, so on. I met this guy, Brian Minden, a stockbroker, rising young executive type. It was one of those lust at first sight things. That night we were in bed together, within thirty days we were married, within two months I was pregnant."

For some reason, Fane was surprised. "You have a child?"

"Yes." She blew smoke up toward the ceiling and glanced down the tier. "A daughter. She's eleven going on thirty. My nickname for her is Miss Attitude."

Fane smiled one of his rare genuine smiles and Camille was struck at once by how quickly he became handsome.

Finishing her cigarette, she handed it to him, saying, "Toss this, will you?" He tossed it into the toilet and when he turned back around, she had stood up.

"I don't see a wedding band," he said. "What happened to marriage number two?"

"It lasted three years, then, like all my other relationships, it crashed and burned. He's remarried. To a Barbie doll, according to Miss Attitude."

Fane could not help smiling again. "I'll bet Miss Attitude is a lot like her mother."

Camille cloaked a smile of her own. "Let's not get too personal. I've gone way over the line with you already. All you asked me was how I became a prison cop." She tilted her head a fraction. "How'd you become a bank robber?"

"Somebody told me there was big money in it."

"I'm serious. I want to know."

Fane quietly studied her for a moment. It was a question no one had ever asked him before. "Okay," he said then. "Go to one of your computers and pull up my FBI sheet. After you read it, ask me again."

Camille nodded curtly. "I'll do that." She walked away.

"Hey," Fane called.

"What?"

"Is there another name that goes with Minden?"

"Yes, but our rules don't allow us to give inmates our first names. It encourages familiarity."

"Okay. Don't want to break any rules."

She walked a few steps farther, then said over her shoulder, "Camille. My name's Camille."

Later, a food cart was pushed up to his cell and an inmate kitchen steward, supervised by Camille Minden, passed Fane a tray of hot food from the staff dining room. Dismissing the steward, Camille again drew up the metal chair and sat with Fane while he ate.

"Cigarette smoke bother you while you eat?" she asked. He shook his head and Camille got one from her sock and lit the tip. "Answer a question for me?" she said, exhaling.

"Maybe."

"What made you give Warden Dixon your word you wouldn't try escaping from here?"

"Off the record?" Fane asked, chewing meat loaf. She nodded okay. "Can I trust you?" he wanted to know.

Camille shrugged. "Trust me, don't trust me. It's up to you."

Fane thought about it. Briefly. "I like you, Camille Minden. I like your style. So I'll level with you. I don't have to try to escape from here; I'm going to escape from the federal courthouse on Monday."

Camille's eyebrows went up, almost tantalizingly. "Can you make it?"

"If everything goes according to plan, I can."

"Will there be any violence?"

Fane looked steadily at her. "I thought you were going to read my FBI sheet."

"I haven't had the privacy to do that yet." Her eyes were as steady as his. "Will there be any violence?"

"Read the FBI sheet."

Camille rose, handed him her cigarette, and walked away.

Fane began to wonder if he had gone too far with her.

When the kitchen steward came to retrieve Fane's supper tray, there was an ordinary guard as the escort. Camille Minden did not return until mid evening. Fane was watching a Western movie on the little TV. Camille turned it off and sat down.

"Okay, I've read your FBI sheet."

"Find any violence?"

"None. Does that mean there won't be any at the courthouse on Monday?"

"It does."

Camille looked at him almost in wonder. "How do you do it? I mean, you've robbed thirty-one banks in twelve states, escaped from federal lockups *and* federal prisons—and all without using violence of any kind. You use weapons, you threaten, you neutralize bank security and prison staff by putting their own handcuffs on them, you probably frighten people half to death—but you never actually *hurt* anybody." She shook her head almost in frustration. "I don't understand why someone like you is even a criminal."

Fane did not say anything. Camille waited for what she determined to be an appropriate pause, then bluntly challenged him.

"Well?"

"Well, what?"

"You know what," she said impatiently. "Why *are* you a criminal? Why are we sitting here with a rack of bars between us instead of having a drink in some nice cozy lounge out in the free world?"

Fane moved to the end of his bunk nearest the bars and sat leaning forward with his forearms on his knees. "I don't really know," he said quietly. He smiled almost shyly at her. "Nobody's ever asked me that before. Not even Eddie Revere, the FBI agent who brought me here. He and I were once best friends. For years. Went to elementary school together, high school, served in the Marine Corps together in Vietnam. Hell, we even dated the same girl from our old neighborhood for years. Girl named Jenny. We both wrote to her from 'Nam. Started dating her again when we got back. Both of us were crazy about her. She ended up choosing him. I didn't blame her. He was the steady one. Good old steady, ever-ready Eddie. Became a cop in Chicago, went to school nights on the GI Bill, ended up joining the FBI. I was just letting the years go by, bouncing from job to job, not really getting anywhere. Then one day I ran into a guy that Eddie and I had known in the service.

We had a few drinks together and he told me how things hadn't worked out well for him either after he came home from 'Nam. Couple of divorces, a few jobs lost, lots of debt—that sort of thing. Then he laid it on me that he and another guy were planning to stick up a small branch bank for money to make a new start. And they needed a third guy. So I got to thinking about Eddie and Jenny, happily married, a little girl, another baby on the way, house in the suburbs and all that. And me, my life going nowhere, no future, no family, no nothing. So I said sure, why not." Fane rose and paced to the rear of the cell and back. He did not like what he was talking about, and Camille could see that in his expression, his body language. She got the feeling that he was almost embarrassed by it all.

"Anyway," Fane continued, "we dumped the bank and got away. It was almost too easy. So we did another one, then another. I began to see little things that we were doing that could be improved on, and before long I was running the show. One thing led to another, and—I don't know, I seemed to have a natural flair for it. By the time I got caught, after the eleventh bank, I had developed into a professional bank robber, a regular Willie Sutton. Naturally, I got sent up for it. I might have been rehabilitated during that first spell in the joint, but I discovered that I had a flair for something else, too: escaping."

He came up to the bars and stood with both hands dangling through them, a look of resignation on his face.

"After the first escape," he said finally, "there was no turning back."

Camille shook her head slowly. "The tricks life plays on us," she said quietly.

"Amen," Fane agreed.

Camille left for a while, but came back later that night. "I'm off shift at midnight," she said. "Anything you need before I go?"

"No, I'm good," Fane said, coming over to the bars. "When do you come back on?"

"Noon tomorrow. Overnight an older officer named Vern Addy will be in charge of you. He's a good guy, not an asshole like Woody." She turned to go, then paused. "Remember the deal."

"Sure."

"See you at noon tomorrow."

"Sure. See you."

Walking away, Camille knew he was watching her. She did not care. Even if she was a few pounds too heavy. Gerry Fane made her feel almost like—well, Barbie.

When Camille came back on shift the next day at noon, Fane frowned at her through the bars.

"What's the matter?" he asked.

"What do you mean?" she all but snapped back.

"I mean, there's something wrong with you. What is it?"

"What the hell makes you think something's wrong with me?"

"I can see it in your face."

"You've known me for twenty-four hours," she said in exasperation, "and you think you can read my *face!* Get real!"

"Fine. Then tell me nothing's wrong," Fane challenged.

Camille fell silent. Her shoulders sagged an inch. She looked away down the tier. Fane let the quiet lie between them for a full minute. Then he stepped close to the bars and said quietly, "Tell me."

Camille sighed wearily. "When I got home last night, a process server was waiting for me. My ex is taking me to court to get custody of my daughter." She shook her head dejectedly. "I'm barely making ends meet as it is. Now I've got to hire a lawyer, probably take unpaid time off work—"

"Listen," Fane began, but Camille immediately held up her hand.

"Don't say it," she warned. "Don't even think it."

"I just thought—"

"*Don't* think. Forget it." She paused a beat. "Please."

"Whatever you say," Fane conceded.

At that moment, Camille's hand radio beeped. "Lieutenant Minden," a scratchy voice said, "this is A.C. Control. There's an FBI agent here to see Gerald Fane."

Camille's eyes met Fane's for an instant, both curious. Then she responded, "Escort him up, Control."

Several minutes later, an officer escorted Special Agent Edward Revere down the tier to Cell AC-30. Revere nodded to Camille, then stood looking through the bars at Fane's accommodations.

"Hello, Eddie," said Fane, smiling.

Revere turned to Camille. "I thought," he said coldly, "that this prisoner was going to be kept in deep lock. An isolation cell."

"This is an isolation cell," Camille replied, clearly not liking Revere's tone.

"Like hell it is! It looks like some kind of V.I.P. cell!"

"Agent Revere," Camille responded evenly, "this cell, as you can see, is totally isolated; there are no other inmates on the entire tier. The prisoner is monitored every hour around the clock. He has been let out of his cell only once since we received him, to shower, shave, and change out of the filthy jumpsuit you had him in—"

"All that aside, Lieutenant Minden, he is obviously being given some kind of special treatment! You may not be aware of it, but he has an incredible ability to take advantage of the slightest privilege and turn it into an escape device of some kind. I want him transferred into a strip cell at once!"

"Agent Revere," Camille said, stepping very close to him, "let me remind you that this is a California state facility in which you have absolutely no authority. You are a visitor here—and *only* a visitor. We have official, written custody of this prisoner until Monday morning at eight o'clock, and we will house him in any manner we wish as long as it is secure. If you'd like to debate this issue further, I'll have you escorted to Deputy Warden Shaner's office and you can take it up with him. I guarantee he'll tell you the same thing that I just did."

Revere did not respond at once. For a long, heavy moment he simply stood there, closely facing the uniformed woman with the deeply severe face, long sculptured nose, flared cheekbones, and piercing green eyes. She did not blink. Revere began to feel as if he were facing a statue.

"Okay, Lieutenant," he said at last. "It's your shop." He looked at Fane through the bars. "Let him have his little vacation. Just make sure you don't get burned." Then he smiled. "Actually, Gerry, I just stopped by to tell you that we arrested a friend of yours last night. Sid Bierko."

Gerry Fane frowned. "Who?"

"Sid Bierko. You worked in the furniture shop with him in Leavenworth."

Fane shrugged. "Maybe. I don't really remember him."

"I suppose," the agent said, "it could be just a coincidence him being in San Francisco this close to your going to court for sentencing." Revere paused and his smile faded. "And maybe it was just a coincidence that he had in his possession a federal handcuff key."

Fane shrugged again. "Means nothing to me, Eddie."

"Good, Gerry." The agent smiled again. "Very good. Glad to hear it won't upset any plans you may have had." Turning back to Camille, he said, "I'm ready to leave now, Lieutenant. Thanks for the hospitality."

"No sweat." Camille radioed down for an escort to take him out.

After Revere was gone, Camille said to Fane, "He ruined your escape plan, didn't he?"

Fane shook his head. "No."

"Yeah, he did. I can see it in your face."

"You've only known me for twenty-four hours and you think you can read my *face?* Get real."

"Look, I leveled with you when you asked what was wrong with me," Camille countered. "But you won't trust me, is that the drill here?"

"Camille, it's a whole different situation with me—"

"No, it isn't, Gerry."

Suddenly they fell silent, disconcerted, their eyes locked. It was the first time they had addressed each other by their first names, and they both realized it in the same instant. Camille softened first.

"Okay, you're right," she said. "This isn't going to get us anywhere. There's no way we can help each other. No way."

"I didn't ask you to help me," Fane said.

"But you will. You'll have to. You'll ask me to get you a handcuff key."

Fane shook his head. "No, I won't." He held a hand through the bars. "Let me look at your handcuff key."

She was astonished. "You want me to hand you my cuff key? I don't believe this."

"Who's not trusting who now?" he challenged.

Camille stared hard at him, an intensified look she had developed and perfected to use in any serious confrontation with an inmate. Without changing that countenance in any way, she removed her handcuff key from a carrier on her duty belt and held it out to him.

"You're probably thinking I'm going to swallow this, but I'm not," Fane assured her. He studied the oddly shaped chrome key, turning it back and forth, over and back, his fingertips feeling its body for rolls and edges. He hefted it once in his palm, as if weighing it. Then he handed it back to Camille.

"Wouldn't do me any good if I had it," he said easily. "Federal handcuff keys are smaller, not as long, and have two tumbler teeth instead of one."

"There's no way I could give you one anyway," Camille said. "Every key in this place is numbered and kept under strict inventory." She drew the chair over and slumped down in it. "Not a real thrilling day for either of us, is it?"

"I've seen better," Fane allowed. "In a way, we're both in deep lock: you with your ex-husband causing you custody problems, me with a couple hundred years behind the walls hanging over me. Why don't we just run away some-where together? You, me, and little Miss Attitude."

"I'm game," Camille Minden said glumly.

Fane stared levelly at her.

"Are you?"

Their eyes met and held.

"Are you really?" he asked in a dead-solemn voice.

Later that night, a couple of hours before Camille was to go off shift, she and Fane sat talking quietly in the dimly lighted tier.

"Tell me what's involved," Camille said, her voice tentative.

"Okay. But first you tell me a couple of things. Your little girl: How do you think she would react to leaving her father behind and starting a new life in a foreign country?"

"I think she'd be all right with it. She's not close to her father, not at all, especially since he's had his two sons." She bit her bottom lip briefly. "But what about school for her?"

"Not a problem. We'd be less than fifty miles from one of the most cosmopolitan cities in Central America. There are bound to be two or three upper-class English-language schools there. We could have an apartment in the city during school term. Go to the beach home on weekends and during the summer."

"Gerry, that would be heaven for her; she *loves* the beach." She caught her breath. "This isn't just a dream, is it? Or a con?"

"No. This is on the level. But I have to ask you about yourself. Can you just drop out? Leave everything behind? And I mean *everything*."

"To get out of this deep lock?" She nodded grimly. "Yes, I can."

"What about friends? Relatives?"

"I only have a couple of real friends, both here at work. And the older lady who looks after Abby for me. Relatives—there's a sister back in Wisconsin, but we've never been close. I could make a clean break, Gerry, I really could. You'd just have to tell me how."

"It's not difficult. What kind of place you live in now?"

"It's just a one-bedroom furnished apartment."

"Good. You have vacation time coming here?"

"Couple of weeks, yes."

"Okay, make arrangements to take your vacation as soon as you can. Tell your landlord that you and Abby are taking a vacation to Arizona. You have a car?"

"Yes."

"Paid for?"

"Yes."

"Okay, when you get your vacation, pack everything you own and you and Abby drive to Phoenix. Tell your landlord and everybody you work with where you're going. Send postcards when you get there. Check into a motel. Call your ex, tell him where you are. Stay there a few days so he can call Abby and talk to her. Then tell him you're going to drive over into New Mexico for a while. Check out of there and go across town and check into another motel. While you're there, do two things: First, get forms from the post office and apply to the State Department for passports for both of you, using the motel as your address; second, sell your car.

"Next, check out of that motel and fly to Albuquerque. Check into a motel there. Call your landlord and tell him that you won't be returning, that you've decided to settle in New Mexico. Check out of the Albuquerque motel, rent a car, and drive to San Antonio, Texas. Check into the Riverwalk Hotel. Look in the Yellow Pages there and write down the names of several private security firms. Then call your boss here at the prison and tell him you're resigning. Say you've been hired by a security firm in Phoenix and sent down to Texas for training. Tell him your first assignment is going to be in Albuquerque. Tell him to send your last paycheck to you at the Riverwalk Hotel. Go to the post office and fill out a card having all your mail forwarded from San Francisco to you at the Riverwalk—"

"Gerry, I'll never be able to remember all that," Camille said wearily. "Besides, I don't have the money to do it."

"Get me a pencil and paper before you go off shift tonight and I'll write it all down for you. And I'll see that you get some money."

"But how—?"

"Never mind how. Just keep listening. Okay, where was I? Oh yeah: the Riverwalk. You stay there until you get your last paycheck and all your bills are forwarded. Then use the rented car to drive *back* to Albuquerque. Mail your final bill payments from there, using postal money orders. While you're doing all this, make sure Abby calls your ex every day or so to keep him from getting suspicious. Then, after all your bills are paid and you have no more mail being forwarded to the Riverwalk, call your ex and tell him you and Abby are starting home to San Francisco. Say you'll call him when you get there. Turn in the rented car and go to a different company and rent another one. Drive back to Phoenix to the second motel you stayed in there.

Your passports should have arrived by then. Stay there overnight. Drive back to Albuquerque. Turn in the rental car. Take a taxi to the Greyhound depot and take a bus to El Paso. There, rent another car and drive to Houston. Turn the car in there. Take a plane from Houston to Mexico City. Check into the Baristo Hotel on the *zócalo*. It's a nice place, very comfortable. Stay there until you hear from me."

"Hear from you?" Camille frowned in confusion. "How can I hear from you? The FBI agent said they'd busted the guy who was supposed to smuggle the handcuff key to you. I don't understand, Gerry—"

"*You're* going to get me a key."

"But you said the handcuff keys we have here won't work on federal cuffs—"

"They won't. But there's another key that will."

"What key?"

"The key that Villemaine Luggage puts in the suitcases it sells."

Camille looked incredulous. "Villemaine Luggage—"

"It's a French company that makes classy, high-ticket bags for movie stars and crooked politicians. The keys to their luggage will unlock federal handcuffs."

"I can't believe it."

"Believe it."

"And the feds don't know about it?"

"Not yet."

"So all I have to do is—"

"Go to a luggage shop in the morning, buy the cheapest Villemaine bag they have, and bring me the key when you come on shift tomorrow."

"You're sure it'll work?"

"Positive."

Fane reached through the bars and took Camille's hand.

"One little key," he said softly. "And it'll get both of us out of this deep lock we're in."

Special Agent Edward Revere, accompanied by the same two U.S. marshals who had brought Gerald Fane to San Quentin, came back for him at eight o'clock Monday morning. Fane was given the orange federal-prisoner jumpsuit, now cleaned and pressed, that he had arrived in, as well as the Velcro-fastened shoes with no socks.

"Sorry to make you leave these luxurious accommodations of yours, Gerry," the FBI agent said sarcastically.

"I know it must be breaking your heart, Eddie."

"Take off your clothes for a strip search," one of the marshals ordered. It was the same marshal who had "accidentally" kicked Fane in the ankle when they delivered him.

Fane stood naked in his cell while the marshal, wearing plastic gloves, meticulously searched every inch and orifice of his body, even shining a penlight into his mouth and ears, and having him bend over for a finger probe. Then he was allowed to dress in the orange jumpsuit, and Deputy Warden Shaner transferred custody back to the federal officers.

After a short drive into San Francisco, the prisoner was booked into the federal lockup in the basement of the United States Courthouse, where he was strip-searched for the second time, then given a civilian suit, shirt, necktie, and shoes for his formal court appearance, which was scheduled for two o'clock. Afterwards, he was reshackled, belly-chained, and handcuffed.

He was put alone in an isolation cell to wait his turn on the court docket.

Camille Minden checked into San Quentin later that morning for her regular ten-to-six shift, and was in the Adjustment Center control room at one-fifteen when the telephone rang. It was Deputy Warden Fred Shaner.

"Warden wants us in his office on the double, Camille."

"What's up?" Camille asked.

"Gerald Fane has escaped from the federal courthouse."

When Camille got to Warden Dixon's office, Lieutenants Keith Woodbury and Vern Addy, along with Shaner, were already there.

At his desk, Earl Dixon's expression was grim.

"You know about Fane's escape?" he asked Camille.

"Yes, sir. Deputy Shaner told me. How did he do it?"

"We don't have any details yet. The alert just came from the Highway Patrol."

Camille shrugged. "We can't be involved. We transferred custody early this morning, didn't we?"

"That's true. But Lieutenant Woodbury here suggests that because of the, ah—extra amenities, shall we say—that were provided while Fane was in our custody, we might have given him something that somehow facilitated his escape. You and Lieutenant Addy were the only two officers in charge of Fane while he was here. Can either of you think of anything we might have inadvertently done that could have aided in his escape?"

Addy shook his head. "Not me, Warden."

"Me, either," said Camille. "All we did was make him a little more comfortable."

"You seemed to get pretty friendly with him," Woodbury pointed out.

"That's not true, Woody," she said. "I was cordial to him. I wanted to stay on congenial terms with him to emphasize the agreement he made with Warden Dixon not to try and escape while in *our* custody. He kept his word on that."

"I was on duty when he was transferred this morning, Warden," said Addy. "A complete inventory was taken of everything in his cell. And he was strip-searched by the feds. Nothing left the prison with him."

"The day we received him," Deputy Shaner asked, "after his cell was cleaned by the trusties, did anyone else have access to him?"

Camille and Addy both said no. Then Camille added, "Except Lieutenant Woodbury."

"I didn't have access to him!" Woodbury vehemently denied.

"Not authorized access, no," Camille admitted.

"Exactly what do you mean, Lieutenant Minden?" the warden asked sternly.

"I came onto the tier one time during my shift and found Lieutenant Woodbury at the door of Fane's cell with both arms inside the bars."

Woodbury turned beet red.

"Is that true?" Dixon demanded angrily.

"Well, yes, sir, but that was an isolated incident and—"

"That's enough!" Dixon snapped. He rose from his chair. "I don't know if we're going to be dragged into this escape or not, but I intend to be fully prepared to answer any inquiries if we are. Lieutenants Minden and Addy, you are excused for now; I'll take separate statements from you both later on. Lieutenant Woodbury, I want you to remain. Deputy Shaner, get a stenographer in here."

Camille returned to the A.C. control room. Several A.C. officers were listening to news of Fane's escape on a portable radio. Details about the incident were just coming in. Apparently Fane, dressed in street clothes for his court appearance, was being escorted from a federal lockup in the basement of the U.S. Courthouse in order to be in court fifteen minutes before his turn on the sentencing docket. Getting off the elevator on the main floor where the courtroom was located, Fane complained to the two federal marshals escorting him that he had contracted diarrhea from the San Quentin food over the weekend, and urgently needed a bathroom. The marshals, fearing that it would disrupt the courtroom and anger the federal judge if Fane's problem was not alleviated before entering the court, quickly escorted him to an employee restroom in the main-floor corridor. There, his right handcuff was removed, his left hand cuffed to the belly chain around his waist, and he was put into a toilet stall. One marshal remained in the restroom while the second stood outside the corridor door to keep other people out.

"Reports," intoned the news broadcaster, "indicate that Fane somehow managed to unlock not only the handcuff on his left hand, but also both shackles on his ankles. He then flushed the toilet and opened the stall door. Before the marshal inside had time to notice that Fane now had both hands and both feet free of restraints, the prisoner snapped a handcuff onto the officer's right wrist, twisted his arm behind his back, and snatched his revolver from a belt holster. Fane then ordered the marshal to summon his

partner. When the second escort officer entered, Fane con-
fronted him with the revolver and relieved him of his own
weapon. The notorious bank robber and escape artist then
used handcuffs and shackles to chain both officers to the
urinal plumbing, and took their own handcuff keys,
badges, and wallets. Before departing, for no apparent
reason, he viciously kicked one of the marshals in the
ankle, saying, 'Hurts, doesn't it?' Then he left the restroom
and fled."

In the A.C., San Quentin officers listening to the news
were astounded.

"How in hell did he get out of his cuffs and shackles?"
Lieutenant Vern Addy asked. "The guy didn't even have a
stick of chewing gum on him when he left here this
morning. I watched the feds strip-search him myself. They
even made him bend over and gave him a finger check.
Shined a flashlight up his nose, in his ears, in his mouth.
They covered every inch of him!"

*Every inch except the false hollow second lower molar on
the right side,* Camille thought.

The false tooth containing the key to the small Villemaine carry-on bag she had purchased the previous
morning.

Camille could not help feeling elated for the rest of her
shift, although she managed to contain any outward
expression of her buoyancy.

He did it! was all she could think about. And without
any violence—except for that kick in the ankle one of the
marshals sustained, and that was certainly not serious.

Now all Camille had to do was wait to hear from him. It

would give her time to memorize the meticulous travel instructions he had written down for her. And, too, she had to wait for the money she was going to receive from him for her and Abby's expenses.

Abby was going to love Gerry, Camille was certain of it. Her daughter had lost all feeling for her father and his Barbie wife and her two little half brothers, whom she had never liked in the first place. Plus, she resented the plush suburban lifestyle that her father provided for his second family while she and Camille barely managed, even with child-support payments, to get by. What Gerry Fane would give them in Central America—the beach home, the boat, the garden and swimming pool, the custom-made SUV, the upscale private school—all that would suit little Miss Attitude just fine.

Me, too, for that matter, Camille thought, suppressing a smile.

Later in the day, Camille was again summoned to Warden Dixon's office to give a formal statement on the matter of Gerald Fane's escape.

"Camille, we've been pretty good friends over the years," the warden said before calling in the stenographer and Deputy Shaner to witness her statement. "I want you to level with me on this. Do I have any worries about being implicated in aiding Fane to escape?"

"Not as far as I know, sir," she answered. "I've done nothing to make you vulnerable in any way."

"You're sure?"

"Yes, sir. Positive." Camille knew in her heart that Gerald Fane would not betray her in any way—not even if he got caught. And if Gerry did not betray her, there was no way the warden would ever have to take any heat.

"What about Addy?" Dixon asked.

"As straight as they come, Warden. I'd vouch for Vern Addy all the way."

"And Woodbury?"

Camille hesitated just long enough to give Dixon time to attach an addendum to his question.

"I'll be frank, Camille. Woodbury wasn't exactly supportive of you in his own statement."

"Well," Camille said, sighing, "Woody and I had a personal thing going for a while. It didn't work out. There's been an edge between us ever since. I think he resented my being put in charge of Fane. I know, as you do, that he thought we were coddling him with all the perks—and, of course, that had been my suggestion. Fane sensed the tension, I think. He baited Woody, and Woody made a grab for him through the bars—at least, that's the story I got. I don't think it was anything more than a burst of anger. If you want to know whether I think Woody intentionally or negligently did anything to help Fane escape, I'd have to say no. Definitely not."

Dixon sat back in his chair and nodded. "All right. Thanks for your candor, Camille." He summoned the stenographer and Deputy Shaner.

When Camille got home that evening, she collected Miss Attitude and they went out for pizza, then to see a Leonardo DiCaprio movie they had already seen twice. Abby had a real thing for Leo, as she referred to him. The walls on her side of the bedroom she shared with her mother were covered with pictures and posters of him. They had only recently replaced photos of Tom Cruise, whom Abby had decided one day was not tall enough for her.

Back home, mother and daughter showered together, scrubbing each other's back, then put on fluffy matching robes and fooled with their hair in front of a mirror they shared. Afterwards, they made hot chocolate with marshmallows, and cuddled up next to each other to watch TV. The first thing that came on was an update on Gerald Fane's escape.

The news anchor said solemnly, "It has now been reported that bank robber Gerald Fane may have had outside help in his sensational escape this afternoon from the San Francisco federal courthouse, where he was due to be sentenced on numerous charges. Two eyewitnesses in the courthouse parking lot told investigators they saw a man matching Fane's description leave the courthouse building by a fire exit and get into a waiting car. The car, unidentified except that it was either black or dark blue, was driven by a female with blond hair, wearing large sunglasses—"

"What's the matter, Mom?" Abby suddenly asked her mother.

"Nothing, why?"

"You just got real stiff next to me, and the look on your face got, you know, like, serious."

"It's nothing, baby. I've just got a headache coming on."

"You're not having your period early again, are you?"

"No, baby. Just a headache."

"Probably all those long hours you've been working," Abby declared clinically. "At least you got rid of that high-risk guy, whoever he was."

"Yes, at least I got rid of him," her mother said quietly.

In Camille's head, the news anchor's words were ricocheting like shrapnel: ". . . *may have had outside help . . . blond hair . . . large sunglasses . . . a female . . .*"

Camille worried about it for a week. The thought was constantly on her mind: at work, at home, in between, even when her ex telephoned about the custody suit for Abby. "Brian, I can't discuss that right now," she told him. "I have other things on my mind right now, and I've got a raging headache."

"I just don't want to have to take this thing to court if I don't have to, Camille—"

"Take it to court, don't take it to court," she cut him off. "I can't discuss it right now!" She hung up.

Another woman. The thought kept eating at her mind.

Why hadn't he told her there was someone else in on the plan? Had he thought it might prevent her from helping him? That she might be afraid that his starting a new life might be with somebody else?

Or was that story about a new life just a con? Was there really a beach home in Central America, and all the other things that went with it? Or had she simply fallen for a guy who was undeniably one of the smartest, slickest career criminals of his kind?

The whole thing was driving her crazy. She now had less than three weeks before she had to get a lawyer and respond to the summons that had been served on her in the custody suit. If she failed to respond altogether, Brian could go into Domestic Relations court and ask for—and probably *get*—a default judgment awarding him full custody of Abby. Yet Camille was totally unable to focus on that issue.

Why? she asked herself. Guilt? Was that it? Not worry about whether she had been duped by Gerry Fane, but the knowledge of what she had allowed herself to *do?* She had

violated the oath of the state she worked for, betrayed the
superiors she worked for, peers she worked with, and,
worst of all, she had committed a major felony by con-
spiring with a convicted criminal to help him escape from
custody. Not only could she lose her job, she could actually go to prison. *Then* where would Abby be?

Nights, after her daughter was asleep, Camille rose from
bed and paced their little living room. What could she do
now? What was done was done. She had a choice of riding
out her mistake, living with it, hoping for the rest of her life
that it never came to light, or going to Warden Dixon and
confessing everything.

If she went to Dixon, he would take the matter to the
Director of the CDC—the California Department of Corrections. Dixon would have no choice: He would *have* to do it:
Maybe the CDC would be lenient, cover it up to keep the
department out of a scandal. In that case, she would just
be terminated—or even allowed to resign. Then, without a
reference, what would she do, where would she work, how
could she live? And with an unemployed mother, what
would happen to Abby?

In the bathroom one night, she splashed cold water on
her face to cool down the puffiness of an allergic reaction
she was having because of all the stress. As she dried her
blotched face, she looked at herself in the mirror and
slowly shook her head. What in the hell, she wondered,
had even made her suspect that a relationship with Gerry
Fane would turn out to be different from any of the other
relationships with men in her life? How many times, when
she started seeing a man, had she thought: *This could be
it, this could be the one*—only to have it crash and burn,

leaving her with the ashes of unfulfilled hope—how many times?

"You're a fool," she said to herself in the mirror. "When it comes to men, you've always been a fool."

Several nights later, when Camille parked her car after work and was walking down to her building, a woman stepped out of a shadowy doorway and said, "Camille Minden? May I speak with you, please?"

Startled, Camille stepped away across the sidewalk. "What do you want? Who are you?"

"I'm a friend of the person you're supposed to meet in Mexico City."

Camille studied her in the haze of the streetlight. She was on the petite side, nice-looking, dark haired. *Not blond,* Camille caught herself thinking. "What do you want?" she asked again.

"I was sent to give you something—" The woman unslung a large purse from one shoulder and handed it to her. Camille accepted it instinctively. "There's fifty thousand dollars in there. You can use it to get to Mexico City, or you can back away from that and use it to fight to keep your daughter and make your lives a little better. The person who sent me said you'd probably be having second thoughts about now. He wants you to know you're free to go your own way. Just like he's doing."

"Where—where is he?"

"In a motel owned by an old friend of his, about fifty miles downstate. He's growing a beard, eating six times a day to put on as much weight as possible, and waiting until a complete set of new identification cards can be printed and chemically aged. He'll be moving on in a few weeks."

"Where to?"

"His place in Central America. The one he told you about."

"I'd started wondering whether all that was true."

"It's true. He doesn't lie to people he cares for."

Camille tilted her head curiously. "Who are you, anyway?"

"My name is Jenny Revere. I'm Special Agent Edward Revere's wife."

"*What?*"

"Look, you know about how Eddie, Gerry, and I grew up together in Chicago, how the two guys went off to Vietnam together, came back together, how I used to date both of them. But there's more to the story that you don't know. One night Gerry asked me to marry him. I told him I'd think about it. The next night Eddie asked me. I didn't have to think about it then. We drove across the state line to Indiana and got married.

"Gerry pretended to be happy for us, but inside I knew he was shattered. The three of us stayed friends for a while, then we started drifting apart, going our separate ways. Eddie and I had no idea where Gerry's life was leading him until one day when Eddie was a Chicago policeman he brought home a federal Wanted poster on Gerry. We were both stunned.

"Years later, when he was a fugitive, Gerry started telephoning me. I could tell by his voice that he was very lonely. He said he just wanted to talk. He asked me about Eddie, our children, the life we led, things like that. I felt sorry for him, so I let him keep calling. I never told Eddie about it.

"Eventually, Eddie joined the FBI. Because he was from the same neighborhood as Gerry and had served in the Marines with him, he was assigned to the task force tracking him down. He didn't like it, but it was his job and he was determined to do his best at it.

"Not long ago, Gerry called to tell me he was sure he was about to be captured again. He sounded very tired, depressed, weary of it all. He wanted to quit, go away, start a new life. He asked if I'd help him do it. He knew he'd go on trial in San Francisco and he needed someone to pick him up behind the courthouse and drive him out of the city. For years I'd been feeling guilty about not telling him before Eddie and I eloped. I knew he was waiting for an answer from me to his own proposal. I felt like I'd stabbed him in the back, that in some remote way maybe I'd been partly responsible for his life turning out the way it did. So when he called, I couldn't say no. I was the blonde who picked him up the day he escaped. A cheap wig. Afterwards, I got some money for him from someone who was holding it. And now I'm doing him one last favor: bringing this money to you and telling you that he'll understand if you want to go your own way."

"Your husband never suspected any of this?" Camille asked incredulously.

"No." Jenny Revere smiled slightly. "I don't think he'd believe it in a million years even if someone told him. And, of course, there are only two people who know: Gerry and you."

"Aren't you taking quite a chance telling me?" Camille could not help thinking how much easier it would go on her if she blew the whistle on an FBI agent's wife.

"I trust you because Gerry trusts you," Jenny said. "If he didn't trust you, he could be long gone and you'd never hear from him again." Her voice softened. "He wants you with him in his new life, Camille. You and your daughter. You can't imagine how much he wants a family. That's why he's taking this chance. That's why *I'm* taking this chance. I *want* him to make it." She glanced at her watch in the dim light. "I have to run. Eddie's flying back from Washington tonight. He's been there for a week. Big investigation over the escape." She sighed quietly. "We'll probably never see each other again."

"Probably not," Camille said.

Instinctively, after a tentative pause, the two women embraced.

Then Jenny Revere walked off into the night.

Camille walked down the street to her building and went up to her apartment. She took off her coat before she got there and draped it over the purse full of money.

"Sorry I'm late," she told the older lady who sat with Abby after school.

"No problem, dear," the lady said. "You two want to come to Bingo with me at the church tonight?"

"I don't think so, thanks anyway," said Camille. "See you tomorrow."

Abby was at the kitchen table, cutting out pictures of Val Kilmer from a movie magazine. "What do you think, Mom?" she asked, holding one of them up for her to see. "Isn't he cool?"

"A dream," said Camille. "What happened to Leo?"

"He grew a moustache—yuck!"

"You're a fickle kid, you know that?"

"Nobody's perfect, Mom."

Camille went into the bedroom and hid the purse on her side of the closet—the neat side. Abby's side was a disaster.

In the bathroom, she looked at herself in the mirror.

Well, she thought, *this is it, honey.*

Now or never.

Do or die.

It's showtime.

Taking a deep breath, she went back into the kitchen and sat down across from her daughter.

"Sweetheart, how'd you like for us to go on a nice, long vacation?"

"Where to?"

"Lots of places."

"Fun places?"

"Definitely fun places."

"Cool," said Miss Attitude.

Mother and daughter smiled perfect smiles of love at each other.

Scrogged:
A Cyber-Christmas Carol

Carole Nelson Douglas

Carole Nelson Douglas's *Good Night, Mr. Holmes* was a *New York Times* Notable Book of the Year and "ushered in a 1990s explosion of women-centered history-mystery reschooling us about the ornery presence of women in both social and literary history," said *The Drood Review of Mystery*. Douglas's Irene Adler Sherlockian suspense novels and the Midnight Louie feline PI contemporary mystery series comprise half of her fifty novels, but she's also written high fantasy and science fiction. Her short fiction has been reprinted in seven year's-best collections, and her work has been short-listed for or won more than fifty awards. Her latest novels are *Femme Fatale* and *Spider Dance* and Midnight Louie's *Cat in a Hot Pink Pursuit*. A former daily newspaper reporter covering women's and social issues, Douglas has written fiction full-time since 1984 and lives in Texas.

Stave the First: The Ghost in the Machine

"A bark as bitter as any gall"
—*The Holly and the Ivy*

Marlowe was dead, that much was certain. Dead certain. The TV news channels had harped on that fact for almost a week now. Dead by his own hand.

Ben Scroggs could hardly believe it, although much that was shown on the TV news was pretty unbelievable these days. Marlowe dead. Killed instantly when he threw himself from the balcony atop the three-story entry hall in his Rivercrest mansion, his brain smashed to smithereens on imported Italian marble, a brain that had been so agile in life, so admirably ordered.

Not that Scroggs had been a particular friend of Marlowe's. Scroggs had few friends at the company. Better not to get involved in office politics during off-office hours, especially the frivolous socializing that led to overdrinking and sometimes even adulterous affairs. None of that nonsense was for Ben Scroggs. And, of course, if he *had* been a particular friend of Marlowe's, it would be *his* figure the news cameras would be tracking as he left the police station after questioning, instead of his higher-ups, dashing in and out amid clusters of high-powered lawyers, their Society Page faces now hidden beneath hasty tents of Armani camel-hair trench coats and *Houston Chronicle* Lifestyle sections.

No, Ben Scroggs was a very small fish in the corporate shark tank, thank Anderson Accounting, and dedicated to doing his job (and saving it) by getting small notice. That strategy—and, honestly, it was more a temperamental preference than a strategy—stood him in good stead now that the nation had its hungry eyes on Axxanon and its executives and all their works. And especially all their *workings.*

That was why at this dread time of unprecedented corporate accountability, Scroggs, the quintessential accountant, still sat at his old mahogany desk, enduring among the husk of stricken employees and absent executives that Axxanon's self-important skyscraper had become. He was working this Christmas Eve as he had all the others, even while the lower-level employees scurried away like mice for their foolish materialistic celebrations they thought honored an infant, but instead honored only the Bottom Line that is the true heart of all business and industry in the civilized world as Ben Scroggs knew it.

His own "personal assistant"—what a ludicrous and largely untrue title! Scroggs allowed no one to become personal with him, and no one could assist him to his satisfaction—was just visible through the open office door, her broad back clothed in cheap Kelly-green polyester.

She was on the telephone, as usual, and on a personal call, as even more usual.

He shook his head. Why would a woman in these enlightened days allow herself to become the mother of four young children with no legal father—or should he say *fathers?*—in sight? Small wonder one of them had been born with some exotic disease she was forever on the phone about. She was, of course, the politically "correct" profile for a corporate personal assistant these days: black and female. At least the pittance they paid her reflected reality.

"Sir," she was saying on the phone to some harried banker, as were most of the support staff at Axxanon these days, "there must be some way to save my 401K."

Four-oh-one Kayo! What did these financial dunces

know, except that the Company was supposed to bail them out of their own ignorance? Scroggs felt no pity for them. He had not opted for employee stock options or any of that slippery nonsense. He kept what he had squirreled away where only he knew about it, and none of it was in get-rich-quick schemes, even if they were disguised as a corporate pension program.

"Merry Christmas!" cried a voice in the outer office. *What?* Was there still some idiot in Houston who could possibly think there was anything to celebrate this December of 2001?

With chagrin, Scroggs recognized the upbeat voice: his own dead sister's son, a ne'er-do-well as seasoned at it as her late husband, the trailer trash from Biloxi. Ah! Nephews.

The fool came barging in to his inner sanctum, spouting, "Merry Christmas!"

"Screw Christmas!"

"Say, Uncle! You don't mean it! The kids love it."

"I don't love the kids, so how is it my affair? Christmas is social extortion, and you ought to know it, Jimmy Joe Scroggs. It's a scheme to keep the poor thinking they have a future, and spending it on gimcracks of the season. Great business, but worthless sentiment. What a scam! You and your naive wife from the wrong side of the tracks are some of the poor who happily will be plucked buck-naked as a turkey this season, all in the name of that ancient invitation to bilking the public, 'Merry Christmas.'"

"Aw, Unc, have a heart. You're welcome to come over and eat brisket with Bobbie Rae and me and the kids."

"Brisket! I can't believe they chose to serve that lowbrow

stuff at Disneyland France. Meadow Muffins! Might as well sit in a pasture and swill what the bulls put out. Eat barbecue with sticky-fingered brats and their stupider parents? I'd rather rot in hell first. And a Happy New Year to you, too, Jimmy Joe."

"I know this scandal must be freezing your pumpkin patch, Uncle Ben—"

"Do not call me by that commercially compromised brand name! No pumpkin pie for me, either, overrated slush! Out of my sight! I've bigger things to tend to."

"Nothin's bigger than a time when people reckoned themselves small in the face of a miracle. I'll still lift a home brew in your honor on Christmas Day, Uncle, for my maw was your sister and she was all right through and through. We're sorry for your trouble. It can't be fun to be an Axxanon employee these days. And I'll say it again, 'Merry Christmas!' We'll keep the hot sauce warm for you tomorrow besides."

At this the young man was on his way, pausing in the outer office to plant a yellow rose on Lorettah's desk.

"There's a pair of idiots." Scroggs offered his opinion to the air. One was about to be goosed and loosed by her employer, and the other had no employer, not even a defaulting one, to speak of. Odd jobs, indeed.

He was appalled to see two more holiday mendicants entering against Jimmy Joe's departing tailwind: a pair of Houston society grandes dames, lacquered and enameled and furred to their spa-applied single eyelashes. They looked like Carol Channing moonlighting in a *Star Trek* movie. But Seven of Nine they were not. More like Majel Barrett.

"Mr. Scroggs," one said cheerily, entering his Holy of Holies. "How reassuring to see you at work on Christmas Eve, even though the house around you falls. We have no doubt that your sterling reputation will survive the current deluge, and a bit of prominent local charity could only burnish your community standing."

"My house is perfectly fine."

"Oh," said the other, "Chantelle wasn't speaking literally. We just thought how this was the perfect time for you to put your house on display for charity. Interest has never run so high in executive Axxanon residences. It's a 'New Hope for the New Year' tour at the end of January, and the Children with AIDS project needs support."

"Better their parents had supported them by having the discipline *not* to have them, or what led to having them!" Scroggs grumbled.

He was pleased to see Miss Personal Assistant Lorettah Craddick stiffen at her desk. Overpaid and underfunded. All this indignation at lower-level employees' losses was bleeding-heart liberalism. What about his investment of every minute of his life in the company? What was he to get out of it but early retirement?

"But they are here, and suffering, Mr. Scroggs."

"Send them back."

"To where? They did not ask to be here."

"To wherever this foul disease originated. Not in my house, I assure you, ladies. Good day."

"It is a good day," one called back as she was ushered out by Scroggs's determined advance. "It's Christmas Eve and I know that there will be happy children tomorrow morning under every Christmas tree in Houston, no matter how poor."

" 'The poor ye have always with you' . . . forget changing things! Good-bye and remember, Christmas is not merry, it is a marketing opportunity!"

Scroggs retreated to his den of an office. When Axxanon was not being besieged by the media, it was having its bones picked by do-gooders. No doubt someone was already on eBay, coveting Scroggs's Aeron chair, not that he had wanted the blamed thing, an obligatory Axxanon office toy, more like a blown-up mesh kitchen implement than a seating piece.

A hulking presence on the threshold to his office interrupted his reverie.

"Everything's done, sir. I was hoping to leave a bit early."

Scroggs regarded what passed for secretarial help in these days. "Four-thirty P.M., Lorettah?"

"My sitter has family and Christmas doin's of her own. I thought—"

"If you thought, you would not still be in such a menial position. Why should you go home while I remain working at the office?"

"You don't have much family, sir, and I do."

"And that is what's wrong with society! You have an armful of brats that a high-earning man like myself must pay taxes to support. All right, but I don't have to let you short-sheet the company, and I won't, even though it's sinking like a stone."

"I lose a lot, too. My job, my pension—"

"Piddlywinks! Nobody's put in more hours than I have. That's the key to success. And will you be in the day after accursed Christmas, asking for more handouts?"

"I'll be in, sir. This is the only job I've got."

"For now. Go on, then! No one has any dedication any-more. There are Kmart trinkets to shower on your brats, no doubt, and I wouldn't get half a minute's attention from you anyway."

She paused before stiffly saying "Thank you," then turned in the doorway before she left. "There's no one waiting at home for you. I can see why you'd be reluctant to leave. Still, I wish you . . . joy of the season."

She had scooped her overstuffed cheap purse from the desk and left the outer office before he could muster a retort: "Joy is not a seasonal thing, it's a delusion!"

He muttered it anyway, fully deserted now, by the highest and the lowest of his fellow employees.

And so Ben Scroggs went home in the December Houston mist, cursing traffic and department-store Santas and vehicles with last-minute trees tied on top by fools who should have saved their dollars, and bottom lines that somehow became lethal when they were only pretty num-bers, all in a row, like Christmas-tree lights—no!

There was nothing light about the Christmas season, a ridiculous concept in Houston anyway, he thought as he motored through neighborhoods sodded in dry yellow grass. Christmas-tree lights draped houses like ersatz ici-cles and outlined every gabled, overdesigned detail on each massive facade (which is what Axxanon had proven to be, a massive facade of the business sort) until the Lodge seemed a gingerbread development inhabited by witches awaiting gullible Hansels and Gretels.

"You kids will get sick on Christmas!" Scroggs shouted to the upscale mansions as he drove by in his Volvo. "You will overeat and die!"

But the kids in the Lodge had never died yet, and still ran over his lawn in summer and shouted names at him all year round.

Scroggs hit the remote control for his driveway gate and drove his elderly black station wagon through. The other Axxanon executives had sniggered at his modest choice of vehicle, but he had never risked a carjacking in it. No, he had been immune to all their easy and obvious temptations now so much in the news: expensive cars, clothes, houses, women, and wine.

Still, he had been forced to buy a home in the "right" neighborhood. His corporate peers and superiors wouldn't have tolerated that much eccentricity. Yet his house was a remainder of the days before the land became an exclusive gated community called the Lodge. It had been built in the 1930s, and the only pleasure Ben got out of owning such an overpriced property (for its neighboring estates were worth multimillions) was equipping it with all of the high-tech devices his computer-nerd's heart desired.

He paused to gaze up at its Art Deco Italianate two-story facade. The city's most chichi decorators of dubious gender and the annual Designer House committee makeover hags had been itching to get their French-manicured hands on Scroggs's house to "reinvent" it. From the outside, it looked shabbily elegant, neglected almost to the point of a visit from the Lodge's Community Aesthetic Standards Committee, but not quite. Ben had learned long ago never to let his personal habits show enough to invite meddling from outsiders.

He was considered a business genius, and a certain eccentricity was tolerated . . . in him, at any rate. He kept the numbers dancing the cancan in their designated rows, just as the CEO and CFO and all the other high muckety-mucks had liked and wanted. He had never looked up to see the bigger picture, and that's what he would tell them if subpoenaed. He had seen only his pixels and his numbers and what wrong was there in that? That is what a Chief Accounting Officer is supposed to do: keep an eye on the bottom line. CAO. That was Scroggs. . . .

He paused at his front door, a copper-painted coffered affair with a showy brass knocker of the masques of comedy and tragedy. (The home's builder had been a Hollywood silent star who had married a Texas businessman and retired to Houston to haunt charity affairs and install her dubious Cecil B. DeMille taste wherever she could.)

Odious things, those twin masques of twisted features. Even the masque of comedy seemed to be screaming.

Scroggs reached for the keypad at the door's right. He needed no primitive knocker or key to enter, for he kept no servants, despite the house's size. It was bad enough that he had to overpay the Merry Maids every two weeks. He punched in his code, and the thing burped it back at him. The LED numbers looked utterly alien until he realized that they broke down into a date: 12/24/01. 122401. Ridiculous. He punched the keypad again, harder. Again: 122401. 12/24/01. That was today, the date that employee 401Ks officially dissolved, though even now their assets were frozen, what there was left of them, as their salaries would be frozen soon.

Scroggs made a fist and punched the entire contrary keypad with his bare, cold hand. Investing in costly leather gloves in a climate such as this, which only flirted with winter now and again, was ridiculous. It was cold this night, though. Maybe that's what made him shiver when his punch delivered a response . . . a deep, distant tolling of bells. It sounded as if it came from inside the house, but of course it was some stupid church calling the ovine faithful to some Christmas Eve service. Near him, someone groaned. He studied the Hollywood twists bracketing his door for lurkers, but the pines with their jagged arms remained still. An odd phosphorescence played over his front door, brightening the age-blackened brass of the grotesque masques for which Houston's leading interior designer had offered him $5,000. . . . They seemed to spring to life and, despite their distorted features, resembled somebody Scroggs couldn't quite place, but whose features frightened him.

Heartbeat thumping through his spare, computer-stooped frame, Scroggs heard them groan and scream with pain and searingly hysterical laughter, like living things being tortured beyond even the dead's endurance. . . .

He shrank back from his own door, but suddenly it popped ajar as it was supposed to. The keypad's red warning light had turned green, and the alien numbers had vanished.

"Nerves," Scroggs muttered to himself.

He moved through the house, past spare rooms with polished wood floors furnished in leather and steel Barcelona chairs and other minimalist modern pieces. As he passed through the rooms, the controlling computer system switched lights and music on and off. The house's sleek, impersonal interior reminded him of the clean electronic order inside a computer. An interior elevator door was open to waft him up one floor to where he really lived, the master bedroom suite. Instead of piping in Muzak, the elevator sound system offered the high-pitched bleeps of high-tech equipment chattering to itself.

Scroggs moved into the carpeted upper hall, passing the home theater . . . passing, then stopping and returning to stare through its open, padded double doors to the huge screen on which black-and-white people moved. The drone of dialogue made him frown. The theater wasn't programmed to go on automatically at his passing. It was operating now, a three-foot-high face in close-up, a dead actor looking troubled fifty-some years after he'd filmed the scene. Who was it now? He didn't watch much anymore, just hunkered down in his bedroom for microwave meals and professional reading material.

Jimmy Stewart, that was it! Mr. Nice Guy. Scroggs blinked at the dialogue. . . . No, not that treacly movie again. Of course! It was Christmas Eve and *It's a Wonderful Life* was a staple of the season! What was so wonderful about being financially ruined through your own fault and attracting the unwelcome attention of some self-appointed guardian angel determined to make you see the bright side of business ruin? This was worse than panhandling socialites in his office. He darted into the darkened room, hunting the controller, but when he found it on the arm of a theater seat, it refused to shut off the movie, or the whining Jimmy Stewart/"George"! Scroggs pressed buttons in a panic, not wanting another syllable of cheap and manipulated sentiment to hit his ears . . . when the image faded. At last.

But the thing wasn't totally off. It showed an office . . .

an office at Axxanon! And seated at the desk was another familiar figure—George Marlowe! In black and white, like Jimmy, but otherwise as live as he could be.

"Marlowe!"

The man stood and came forward to perch on the desk edge like some latter-day Walt Disney selling Disneyland. "This is my last will and testament," he said, staring straight at Scroggs. "I guess you could call it my 'unliving' will."

"That's right, Marlowe! You're dead, so you get off my movie screen."

"Can't. Guess this is my purgatory, or limbo, a limited engagement at your home theater."

"You're seven days dead."

"I suppose you were expecting advanced decay by now. No, I just turned . . . pale. This two-dimensional existence is pretty painful, though."

"You're a delusion."

"But I'm your personal delusion, so you might as well sit down and listen. I've come to warn you, Ben."

"We were never friends in life."

"We weren't enemies, which is saying a lot at Axxanon."

"I don't get it. You were an honest and decent man. You had the least to hide of anyone. Why did you of all of them—?"

"When the truth came out, I saw that I was a part of the conspiracy, unwittingly maybe, but it was all a vast network of links and nodes. I saw in an instant all the thousands of hapless employees whose pensions had been financed in company stock, whose futures were tied to the company's stock-market value, who suddenly had nothing, and all those hundred of thousands of ordinary souls, retired workers whose pensions had been invested in the glittering, rancid bubble that was Axxanon, who'll now be working into their eighties to survive."

"Neither of us had much to do with it."

"We were there!" Marlowe thundered over the high-end Bose speakers, sounding like Charlton Heston's Moses on the mount. "There is no escaping such facts in the after-life. I may not be blue-faced and dripping seaweed or rat-tling chains or sliming unsuspecting mortals like a *Ghostbusters* wraith, but I wear an invisible cloak of regret as heavy as stainless steel. I'm imprisoned in shades of gray forever, mocked by others you thankfully cannot hear or see. So hear *me,* Scroggs! You face the same eternal fate unless you do something about it."

"What?"

"Three spirit guides will visit you tonight. You must go where they take you and face what they show you."

"Spirit guides! I don't believe in that New Age claptrap."

"Believe, or you will linger in a limbo worse than any you could imagine, half-seen, half-heard, but sensing every-thing around you as if it were felt through steel wool. It wounds, Scroggs, to know your own failures so well, to see the hapless, hopeless, helpless faces of your fellow humans and know you put the agony into their features. It is more than I can bear!" Here the figured moaned and wailed with a sound so like a garbage disposal crossed with a demon that Scroggs put his palms to his ears. Still he heard Marlowe's voice even as it descended into gut-tural howls. His image twisted, and melted into that of a Great Dane, an ancient woman, Jimmy Stewart.

"You of all of us did the least wrong, Marlowe! You couldn't help it that our superiors used our cleverness with numbers to defraud our fellow workers and the stockholders."

"I could have helped it! It was my job to have 'helped it.' I answer here not to Axxanon, but to every last one of those faceless fellow workers and stockholders we took no notice of until government investigators and newswriters told us how they had paid for our indifference and arrogance."

"Humankind has always suffered, on the whole. Those people were not our affair. Our jobs were our business, and doing them satisfactorily."

"Humankind was my business! Their welfare was my business! The company existed to supply numberless people with services, and jobs, and some modicum of financial security, not to make its top executives wealthier than Greek shipping magnates. We have sinned, Scroggs, and will pay for it after death, as I should know most painfully."

"I don't know why I should believe the word of a suicide, a man who couldn't face his own music now asking me to face something I don't believe in. Spirit guides! As much mutter about the 'spirit' of Christmas. As you point out, Christmas is only for the rich and the greedy, and as much as you and I were paid for our services, we are minnows in the shark tank. I have nothing to atone for."

"Believe in me," Marlowe's voice thundered again. "And I wasn't a suicide, Scroggs. I didn't kill myself, else I'd be in some even more horrible lower hell. I was murdered."

"Murdered! My God, man! Murdered?"

The image blurred, then Jimmy Stewart was poised on

a bridge, about to leap to his own death, when a guardian angel named Clarence appeared by his side. The only Clarence Scroggs could remember was a clown on some children's show in his foggy, foggy youth. Or was that Clarabell? Either way, the name was a silly abomination, and irrelevant.

Scroggs wrung his hands on the controller as if to break its plastic neck, punching buttons with the same impotence as he had belabored the keypad by his door.

"Murdered," he whispered to himself as the screen went blank, leaving the room pitch dark. "Spirit guides? Hardly. Indigestion, more like it! Too many Taco Bell lunches. I'll go to bed and finish dreaming there."

Stave the Second: Alien Visitors

"A prickle as sharp as any thorn"
—*The Holly and the Ivy*

Scroggs scurried to his bedroom hideaway, ate a can of cold mushroom soup and three Oreo cookies, and called it Christmas Eve. Then he lay down in his bed, a circular affair with a built-in TV in the gray flannel canopy that had cost as much as a good car. Axxanon required its employees of a certain level to live up to a certain level. Scroggs chose his excesses to match his misanthropy.

Marlowe murdered. Now, that was news, Scroggs thought as he muted the nightly news show, leaving footage of his former bosses being paraded in and out of courtrooms silent, like a Keystone Cops short subject from the twenties. Pity no one would know but he. Nor would anyone believe it, if he were so rash as to say such a thing. Scroggs burped, then shook his head. Indigestion. With the cursed season as well as his diet.

The lights in his bedroom brightened like the rising sun. He sat up blinking. He hadn't ordered this blinding, and expensive, blitz of kilowatts. His built-in stereo system was wailing out Christmas carols. And somewhere an old-fashioned clock chimed. And chimed. And chimed. He owned nothing but modern, and quiet, timepieces, but Scroggs thought he counted thirteen chimes of the clock.

A baker's dozen that added up to 1:00 A.M.

On the sleek stainless-steel portable refrigerator that served as a nightstand (and which held what was left of the mushroom soup, for Scroggs's stomach had been a tad unsettled after the Marlowe episode) perched an aged waif, looking rather like a child with that premature aging disease the TV news shows were always showing to revolt people and loosen their purse strings for medical research. Purse strings? That was a strange way to put it. To lift the contents of their crocodile wallets and 401Ks was more like it.

"I suppose you represent yourself to be a 'spirit guide,'" Scroggs snickered. "You look rather old to be a Boy Scout."

"I am a boy and not a boy any longer," the creature answered with a certain melancholy. "I am the Ghost of Christmas Past." A small, wizened hand reached for Scroggs's fingers, which looked knobby and old even to his own eyes, yet clutched the down comforter like a child's. "Come with me."

Before Scroggs could say yea or nay, the ghostly hand had seized his own like icy, oozing Silly Putty and was dragging him toward the metal-blind-shrouded window.

"We'll crash!" Scroggs cried. Instead he felt a cold

bracing wind, and then he was treading thin air hand-in-hand with the spirit. And him wearing only Neiman-Marcus boxer shorts.

Houston's high gleaming buildings—Axxanon's A-shaped mirrored plinth among them—flashed beneath them like a river of fireflies. Only the chill high stars remained. Scroggs took pleasure in their remote placement, as predictable as numbers on a spreadsheet. But soon the pair were plummeting back to earth, humble east Texas earth, pockmarked by stands of piney woods and reedy swamps. Scroggs saw battered pickup trucks plying the rutted country roads—few SUVs here, and no Humvees—and they plunged low enough over the one beacon in the darkness, the lit-up Dairy Queen, to hear arriving and departing diners wishing each other "Merry Christmas" and "God bless."

"Meadow muffins!" Scroggs grumbled, but, as the ghost pulled him on, he recognized more than the terrain. "Why . . . this is my hometown. I'm amazed that toad puddle is still here."

They were plunging down to the very center of it, the Baptist church. This was a simple wooden building very proud of its one dinky spire. It had been a hardscrabble town and life, and the religion had been demanding and sometimes cruel.

"There is a child below debuting in the Christmas pageant; perhaps you'd like to see."

"Oh, God, no! I was just some dribble-chinned Joseph hanging over a manger, not knowing why. Having children is overrated."

But the ghost swooped low and Scroggs with him, until they were hovering over the hovel Scroggs recognized from his youth. Someone was shouting. Scroggs's ears shriveled at that angry din, though he was not the object of it, and instead sat silent in a corner, in some craven way happy to be the observer rather than the object of the tirade.

Daddy was drunk and Daddy drunk was usually mad, but this time he had something serious as the object of his fury. He railed at Scroggs's sister, Fran, a frail girl trying to grow into a woman on too little food and no love. She cowered against the paper-patched wall, her thin arms wrapped around a slightly swelling stomach, like a young pine bent by the wind but not quite breaking. The word *slut* peppered the air.

"Fran!" Scroggs cried out. Now he would go to her defense. She had always stood between him and the Old Man, and seen to his clothes and his snotty face. He didn't understand, then, what the problem was! If only he had been big enough to defend her.

He saw her now, again, while he quailed like the ten-year-old he was at Daddy's big hands and Daddy's big voice. She was sixteen, he remembered, a shy, pretty girl with something stronger beneath their mutual fear. Something in her was better and braver than he ever could be.

"Take me away, ghost! I'll never see Fran again on this earth, and I can't stand seeing her berated again now!"

The ghost bent a sharp eye on Scroggs's face, and saw the horror and unhappiness.

For after that searing scene, Fran was gone forever, and Scroggs heard no more of it or her until he had escaped on a scholarship to Houston and the university. He learned later that he couldn't have defended her that night even if he had mustered the will, that he had a young nephew he never knew, and a dead sister he'd never known was ill. He learned it from his mother, a shadow not much different from a ghost that he'd never paid much mind to, just like everybody else, after his father had died.

By then he had Latin words awarded with his accounting degree. *Magna cum laude.* By then he knew what they meant, which no one in his hometown could claim except the Catholic priest with his tiny congregation among the born-agains of the county. At university his classmates had dismissed him as a "grind," but he landed a good position with a family hardware business . . . until the chain stores of Home Despot put it out of business.

The ghost floated with Scroggs over the dead carcasses of many businesses of his memory . . . the old single-screen theater with the Art Deco marquee . . . Nathan's Drugstore, where you could call in an emergency and a pharmacist would get out of bed to assist you . . . the old hardware store that smelled of oil and rusty metal instead of the modern tang of chrome carts and computerized checkout stations.

"It's gone," Scroggs mourned, "all of it. My sister, my youth. Take me home, ghost. I can't stand to see these places of my past. . . ."

So the ghost did, wafting Scroggs and his N-M shorts over the topless towers of downtown Houston, Axxanon the highest and sharpest, like a paper spike on an old-time desk, except it was made of shining chrome and heartless glass, reflecting only ambition and envy and greed.

"I was not like that," Scroggs wailed. "Once." But he looked at the ghost and saw it had changed, metamorphosized, and now it was as gigantic as a jolly gray giant, a great floating jellyfish of ectoplasm in the sky, wreathed in perhaps six thousand dollars' worth of Christmas icicle-lights. Scroggs's accountant brain knew what his neighbors'

Christmas excesses cost down to the last twinkling Rudolph the Red-nosed Reindeer lawn ornament.

"Ghost, who are you?" he cried, for by now all this nocturnal floating had convinced him that he had either eaten Oreo cookies doctored with LSD, or he was dreaming or dead, and he was beginning to hope for the latter. Better dead than misled.

For the first time he got a glimmer of how Axxanon's employees and stock investors might feel.

The ghost laughed so heartily that the illuminated faux icicles shook like a bowlful of luminescent spaghetti. Scroggs's stomach lurched, a victim of heights, bright lights, and motion.

In an instant they were plunging down again, onto a peaked roof the size of a small county that Scroggs recognized as Chairman Lao's principal residence of some seven luxury hideaways worldwide.

There was no shouting and bullying under that immense roof . . . or, rather, it was disguised under the cloak of jollity and a rather perverse celebration of infamy. For Scroggs recognized the Axxanon Thanksgiving party at Chairman K's he had not attended. Parties bothered him, you see, always had: the noise, the crowds, the loud voices . . . for the first time he saw that it was not festivity he shied away from, but the memory of noise and loud voices from his past. Fran! Why had he never followed her, tried to find her? Being ten years old was no excuse! She had been his champion, and he had shrunk from the idea of championing her.

This ghost was a solid, middle-aged sort of soul. His grip was almost physical as he yanked Scroggs down through the acres of slate roof—*Oof!* That felt like being buffeted by a steel surf on South Padre Island!—and into a massive Great Hall filled with Axxanon employees.

It wasn't really a Great Hall, it was just your average Houston executive mansion of 15,000-square-feet.

They were making merry, though it wasn't Christmas. Scroggs had remembered hearing about this party. He had been invited, of course, but he never went where invited. And well that he had not attended. The event had been the usual extravagantly boring affair designed to celebrate the triumphs of Axxanon's upper-echelon management. Scroggs was decidedly under-upper management and happy to be ignored . . . overlooked as he had been at home when the punishments had been handed out. Somehow that had translated into being ignored when the rewards were being handed out, too. He had to admit that at least he hadn't benefited from these shameless sorts of rewards. He'd always tried to do a day's honest work, unlike most around him. When had that day's work become dishonest, and why had he failed to notice?

They were laughing below him and missing him not at all. The room was full of attractive female support staff and trophy wives, no wonder *Playboy* had leaped to do a "women of Axxanon" photo spread. Scroggs snorted his disgust as the ghost let him drift over a cluster of executive wives with shellacked blond hair and crimson fingernails. "She's asking a hundred and forty thou a month maintenance in the divorce," said one. "That includes ten thou a month on jewelry," another noted. "And," said another, ticking off the items on her clawed fingers, "nine hundred for a personal trainer, six hundred for a makeup person, eight hundred for a hairdresser—"

"She certainly didn't get her money's worth," another hooted with laughter.

"They say his mistress got a hundred and fifty thousand a month."

"The one in Paris or the one in Belize?"

Thankfully the ghost pulled him away. The wives had sounded more like accountants than mates.

There were silly skits and musical interludes that made much ado about nothing, to Scroggs's mind. The president was there, not in the flesh, but on videotape, but he hadn't been president then, only governor. Maybe that's why he'd made the videotaped appearance, he saw the future, as Scroggs was now seeing the past, caught as he was now in the grip of Christmas Present. "This isn't present," Scroggs objected.

"Yes, it is. It's making all the newscasts now. Merry, merry," trilled the spirit.

The men were clustered around the huge plasma TV screen, hearing how much the Axxanon executives had supported the presidential dynasty of the past, present, and future.

Uber alles Axxanon!

Scroggs watched, with an accountant's dismay, a skit showing the departing Axxanon president play a doubting Thomas (though his first name was Rich, a telling abbreviation) as he told his successor, Billings, "I say, old man, I don't think you can pull off six hundred percent revenue growth after I leave."

"Hah!" Billings retorted. "We've got HPV on our side."

HPV? Was that like HIV? Scroggs wondered.

"HyPothetical-future Value accounting," Billings chortled.

"We'll make a killing. We'll add a billion dollars to our bottom line."

Scroggs writhed in the grasp of the Ghost of Christmas Present. "Release me, spirit! Let me fall to my death like poor Marlowe! I see now what he saw! I contributed to the insanity. I made the figures balance on the head of a pin, when there was nothing there but air, as is under me now. Let me drop! I am not worth holding up. Always I retreated to the corner and let the worst do the worst to the best. Let me go!"

"I cannot let you go." The Falstaffian ghost's voice boomed louder than the din of the partying crowds below. "You must face one last spirit, and he may indeed fulfill your wish. But first you must see others celebrate the season, grim as it is for them."

Swooping downward, Scroggs was soon a fly on the ceiling at the cramped but crowded apartment of . . . his nephew Jimmy Joe.

"You actually stopped by the geezer's office?" a plump young man was asking, laughing rather.

"He *is* my only living kin, crabbed as he might be in that empty office of his. I said 'Merry Christmas.' It's no more than I would have said to a Salvation Army Santa outside the mall."

"But that Salvation Army Santa would be doing some good in the world," a young woman dressed in not nearly enough put in, "and your uncle has been part of the worst rip-off of the American worker the century has seen."

"It's a new century now, Bobbie Rae." Jimmy Joe shook his head, with its too-long hair. "He's a weird old bird. Never had a thing to do with family, not that ours was worth much socializing with. But my mother always had a soft spot for him, kept telling me what a rotten childhood he'd had. Hell, the old man's alone in the world, and so am I. I thought I'd say a kind word to my only kin."

"And he snarled at you," Bobbie Rae said, both teasing and lecturing.

"Snarling dogs don't bite. They just hurt themselves because no one will want to go near them. I give up. You're right. Uncle's a lost cause. There is no Spirit of the Season, at least not in his office or house or world. So . . . Merry Christmas to what friends and family care to share it with us!" Jimmy Joe lifted a bottle of Shiner Boch beer.

"I used to drink that in college!" Scroggs cried. "When I drank, which wasn't long. Accountants who wanted to be trusted didn't drink. Or do drugs. Or . . . date. I don't know why I didn't do any of that after a while. It just seemed . . . too much trouble."

The ghost was dragging him down again, under another humble roof that would hardly occupy the square footage of his entry hall at the Lodge. His empty, sparsely furnished, unwelcoming entry hall . . .

"Ghost, I'm beat. I can barely see straight, and this journey has been like riding the Viper roller coaster at Six Flags AstroWorld. Let me rest."

"One last stop, Scroggs. One last visit to the one person who is closest to you now."

"Close to me? Who?" Scroggs couldn't think of a single soul who would fit that definition, and while he was searching his memory banks, the ghost pulled him down into the meanest, smallest domicile yet.

A woman was sighing. She was hanging up a phone receiver.

Why didn't she have a cell phone, like all civilized Houstonians?

"That was M. D. Anderson," she said, referring to the famed cancer facility and turning to show the face of his personal assistant, Lorretah, ridiculous spelling! There was nothing ridiculous about her expression, a sort of resigned despair that Scroggs recognized as his late mother's most consistent mood. "They can't," she was saying, choking on the words, "or won't take Little Lanier. They're sympathetic, they hate the system. But if we don't have the money and we don't qualify under the right pro- grams . . . would you believe, honey, that my 'good' job at Axxanon is an obstacle, as they put it? Oh, I don't know what I'm going to do!"

Scroggs turned away as Lorettah buried her face in her hands and then in her friend's shoulder. "What's wrong with the kid?" he asked the ghost.

"A puzzling leukemia, but not puzzling enough to merit scientific investment."

"Is that the child?" Scroggs nodded at an ashy-skinned little boy sitting close by the artificial fireplace—abominable invention—as if for warmth. The child in the corner, he thought, and shivered despite the image of a flaring fire.

"*Yesss,*" the ghost hissed on a sigh. "You see the walker beside him."

"Poor little tyke! He hasn't a chance."

"But he has a happy family. Look."

Scroggs was gazing down on a tiny, people-crammed kitchen about the size of his guest closet. Friends and family were lifting aluminum foil from a scant few bowls and plat- ters of food. Elbows struck elbows and, er, rears chimed with rears like cymbals clashing as piping dishes were laid out on the chipped countertops. There were candied yams, rich and yellow-orange; beans awash in mushroom soup and bacon bits, the lucky New Year's pot of black-eyed peas; mashed potatoes, collard greens; a snacking bowl of pork rinds, but no main course, no ham or turkey.

"This'll get Little Lanier grinning." A woman who looked like Lorettah's sister bumped hips with her sibling as if they were doing a cha-cha. "Good food will overcome anything."

"No, it won't!" Scroggs cried. "Why do they deceive themselves? I've run the numbers on everything from this year's profits, which are fantasy, to the future in worrying about the future. Nothing computes but losses. I've lost everything, why shouldn't they? How dare they be happy when they have nothing and I have everything and am not!" His cry, however heartfelt, did not appear to impress the Ghost of Christmas Present. In a dizzying instant Scroggs was dropped with a *thump* back onto his massive king-size bed, which he now knew was both oversize and empty. Moaning, he passed out.

A nagging alarm awoke him. Not his pretimed awakening gong via the smart-house computer, but a *bong-bong-bong* like a hammer on a hungover head. Scroggs had not been hungover since freshman year, when he had decided it was not a good career curve.

A skeletal hand attached to nothing else human was reaching out for him.

This time Scroggs was not playing along. *Hell, no, he wouldn't go.* Pity he hadn't said something of the sort to Axxanon years ago, but he hadn't.

"Go away," he ordered the spirit. But ghosts, like hang-overs, leave in their own sweet time.

Once again Scroggs was jerked from his bed and his attuned-to-his-body-temperature electric blanket. Once again the dark of night embraced him like a chilly ebony shroud as he was wafted over rooftops and finally down to a stark concrete building that crouched like a machine-gun pillbox in a hill on some featureless, lightless, unoc-cupied land.

"This is it," Scroggs intoned, trying not to let his voice shake. "Hell at last."

"No, Benjamin Scroggs," a voice intoned, eerily sounding like it came over a loudspeaker, though all Scroggs saw was the bony hand still clasping his wrist like a cold ivory handcuff. "Hell is too good a destination for you and all the things you left undone in life. This is your heritage."

Scroggs gazed around at the featureless dark. Where was there this much undeveloped land near Houston? For the flight had been far faster than his first journey back to East Texas. Apparently even spirits faced transportation traffic jams.

An answer came to him: the city dump.

The grasping hand pulled him down until his icy bare feet touched cold hard ground in front of the austere building.

"Here, Benjamin Scroggs, is your destiny. Here will you go, and no farther." In the distance a bell began to toll. Houston had a good many churches, but the biggest were far too fashionable for anything so downscale as a single bell: ominous, tolling bells. A passing bell, as used to be rung for the dead, one toll for every year of life. Uh . . . this must be three, four, five—

"You are the Ghost of Christmas Future, aren't you?" Scroggs asked, still mentally and frantically counting. His preternaturally developed left brain totaled the bell tolls like a mathematics program running in the background on a computer whose foreground programming had gone buggy and crashed.

"Don't leave me here alone! I know my sins now. I know I have withdrawn from all that is human and humble in myself. I've treated my fellow man—and woman—as if each had only numerical worth, and low figures at that. I may not have schemed to defraud, but my vanity and my self-sufficiency allowed me to be used to shatter the lives of hundreds of thousands. I do not deserve to live, Ghost, I know that! But . . . somehow I still want to, and more than ever. There are things I must do, and foremost among them, I beg you, let me live long enough to testify, as poor Marlowe was never able to! I *will* do good. You'll see." Scroggs gazed entreatingly into the empty air two feet above the disembodied hand. Well, maybe you won't *see* exactly—"

"Silence! You always read numbers, and put your faith in numbers. Now read those."

The hand released him and Scroggs fell to his frozen knees. Where the skeletal finger pointed, he saw phosphorescent lettering on the building's dark plain wall.

December 1, 1933–December 25, 2001

"My God! It's my birthday and . . . my death day. Today! It's too late! It's *too* late." His eyes lifted above the damning numbers, even more damning than the numbers he had calculated endlessly for Axxanon, and saw his name very neatly etched in the bronze plague. At least someone had paid for that, he thought numbly. Who?

Scroggs collapsed on the ground, his fingernails clawing the hard Texas clay. He'd been cremated, burned in hell just the same. No doubt this spirit and he were the only people, souls, who had yet come or would ever come to mark this proof of his presence on earth. There was nothing left to lose. He bawled out his horror and sorrow. He moaned like a ghost—would he become one now and drift like poor tortured Marlowe? He bewailed the past he could not change a jot or tittle or decimal point of. He bid life adieu like a mewling baby, but all remained dark and cold and unutterably lonely.

Finally, exhausted, he opened his eyes.

Stave the Third: Spooked

"A blossom as white as the lily flower"

—*The Holly and the Ivy*

He lay on a hard cold surface . . . but—He pushed himself up on his elbows, looked around. It was his bed! The computer system had failed and the air mattress had deflated to granite-hardness and the electric blanket was stone-cold dead.

There was no wall before him but the blank, giant liquid-crystal TV screen on which he ran accounting programs.

On it he saw, in his mind's eye, himself groveling before his own epitaph, an epitaph that recorded only name and dates, nothing of his life but the factual parameters of it. And why should it? He had never lived beyond his factual parameters. And he heard his slobbering self sob, "Is there nothing I can still do, to help others if not myself?" And the bony forefinger pointed to an adjoining bronze rectangle. Those almost-forgotten phosphorescent letters and numbers glowed again on the dark unactivated screen before his eyes.

George Marlowe
April 23, 1948–December 17, 2001

Now, in his unheated, unfriendly bedroom, where even the resident computer program had deserted him, Scroggs understood the mute message. He must testify as poor Marlowe had intended, testify against his superiors who had turned out to be so morally inferior.

This he could do, if he could live. Scroggs pinched his forearm flesh. It was icy but registered the burn of pain, mortal pain, something he had not felt in the flesh or in the mind or in the heart for decades. Yes. Perhaps he would die as soon as he completed the task, but then there would be something to put on his bronze marker besides name and dates: whistle-blower. Well, after the fact, but better late than never. Scroggs struggled upright in the icy linens, rubbing his upper arms, and wiggled his numb toes.

No, there was something else to do. Something that nagged at him, that had nothing to do with spirits and other bad companies. *Heh.* A small joke. *Heh. Heh-heh-heh.* He was alive. Cold as hell, but not *in* hell.

He clapped his hands at the screen and saw the opening image blossom to fill the frame like a painting. A spreadsheet. Scroggs pulled the portable keyboard he always kept by his bed onto his thighs—*oooh,* cold!—and began clicking keys, going into the operating-systems-desktop-properties menu.

Clickety-clickety. He'd never noticed it before, but a key-board had a cheerful chirpy sound. Snickering, he raced through all sorts of options. Nothing quite matched his mood, but he found an image of falling snowflakes on a sky-blue background to use as new "wallpaper." It would have to do until he could customize something . . . perhaps photographs of friends and relatives. He hardly had any. Well, he would.

He went into the house's programming and turned on everything again, everything that ghostly hands had somehow turned off. Last, he brought up *It's a Wonderful Life* on the big screen and programmed it to play the last few minutes, the happy part, on a loop. Around him the house whirred into its low-key electronic life, heating, humming, breathing. He could hear an echo of the *Wonderful Life* sound track from the big screen in the home theater.

"Good old house!" Scroggs chortled. "I've kept you to myself too long. How'd you like some company? Not just decorators, but parties all year 'round! Party, party! They wanted in, I'll let them in, but only if they donate to the charities I back."

He finally had the courage to push his cold feet down to the rugs on his floor. They felt warmer already, but still chill enough that he hotfooted—that expression made him titter despite his bitter coldness—his way to the big window overlooking the street, where he pushed the button that opened the metal blinds.

They obediently swiveled to reveal no winter wonder-land, but the cool pale pink glow of dawn breaking over the slate rooftops as high as mountains. Christmas lights still twinkled over every surface, as did stars above, for the moment vying with each other. Both would soon fade and grow as invisible as the warmth of a man's heart when the sun came fully up, but the sun was indeed coming up. He cracked a door to the balcony that he had never opened (it was not computer operated because Scroggs never intended to open it, never feeling the need to look out on his neighbors and neighborhood and the world, but today he did). The facade of the house was old if the contents were not, and he had to fight the latch and push against time and disuse to get himself out in the crisp predawn air. There was no snow on the ground, but the rising sun had painted the yellowed sod a gracious shade of pink, burnishing everything like a blush.

Scroggs inhaled such a deep gasp of fresh air that he choked on it and coughed and realized that he'd attracted the attention of the sole person outside right now besides him: a woman below in a red velour sweat suit and stocking cap and white earmuffs with white angora gloves and black hiking boots, her cheeks flushed cherry-red.

Why, it was a lady Santa Claus!

She stared up at him, gaping. For one thing, no neighbor had ever seen hide nor hair of him. For another thing, he realized he was wearing nothing but his Neiman-Marcus shorts.

"Mr. Scroggs?" she said as if she'd just seen a ghost.

He laughed. "Out for a walk so early on Christmas Day? It *is* Christmas Day?"

She seemed befuddled at what to answer first. "I always walk at six-thirty, and, yes, it's Christmas Day, and aren't you going to catch your death?"

"What? Oh, my, no! No, I'm not going to catch my

death." Scroggs couldn't help laughing, but he could tell it
was an unprecedentedly merry laugh and, wonder of won-
ders, the woman started laughing with him. "Catch my
death? Not now, no, sir! Er, no, ma'am!"

He clapped his hands on his skinny arms and reflected,
a bit mournfully, that he was at an age and in a condition
when the sight of his bare upper torso would not frighten
strange women but inspire concern. He'd better retreat,
but before he did . . .

"Merry Christmas, neighbor!"

She waved a red-mittened hand as he ducked back
inside, still chuckling.

He had plans to make for the day. Many plans.

Jolly old elf. That's what Mr. Claus had been called in
that delightful Christmas poem he had used to hate the
sound of. Mice and sugarplums, indeed. But that's what
Scroggs felt like, a jolly old elf, after he dressed and began
planning his first Christmas Day party schedule.

First he hacked into the company computers . . . for the
employee information. Then he hacked into the city hall
files, for more information, laughing all the way. He had no
time for regular channels, and besides, they were all closed
for the Christmas holiday. *Halloo, hooray!* That suited his
plans perfectly.

It was 10:00 A.M. when he and a crew from Delectation
Catering showed up on the Craddick doorstep. The apartment building was as shabby as the side of town it occupied, but on the door a ragged wreath's candy canes
crossed as spiritedly as swords.

Scroggs wore his best suit and had insisted on buying a
festive red muffler from the catering manager for fifty dollars,

although she had kept muttering "Target" as if they were in a shooting gallery. The catering crew was grinning, because he'd paid twenty-five hundred for their food and the service and had promised they'd be home to their families by noon, cab fare on him.

A small child opened the door, clad in pajamas. A small black boy who looked too small for his age. An older child, a girl of twelve or so, came up behind him fast. "Lanier," she was starting to rebuke him and then she spotted Scroggs and his party of five, not to mention the wedding-reception-size pans and dishes and trays they bore. "Mama!" Behind her appeared Lorettah, wearing a caftan in some African fabric and long wooden earrings that dusted her shoulders and looked pretty impressive.

"*Mis-ter* Scroggs!" she said, half-exclamation, half-question.

"Call me Ben," he said. "May we come in? I've got a bit of Christmas cheer."

She glared over his shoulder at the corps de kitchen. "Delectation Catering? But aren't they closed for Christmas?"

"They were." He peeked beyond her to a living room with a decorated pine tree straight ahead and a floor strewn with wrapping paper. "Just show us the kitchen and the crew will get you set up and be out of your way in a twinkling. As will I."

"Scroggs?" asked the preteen girl behind her mother. "Isn't he the old grouch who kept you overtime and never paid it?"

"Be quiet, child," her mother ordered, and was obeyed.

"What a delightful girl. Frank and not afraid to speak up. Yes, my dear, I am that old grouch, but I've had a

change of heart. Christmas dinner is on me, and, Ms.
Craddick, a raise is long overdue for you. It may not be at
Axxanon, I'm afraid, but I'm sure another position can be
found at a more upstanding company. In fact, I will make
that a condition of my testimony."

"Testimony?"

"I'm going to blow the whistle . . . after the fact, perhaps,
but blowing nevertheless. I never meant to participate in
such heartless and illegal doings, and I *am* Mr. Numbers,
aren't I? I am liable for much ignorance and indifference,
but I can do a lot of damage to those who actually meant
to harm in their hearts."

"Mr. Scroggs," she said again, only this time she
sounded like a stern but—was it possible?—loving aunt.
"You just get your skinny ass in here and let your people
go to work and stay out of my kitchen and take a look at
our Christmas tree and such. Now sit."

And he did, and was besieged with a lot of what he had
used to call "brats," who, it seemed, had no preconceptions
about him at all except that he was responsible for the fra-
grant smells coming from their kitchen.

The little one, whom he knew must be the sickly child,
leaned against his knee and watched him like a hawk. "We
said grace for you last night," he finally confided. "Everyone
said it was a loss but Mama, who said you were the means
of our money no matter what and we should be thankful.
And I sincerely tried to be thankful and I guess it worked."

"Being thankful always works," Scroggs said, lifting the
boy gingerly to his lap. He weighed hardly more than an
inkjet printer. "And we should be thankful that Houston
has so many first-rate medical centers, for I'm sure that
they'll find a present for you in the near future."

Meanwhile, Lanier's siblings crowded around, proudly showing plastic gewgaws from Wal-Mart. Scroggs discovered he had a sneaking desire to play with some of them, although it would be beneath his dignity. Dang dignity!

And so he was happily playing with some fool computer game on the floor amid the wrappings when the Delectation staff marched out and Mrs. Craddick invited him for Christmas dinner, for now there was a clove-dotted ham, a glazed turkey, roast beef, and fried chicken.

"Just a smidge," he said, standing and looking abashed. "I'm expected elsewhere."

But he hadn't been expected elsewhere, his only lie so far, and a benign one. Knocking on Jimmy Joe's apartment door late that afternoon was the hardest thing he'd ever done. He brought nothing but himself and his goodwill for the future, which didn't really show, as the best goodwill doesn't.

He brought humble pie, he supposed, and that was invisible, too. The girl opened the door, and her face fell. Amazing, he'd never met her, but his reputation had preceded him. Well, his disapproval. How was she to know that he had disapproved of everything?

"Jimmy Joe," she called, like a woman asking her man to banish some disgusting vermin that had gotten into the house.

Even in his new good humor, Scroggs could hardly muster a sheepish grin. He wasn't welcome here, and why should he be? Beyond the door he saw a roomful of young people. Young people? When had they become "they" and he had become so opposite to them, so full of sour instead of sweet, fatalism instead of hope, drudgery instead of enthusiasm?

He was an old, cold man. He didn't belong here.

"Uncle!" Jimmy Joe was standing before Scroggs like a portrait of his dead mother, face flushed with Christmas cheer. "Good God!"

"I've . . . come to wish you Merry Christmas. That's all." He wanted to do more than that for his nephew, but realized that he would have to earn the right. Just saying you were sorry was not enough.

"Merry Christmas? Well—"

"You young folks need to get on with your partying, but I wanted to stop by."

"Stop by and, and step in, Uncle. We're playing Trivial Pursuit and I suppose . . . someone your age might be pretty good at it."

"You mean an old geezer like me."

Jimmie Joe clapped him on the back and shot a glance toward his girlfriend that was half-plea, half-command. "Christmas is a time for all generations, and we are a solid bunch of Gen-Xers. I guess we could use some mixed company. Want something to drink?"

"I don't dr—" Scroggs looked around. "Beer would be good."

A young guy in a Harley-Davidson T-shirt jumped up. "Beer for the geezer! Ebenezer Geezer has arrived."

Ebenezer Geezer. Nobody had ever bothered to give him a nickname before. He liked it. Might have a T-shirt made with just that on it. Yes, sir.

Finally, full as a tick but sober as a judge, he drove back to the Lodge. It was the short end of Christmas Day, and dark had fallen.

He entered a gated community transformed into a fairyland of blinking lights. He'd driven past the displays before, but he'd never seen them, or believed in them.

Poor nerdy Rudolph's red nose beamed from several rooftops, leading the leaping reindeers and Santa's sleigh. *A little child shall lead them.* Sometimes the little child that led them had to be the lost little child in ourselves.

Scroggs thought of Lanier Craddick and prayed that he would grow from a little child into a man who had not lost himself, as Scroggs had.

His own house stood dark and unfestooned. This year. Next year would be a different story.

But there was another house he needed to visit. This was the last visit of Christmas Day. He had become the Ghost of Christmas Future, with a new role to play.

Now, Scroggs's heart ached, for he knew that numbers no longer sufficed. Every "one" had a human being at the other end of it.

Stave the Fourth: Dead Reckoning

"A berry as red as any blood"
—*The Holly and the Ivy*

He drove to the only other dark house in the Lodge and parked out front.

Had the spirits who visited him felt this sad, heavy lassitude? This reluctance to bring retribution on a day made for salvation?

But retribution *was* salvation. He saw that now. Only repentance would redeem, and people were astoundingly willing to forgive if you admitted that you needed forgiveness.

Scroggs slammed the car door behind him and approached the door. He thought he saw three spirits cavorting on the roof, drawing a sleigh bearing a fourth spirit burdened, not with Christmas presents, but bound with electrical cords trailing computer monitors of guilt and regret.

Only Scroggs could liberate that fourth spirit from the terrible death and afterlife it had experienced.

He rang the doorbell and glanced at the redundant knocker, a pretentious mass of costly brass. Pretension. That had been the sin of Axxanon. Everyone pretending to greater glory and more money and vacation homes and high-end cars and power and a hard, glittering diamond of interior emptiness that was as big as the Ritz.

After a long while a light came on, shining through the glass sidelights on either side of the impressively coffered double doors. The door cracked open. "Yes?"

"Mrs. Marlowe?"

"Who else would it be? I can't afford servants anymore."

"It's Ben Scroggs."

"You weren't at my husband's funeral."

"I'm . . . I was . . . a recluse. But I was at his funeral. His real funeral. May I come in?"

"Sure. Share a Christmas toast. I'll be outa here in two weeks. Foreclosed. The bastard's life insurance doesn't pay for suicide, and the bastard police are sure that's what happened."

"I'm sure it wasn't."

The door swung wider. The woman standing there held a wide-mouthed martini glass tilted in one hand. Her figure was as svelte as liposuction could make it, and her hair was streaked to the color of champagne. She looked no more than thirty, yet her face sagged with four or five decades' worth of unhappiness. Scroggs would guess that it had mostly showed up in the past month.

"So who are you?" she asked, her words slurred.

"Ben Scroggs," he repeated patiently. "I worked with your husband at Axxanon."

"You and eight thousand others. Who cares?"

"I do. I believe George's death wasn't suicide."

"Wasn't a suicide? Then . . . then the insurance would pay off, and I wouldn't lose the house and . . . everything."

"If the policy regards murder as payable, no."

"I'd keep the house?"

He nodded cautiously, but she waved the hand holding the almost-empty martini glass and welcomed him in.

The entry hall had a domed ceiling three stories high and a marble staircase winding along it to a skylight high above and black with night.

"My God, Scroggs, is it? He may have mentioned you. Yeah, you're the numbers nerd with your head in the clouds. My George had his head in the clouds, too. He was going to rat on them, all the big cheeses. The top executives who sold every little investor and employee down the river. Why not? It's just get all you can and flash it. If you don't have the house or the car or the best hairdresser or twelve residences all over the place . . . George was a loser, you know? But if I get the insurance money, I won't lose. I'll keep the house and the address and my hairdresser—they're the ones that know for sure, they say?—and I'll be all right. I'll keep my friends. So you can prove he didn't off himself? You're a godsend, Mr. Scroggs, a damn godsend. Let me call the insurance-company investigator, irritating prick. You talk to him. You tell him."

She snatched a cell phone from the entry-hall table, a slab of glass that balanced atop two stag heads, with antlers. She barked her name at whomever answered.

"Arlene Marlowe. I don't care if it's Christmas. I don't care where you are. Listen to this. I got proof."

Scroggs took the phone, pressed it to his ear. Somewhere, perhaps with angels we have heard on high, he heard—saw—the three spirit visitors of his Christmas Eve.

They had come on a deadly mission, with bad news, but somehow it had become the Good News.

And the last figure he saw was Marlowe, dragging his lost life and opportunities behind him through eternity.

Scroggs took the phone. He introduced himself. He explained his position at Axxanon. He found a plausible way to mention what he knew to be the truth.

Mrs. Marlowe screamed. She dashed the martini glass against the marble floor. She collapsed on the first step of the grand spiraling staircase to the second and third stories, and to the unlit Santa sleigh on the roof and to all the ghostly overseers up above, including her late husband.

Scroggs slowly explained to the insurance investigator. "She couldn't stand to lose the status that her husband's money and position gave her. She was terrified what his testifying to his boss's malfeasance would do to her social standing, their worldly goods. She killed him. It was her bad luck that it was presumed to be a suicide. Even the wives at Axxanon were infected. It was an epidemic of greed. Scroggs. Ben Scroggs. I'll be testifying for the prosecution. You're welcome. What? Oh. Merry Christmas." He looked at Mrs. Marlowe, sprawling across the bottom step of her Cinderella staircase, behind the massive facade of a Rivercrest mansion, under the unlit ghost of a Santa sleigh, and he felt as sorry for her as no one had ever felt for him. Behind every cold grasping soul is a fearful lost child with a heart as chill and deep as death.

Suddenly the silence was broken. Distant voices echoed in the entry hall. The noise startled Mrs. Marlowe out of her stupor. She looked around wildly, then laughed.

"Just the damn home theater. George must have preprogrammed it before he died. He was always doing things like that. A gadgets geek. I suppose I'll have to listen to *that* all night."

Scroggs listened, expecting *It's a Wonderful Life*. The lines were familiar, but were being spoken by British actors, not *Life's* all-American cast.

He left and shut the double doors behind him. He could hardly expect the police to bring charges on the basis of a hunch and a drunken confession. Marlowe would remain unavenged.

He looked over his shoulder. The Marlowe knocker was glowing phosphorescent green. For an instant Scroggs saw an anguished face. The brass must be reflecting the neighbors' outdoor Christmas lights, he concluded.

And then he realized what film had been playing uninvited on the Marlowe's expensive, oversize television: the old Alistair Sim version of *A Christmas Carol* that he had seen at the college dorm one year.

He glanced up at the dark and star-sprinkled sky. Empty.

Still, could unwanted spirits pay unexpected visits on Christmas Day, too? The night *after* Christmas instead of the night *before!*

Smiling, Scroggs walked to his car. He began humming a tune he was barely conscious of. It was, of course, a Christmas carol.

The Widow of Slane

Terence Faherty

Terence Faherty is an Edgar Award–nominated author who currently writes two mystery series. The Owen Keane stories are a contemporary series of novels detailing the life journey of a failed seminarian who searches out mysteries in the hope of finding answers to the metaphysical questions that still haunt him. Recently all of the short stories about Owen were published in *The Confessions of Owen Keane* from Crippen & Landru. His second series is the Scott Elliott books, which are Hollywood historicals set after World War II. Elliott, a former actor and soldier turned private security operative, fights a rearguard action throughout the series, trying to protect the dying Hollywood, and uncovering mystery and villains along the way. Faherty's latest novel is *In a Teapot*.

1.

"It can never have been murder. Never in life. You don't murder a man by dropping a stone on his head. It's too uncertain. You can't aim an awful great stone. It was an accident, surely. A freak accident. That stone's been teetering up there since Cromwell's men burned the friary. And three months ago this very night it fell. It fell and hit poor Timothy McKinney on the head."

The speaker was a tiny man in tweeds of muted colors and sharp aromas, one of which was pipe tobacco. He tapped out his briar into an empty glass and repeated, "It hit poor Timothy McKinney on the head."

"God rest his soul," said the passing bartender, a very busy man. "And use the damn ashtray."

A second man at the crowded bar, this one standing to my right, observed, "Sure, it would have been like a bad mystery novel, where the victim has to do exactly what the murderer wants him to do, where he wants him to do it and when, for the plot to work."

The tweedy man snatched this up. "I know the very one you mean. By Dorothy something Sayers. Man killed by a swinging weight, a booby trap he trips himself at the appointed place and hour. Stage business. Not real life. Not real murder."

I was familiar with the book in question, though my tastes ran to more worldly investigators than Sayers's Lord Peter Wimsey. I was even familiar with the criticism of the murder method used in that book, and I'd always considered that criticism to be nine-tenths carping. The act the murder victim had to perform at a specific time and place for the booby trap to work was switching on a big console radio for the evening news, a perfectly ordinary thing, and one that could only be done at a specific time and place.

The tweedy man's dismissal of the murder technique as stage business was truer than he seemed to know. Sayers had based her book—murder weapon and all—on a successful stage play. Observing that aloud would have been a way to inject myself into the conversation, but I didn't do it. I was feeling a little too dizzy.

It wasn't alcohol, either, though I had a pint glass before me on the bar. It was the unreality of the moment. Of being in Ireland, a country I'd always dreamt of visiting without ever expecting I would. It was the coincidence of hearing Dorothy Sayers discussed while I was sipping a Guinness, a product she'd helped to advertise as a young copywriter. It was the further coincidence of hearing a discussion of an unsolved mystery. I'd sworn off mysteries almost as often as I'd sworn off drinking.

"The coincidence, though," the man on my right said, yanking me out of my reverie by seeming to read my thoughts. "The coincidence of Tim's being in that spot when the stone fell. It's too much entirely." He was a tall man with a nose like the dorsal fin of a shark, the prominence topped by tiny steel-framed glasses. "Much too much. Whatever was Tim doing up there in the middle of the night?"

"What we all of us hope to be doing in the middle of the night," the tweedy man said, raising a general laugh. "The question is, who was he doing it with? And who found out about it?"

"That's enough," the bartender said, slapping the bar

top with a hand that seemed used to the job. He was a big man, though not young, not even by my middle-aged standards, and his name was Mullin. He had a prizefighter's battered face and a comb-over that was plastered to his scalp by perspiration.

"Tim McKinney was a good lad. He'd be working the sticks here tonight, drawing your precious weekly pint for you, O'Rooney"—he glared at the tweedy man—"if he hadn't been taken in his prime. Didn't I plan for him to run this place for my Margaret when I'm gone myself? I won't have any loose talk about him. Nor about Breda, the widow."

"The black widow," someone behind me muttered.

The big hand came down on the bar again. "That's enough, I said. What must our American, Mr. Keane, be thinking?" he asked, nodding toward me. "And him sleeping under the widow's roof."

I was actually sleeping in the widow's bed. As conversation material went, that would have beaten senseless any observations I might have made on Dorothy Sayers's technique. But still I played mum, unwilling to brag at the expense of Breda's reputation. Even if I hadn't been, I would have feared the scowling Mullin's displeasure.

The beaky man, perhaps counting on his eyeglasses to save his remarkable nose, showed no such concern. "She hasn't an alibi for that night, Mr. Mullin. The night Tim died. I heard that myself from Constable Garvey."

"And what alibi would you expect a respectable woman to have at midnight when her husband's away?" the exasperated pub owner demanded. "Do you expect signed affidavits? Why should Breda McKinney produce an alibi at all?"

"She shouldn't," O'Rooney of the tweeds cut in. "For it can't have been murder. I've reasoned that right off the list. You don't murder a man by dropping a stone on his head."

2.

I was in Ireland in the first place, in the village of Slane in the county of Meath, on a whim. I'd been on my way from Nairobi, Kenya, to New York, stopping over in Heathrow, outside London. It would take a book to explain the Africa trip, so I'll just say that I was sent there by a friend to help another friend. At Heathrow I'd seen a poster for Ireland and decided on the spot to treat myself to a side trip, to spend money I really couldn't afford to spend on a few days in the land of my ancestors.

My first glimpse of Ireland had been through the erased window of a turboprop and a layer of patchy clouds as we'd descended to land at Dublin. Even that suburban land-scape had been so green and lush after the dry brown of Kenya that I'd stated on and on forgetting for once to be afraid of the business of lauding. I'd rented a car and driven north into the Boyne Valley, where my mother's people had lived. I'd ended up in the crossroads town of Slane because it had a ruined friary and because it was close to Newgrange and its massive Celtic burial mound.

I'd stayed on in Slane for a second night because of Breda McKinney, who owned and ran the Hill of Slane Bed and Breakfast. How it had ended up being bed, breakfast, and sex for me, I still didn't quite understand.

I was considering the question as I left Mullin's Pub and started down the hill to Breda's. Though the June night was mild, the air was damp. I turned the collar of my navy blazer up and held its lapels flat against my chest with one hand.

I guessed Breda to be in her thirties, young to be a widow. She looked younger still despite her hard-luck life. She was a very petite woman whose pale skin was set off by almost-black hair, the darkest I'd seen in Ireland. Her eyes were also very dark, very round, and very large. A child's eyes, when they were happy. A doll's dead eyes at other times. Her mouth was tiny and thin-lipped, with a tendency toward wry smiles.

She'd greeted me with one of those smiles when I'd shown up late, with no reservation, the prior evening. She'd shown me to her best room—all of them being empty—and then invited me to share her peat fire in the parlor. That invitation had been stretched to include a whiskey and then another, and we'd sat talking together for hours.

We hadn't talked much of personal things, I now realized. My head had been full of Africa, and I'd shared a little of that story, of the mystery I'd solved there, with this safe stranger. Breda had talked more of the Boyne Valley than herself, of her love for it and of its long history. She'd only touched on her dead husband in passing, never mentioning how he'd died.

As she'd been describing the legendary signal lire St. Patrick had built on the hill where the friary now stood, the lire that had been a challenge to the pagan Irish nobility on the Hill of Tara across the valley, it had occurred to me that the parlor's simple peat fire, when reflected in the dark eyes of a beautiful woman, was as wonderful as any lit by a saint.

Shortly after that, she'd taken my hand and said, "I've one more bed to show you."

Mullin's place was on the Newgrange Road—the High Street, the locals called it—and Breda's stone house on a crooked little lane well down the hill. As I made the left from the street to the lane, a man stepped from a shadowy shop door and said, "We're a priest tonight, are we?"

Anyone surprised like that on a dark corner in a strange town might have jumped, as I did. Anyone might have been disoriented by the nonsensical question, as I was. But only someone who had studied for the priesthood, as I had once done, could really savor the full potential of the moment.

"I said, we're a priest tonight, are we?"

The speaker was a big man who seemed huge just then, an ashen-faced man whose skin seemed to glow. He was dressed as most of the men in the pub had been dressed, in a farmer's version of business casual: a shapeless woolen suit coat over a rumpled, open-neck shirt and baggy pants. The flat cap on his head was pulled low, keeping what light there was from reaching his eyes.

"I bet you treat your vows no better than the old Mars did, the lechers."

Though I couldn't see his eyes, I somehow knew they were fixed on my chest. And I realized that I was still holding my lapels shut against the damp, making a Nehru jacket of my blazer and creating the illusion of a Roman collar around my neck.

I took my hand away, and my coat fell open. "I'm not a priest, I'm a tourist," I said, surprised to hear more Guinness than fear in my voice.

"Staying at the Hill of Slane?" the roadblock asked. "Keeping the lady of the house up all night, are you? With your comings and goings?"

Either this stranger had a gift for firing blind or he was unusually well informed. Supernaturally well informed, perhaps. Though I was no great believer in ghosts, I found myself wishing I'd asked for a physical description of Tim McKinney back at the bar.

"The thing about tourists is," the stranger observed, "they move on. Try the west. Try it first light."

3.

My new acquaintance left me then, not dematerializing but simply brushing past me and stomping off into the High Street. I listened to the sound of his angry steps for a time. Then I made my way down the lane to a stone house whose front windows illuminated the sign for the Hill of Slane Bed and Breakfast.

Breda was sitting up for me, as I'd expected. She had some expectations of her own, which a single glance at me confirmed.

"They told you then, did they, Owen? The Mullin's Pub oral-history society? Told you the whole wonderful story?"

"Not the whole story," I said.

"Enough, though. More than enough, I can see that. You're white underneath your African tan."

She was seated on the little sofa near the peat fire where we'd had our marathon talk. She was barefoot, oddly, since in addition to jeans she was wearing a cardigan sweater as long as a bathrobe, which she held tight around her. The long black hair that had been loose and flowing when I'd left her was now pulled back tight and largely hidden by the sweater's heavy collar. It was her dead husband's sweater, I realized with a little shudder.

"If I'm pale," I said, "it's the work of a guy I bumped into up the block. You might know him. Size of a small house."

Breda considered this while staring into the fire. There was nothing childlike about her eyes tonight.

"But they did tell you," she said. "The drunks in the pub. All about how Tim died. About what he was doing up at the old friary at midnight. And who found out about it and what she did to him. They mentioned the name 'black widow,' I'm sure."

I was still standing one step into the room. Now I crossed to the little sofa and sat down unbidden. Breda made me feel welcome by drawing her sweater tighter around herself and whispering, "The black widow of Slane."

"What was your husband doing up at the friary the night he died?"

"God knows. He was fascinated by the place. By any old ruins. By my old legend. By ghost stories, especially. He was a ghost chaser, I guess you'd say. It was his great dream to see one. I would much rather he'd been a skirt chaser. I could have dealt with that."

She looked from the fire to me. "You have the same something in your eyes; I saw it when you came in last night. The same as Tim, I mean. The look of a man who sees things that aren't there. Who looks for things that aren't there. Mystical things. That's what killed Tim: some mystical thing."

"I heard it was a big rock."

Breda responded to my bluntness with her wry smile. "There's nothing more mystical in Ireland than the rocks. The stones. You went to Newgrange today. You took the guided tour. You went down into the heart of that great pile of stone. Don't tell me you didn't feel anything, any vibrations."

"Only claustrophobia." I was hoping for another smile, however wry. What I got was another question.

"What else did the drinkers say about me, Owen?"

"Nothing. Mullin put a lid on it."

"The least he could do," Breda said bitterly, "for the widow of his pet employee. Three months Tim's been gone and the talking hasn't stopped. Oh me, oh me."

She couldn't expect gossip like that to die in three months. Not in a town without a sports franchise. But I didn't point that out. I'd been struck by another thought.

"It was your suggestion that I go up to Mullin's and get a pint. Did you send me there as a scout, to see if they were still talking about you?"

Breda's pale cheeks flushed. "Maybe I wanted you to hear the gossip so you'd be easier to get rid of. Maybe I wanted to scare you off. Have you figured out yet what your great attraction is for me? Could it be that you're a stranger with a perfectly innocent reason for being in my house? The only man I could take into my bed without starting the tongues wagging, without bringing the constable and his notebook around? Three months is a long time to fast. A woman gets less choosy."

Now we were both flushed. "And here I thought it was the mystical look in my eyes," I said as I stood up.

From the parlor doorway, I added, "I was told something

else at the pub. You don't have an alibi for the night your husband died."

"Oh, I have an alibi," Breda replied. She was staring into the turf fire again. "You met him just now in the lane. Checkout is eleven sharp, Mr. Keane."

4.

I slept alone that second night at the Hill of Slane Bed and Breakfast, but I didn't check out the next morning. I snuck out instead. While Breda was busy in the kitchen, I slipped into the lane and made my way up to the High Street.

It was going to be a beautiful June day in Ireland, which meant that a sweater would be optional. After noon, that is. Noon was hours away and I had no sweater, so I turned up my collar and tugged my lapels together, joining the priesthood again. The irregular priesthood.

My very vague plan was to chat up Mullin, the pub owner, to get an unbiased version of Timothy McKinney's death. But when I neared the crossroads where the pub sat, I smelled bacon frying and coffee and added them to my list of goals.

Unfortunately, the front door of the pub was locked. I went around to the side door, following the breakfast smells. My knock was answered by a woman who identified herself as Mullin's cook and looked like she might be his sister. His older, burlier sister. She told me that the owner was off to market, asked me if I'd had my breakfast, and invited me in.

I decided that the cook might do as well or better than Mullin as a source of information, but she didn't give me a chance to start the interview. She sat me and a mug of coffee at a round table in a very small dining room, asked me how I liked my eggs, and bustled out.

The little room was decorated with photographs. Family photographs, I saw, when I got up to look them over. Mullin appeared in most of them, recognizable at any age due to his mashed nose. He appeared in one with a woman and a young girl and in many of the others with the girl alone. I decided that she was the daughter he'd mentioned—Margaret—and that her mother had either died or taken off. In one shot, Mullin was standing with his arm around a white-haired man. Behind them was the familiar pub, but the name above the door was Carlin and Mullin's.

While I was studying this picture, I heard a foot scuff behind me. A young woman was standing in the kitchen doorway, a thin woman a head taller than Breda McKinney, very delicately featured and lightly freckled. Her long brown hair had a frazzled, overcooked quality, which didn't keep her from chewing on a strand of it.

For a second, I thought I'd guessed wrong about Mullin being wifeless, for this was surely the woman in the group photo, Margaret's mother. Then I realized that it was Margaret herself, grown up. Or almost so.

"Morning," I said. "You're Margaret, right? Your dad told me about you. My name's Owen. I'm from America."

Only the last part of that interested her. She gave off the hair-chewing to ask, "Where in America?"

"New Jersey, the Garden State." The odds were she'd never find out how inaccurate that nickname was.

"That's near New York," she said.

"Yes. I've lived there, too."

Another layer of her many-layered shyness dropped away. "I'm going to New York someday. To live."

"You'll like it." Actually I thought she'd have her hair chewed down to the roots in a week. But I wanted to stay on her good side. She was another potential source of information about the dead McKinney. He'd worked in her father's bar, after all. And Mullin had planned for McKinney to run the place for Margaret when he was gone, according to what he'd told his customers last night. Now that I'd met her, I understood why Mullin would want to make that kind of provision.

It seemed to me that Margaret and I were as friendly as we were going to get, so I said, "*I* guess you knew Timothy McKinney pretty well."

She stood there frozen for a second, only her small blue eyes—very small compared with Breda's—moving. They darted back and forth, scanning the air between us as though she were reading and rereading my words.

Then she was gone, slamming the door behind her.

5.

I didn't get any more out of the cook than I'd gotten out of Margaret. The big woman had observed the girl's flight and blamed me for it, not unreasonably. I was shown out without so much as a burnt piece of toast.

That concluded the planned portion of my day. I was standing in the crossroads before the pub, trying to regroup, when a man rode up on a bicycle. He was wearing the dark-blue uniform of the Irish police, the Guarda.

"Good morning," he said.

"Morning," I said. "Constable Garvey?"

"However did you know my name?"

"I heard it last night in the pub."

Garvey stopped his bike, still eyeing me closely. He was a solidly built young man, not overly tall. His teeth were crooked and prematurely yellow, but his smile looked genuine.

"Heard my name in the pub? Taken in vain, I'm sure."

"Mentioned in connection with Timothy McKinney's death," I said. "With the investigation of it."

"A sad business."

"I'd like to hear more about it."

Garvey had been straddling his bike. He stepped off it now. "Perhaps you'd better put us on an equal footing first, by introducing yourself."

I did, explaining that I was stopping over at the Hill of Slane Bed and Breakfast. I didn't mention having once had my breakfast in bed with my landlady, but something of my concern for Breda must have come through. The constable was nodding before I'd finished.

"I feel for her situation. She's in limbo, you know. True limbo. If only I could have brought the thing to a satisfactory conclusion. Worked out an answer."

He was looking up the hill toward the ruined friary, gray and stark against the morning sky. "Would you care to see where it happened? I have to go up there and unlock the tourist gate."

He stashed his bike in the pub's alley and we started up the road on foot, Garvey explaining that the bike was his doctor's idea and not his regulation ride. Cycling seemed to be working out for him. He spoke without effort as we climbed, while I was breathing seriously by the time we reached the iron gate in the wall that surrounded the ruins. A rusted tin sign informed me that the gate was locked each night at eight.

I said, "Tim McKinney died around midnight, didn't he?"

"As near as anyone can tell. His body wasn't found until the next morning—by a couple from your St. Paul, Minnesota, by the way. Certainly the last anyone saw of Tim alive was when he locked up the pub a little after eleven."

"The sign says the gate's locked at eight. How did he get in?"

Garvey's laugh was in the tenor range. "The sign is for you tourists. We try to scare you out of here at a decent hour so you don't get hurt climbing around in the dark. Any local knows a dozen different ways to get inside. The perimeter wall's only a few stones high in places. The old friary's always been a popular spot for kids learning to smoke and drink and for couples. Courting couples, you might call them."

We started up the hill to the ruins, a much steeper climb than the one we'd made from the pub. There was no path, just very lush grass, well dotted with cow patties though no perpetrators were visible. At this range the jumbled ruins had resolved themselves into two main structures and a fringe of minor ones. An almost-intact square tower dominated the ruin on the left, identifying it as a former church. The structure to our right must have been the friary. It looked to have a bigger footprint than the church's, and one or two of its surviving walls were almost as tall as the square tower.

"Speaking of courting couples," I said between breaths, "was there any talk about Tim McKinney and Margaret Mullin?"

It was an idea I'd been kicking around since the girl had bolted at the mention of McKinney's name.

"Not before his death," Garvey said. "But afterwards, yes. Maggie Mullin's always been a quiet girl, a fey girl. But since Tim died she's gotten almost strange with it. That started people asking themselves whether she hadn't been sweet on Tim. If she had been, it could answer another big question, of course, which is who Tim was hoping to see that night, if in fact he was up here for a tryst."

"Was he—was the body clothed?"

"Completely. Which ought to put the lie to the story that someone caught him in the act, so to speak. That and the fact that he was struck on the crown of his head, proving he was on his feet at the fatal moment."

When we finally reached the top of the hill, I was surprised to see graves around the ruined church, some of which looked quite new.

"Tim's not buried up here if that's what you're thinking," said Garvey, who had followed my gaze. "He's in his family's plot over in Navin. But this cemetery is still used. You'll see that often in Ireland: new graves around an ancient church. Makes for a peaceful resting place, I always think. The spot you want to see is over there, in the old friary."

The closer we got to the friary, the more ragged it looked. The walls were broken off at random heights and the stones they were built from were quite irregular, gathered rather than quarried. Only around the surviving door and window openings was the gray stone finished. Some of these pieces were carved quite elaborately, with twisting vines and flowers.

Garvey guided me into the maze of broken walls, eventually taking me down a little passageway that ended in a cul-de-sac. Here the walls were fairly tall, a dozen feet or more, except for one spot that looked like it had been cleaved by a giant ax, the fissure running almost to the ground.

"He was found right here in this dead end, facing out-ward." The policeman positioned himself in the exact spot. "The stone fell from up there behind me; you can still see the gap."

I looked around for its final resting place, but there was nothing on the ground bigger than gravel.

"We took it away," Garvey explained. "As evidence, of course, but also to keep it from becoming some ghoul's souvenir or a tourist attraction in its own right. It's the size of a small satchel. Small enough for one man to move and big enough to move one man to the next life."

6.

Garvey and I poked around for a time. I even went so far as to climb up to examine the spot where the fatal stone had rested. I was able to do that because of the rough construction of the wall's back side, which provided a wealth of handholds and footholds. I couldn't see any indi-cation that the murder stone had been jimmied free, but several in the top course were dangerously loose, the lichen-covered mortar having been worn to powder in places by rain and wind.

"I checked the ground carefully for some sign that a ladder had been set there," Garvey observed as I climbed down. "I found none, but then, as you've demonstrated, a reasonably active man wouldn't need a ladder.

"Still, as tempting as it is to treat this as a murder, I just can't bring myself to do it. How could the murderer have known exactly where McKinney would be standing? He had to know that or else scramble along the top of the wall like a squirrel, watching McKinney and waiting for his chance. The thing's impossible."

We were walking back down the hill by then, our view the beautiful farmland of the gently sloping valley.

Garvey was lecturing on: "You could say that little passage was where McKinney and his girl, Maggie or whoever, always had their sex, that he'd naturally wait for her there, but that doesn't really answer. McKinney might have stood anywhere in that alleyway waiting. Or he might have paced. And neither of those would have served. The stone could only have hit him in one spot, and there was no way for any murderer to know that McKinney would stand there, no way for an accomplice to maneuver him into position without giving the game away or being in deadly danger herself when the stone came crashing down."

We paused at the gate to take a last look up the hill. I said, "Three months ago it was March. Not the best time of year for having outdoor sex."

Garvey laughed his tenor laugh. "Our Junes may be cooler than yours are in America, but our Marches are milder. And our facilities for conducting illicit affairs are less numerous. But I see your point. For me, though, a greater objection is that the whole hill is sacred ground."

"That didn't stop the friars in the old days, from what I've been told."

"Oh yes? Is that something else you picked up in the pub?"

We started down the road toward town.

"No. I heard it on my way home last night. From an unfriendly guy big enough to juggle satchel-sized stones."

"That could only be Jimmy Kerrigan. He's another one who's been acting strangely since McKinney's death. And, though it's a sin to repeat gossip, his name was once linked with Breda McKinney's."

"Once?"

"They've not been seen so much as smiling at one another since her husband died."

Three months is a long time to fast, I heard Breda say. *Makes a woman less choosy.*

We paused at the crossroads to let a tour bus roar past. When the noise died away, I asked, "Who around here would know the old stories about the friary, the history and the legends?"

"Once upon a time, I would have recommended the dead Timothy. Now he's part of the history of the place himself, poor man. Try Sean O'Rooney."

"Little guy who smokes a pipe?"

"The same. He owns an antique shop, The Cobwebs, it's called, on down the road here, almost to the bottom of the hill."

The front doors of the pub burst open before we were halfway across the road. Mullin charged out and headed straight for me, spilling his words out ahead of him.

"Bastard! Bastard! What did you do to my little girl? What did you say to her? What do you mean, stirring up things you don't understand? You bastard!"

Most of that speech was delivered over Garvey's broad shoulder. If it hadn't been for him, Mullin would have had me under the wheels of the next tour bus.

The breeze was blowing the Mullin combover straight up like an open lid, exposing his pink scalp and making him look more pathetic than threatening. And suddenly he was sounding pathetic, all his anger spent, the small, ice-blue eyes he'd passed on to his daughter welling up with tears.

"How long does she have to be punished for one mistake? For a mistake of the heart? For a simple human weakness? Tell me that."

"Nobody's punishing her," Garvey crooned. He'd gone from blocking the pub owner to propping him up.

"I'm taking her away. To my sister's in Kilkenny. I should have done that months ago. I see that now."

"That's probably for the best," Garvey said, still using his nursery voice. He looked over his shoulder at me, then jerked his head in the direction of the High Street.

I took the hint and hurried down the hill.

7.

Though he'd caused my heart rate to spike, I was in Mullin's debt. The sobbing father had moved a rumor into the fact column: his daughter and McKinney had been lovers. Breda had told me that she would have preferred a skirt-chasing husband to a ghost-chasing one. That she could handle the former, I wondered now *how* she had handled him.

I was also thinking of something Garvey had said. That the killing couldn't have been murder because there was no way a murderer could know exactly where McKinney would stand during his last moment on earth. It was the same point the man I was hurrying to see, Sean O'Rooney, the little antiques dealer, had made during the bull session in the pub.

Now I was twisting that idea around, or rather, standing it on its head. Given as a working premise that McKinney's death had been murder, it followed that the murderer *had* somehow lured him to an exact spot in the old friary. The thing couldn't have worked any other way. So my job was to figure out exactly how it had been done.

If I was lucky, figuring out how would also tell me who. The reason real murderers seldom used the kind of elaborate murder method that Dorothy Sayers had delighted in dreaming up, besides the fact that most murderers were too stoned or drunk or mad with rage, was that a complicated scheme, once figured out, could point the way back to the murderer as effectively as any blood trail.

I found O'Rooney's little house very near the River Boyne. The Cobwebs took up the whole first story, though it might only have counted as half a story, the ceiling of the shop was that low. Low and heavily beamed, the black hand-hewn timbers making me bob my head repeatedly as the proud owner showed me around the place.

O'Rooney remembered me from Mullin's, though we hadn't exchanged a word there. "Mr. Keane from America," he said when he was back in his Windsor chair behind his workbench counter. "Your name in the Gaelic would be O'Cathain, roughly, 'son of battle.' It was anglicized first as O'Cahan, later as Kane and Keane."

"How do you happen to know that?"

"It's one of my hobbies, genealogy." As near as I could tell, he was dressed in the very tweeds he'd worn the night before, though his flat cap was missing, revealing him to be as bald as the sobbing pub owner. "And heraldry, too, you know. It's good for business. Americans especially are always wonderfully impressed when I rattle off a little of their family history. If you don't mind my saying so, you Yanks are a woefully uninformed group."

He had a pipe filled by then, a well-browned meerschaum. While he was lighting it, I started in.

"I came by to ask you about another of your interests. I'm told you're an expert on local folklore."

"So I am. But it's a broad topic. Is there something particular you're interested in? I can see there is by the light in your eyes. If you were as keen on antiques, I'd have a banner day."

"I'm interested in any ghost stories connected with the old friary."

"Are you now? Why would that be?"

"I'm a ghost chaser." I tried to remember the exact words Breda had used to describe her husband. "It's my great dream to see one."

I was curious to know whether Breda had told me the truth and whether O'Rooney would pick up on the echo of McKinney's reputation. He did.

"A dangerous thing to want, Mr. Keane, if you'll pardon the impertinence. The dead past is a dangerous thing to poke at generally."

I knew that from bitter experience, but I didn't say so. I wondered instead about O'Rooney's free advice. Thanks to Mullin, he knew that I was staying with Breda. So he might have understood my real interest in the friary. He might even have guessed the secret intent of my question. If he had, he kept his guess to himself.

"Two stories come to mind," he said. "One involves a headless abbot, the other a poor murdered girl."

"I'll take the murdered girl."

O'Rooney puffed on his pipe for a time. I had an idea by then how the ceiling beams had gotten black. Judging by his expression, the smoke signals meant, "I thought you might."

"She's a legend only, not an historical fact. According to this tale, a beautiful local girl named Catriona caught the eye of one of the friars in the abbey. This was way back in the fourteenth century, when many of the religious weren't as chaste as we expect them to be today.

"The friar was so besotted with Catriona that he hired the girl into the friary after Mass one day and had his way with her. Then, fearing exposure, for Catriona was no girl to he threatened into silence, he killed her and buried her under the friary's stone floor.

"But, his secret came out in the end, as murder always will. Catriona's ghost saw to that. It walked the halls of the friary until the bloody friar went mad and confessed."

"And the ghost still walks?"

"Not that I've ever heard. So it would be a real feather in your cap, were you to be the one to see her. The making of your reputation as a ghost chaser."

8.

On my way back to the haunted friary, I looked in at the tiny Guarda station and was told that Constable Garvey was off taking a report on a missing horse. I decided I wouldn't wait for him to get back, that I couldn't wait for him, in fact. I was too excited even to take my time as I made my way up the hill to the friary's entrance gate. Before I'd reached it, my double-time pace had reopened half-healed blisters from my African campaign.

I'd seen how the thing had been worked, and I was in a lather to verify my guess. Garvey had said that there was no way an accomplice could have lured McKinney to the murder spot without exposing herself to danger when the stone fell. But there was a way. The killer had used Tim McKinney's well-known passion for ghosts as bait, if I was right, if something about the passageway in which McKinney had died was true.

A half-dozen laughing German tourists were coming down the grassy hill as I went up. I was alone on the summit, but down the far slope a farmer was letting a herd of black cows through a second gate in the perimeter wall. He waved to me, and I waved back.

Then I hurried, to the spot where Breda's husband had died. I stood there, as Garvey had done an hour earlier, and took in the view. There was nothing very interesting down the passage and no view at all to my right, thanks to the intact wall. The wall on my left had a break I'd noted on my first visit, when the cleft had suggested the handiwork of a giant ax. That cleft afforded a very narrow view of the interior of the friary, specifically of a fairly intact wall supported in part by the remains of a chimney. This wall also had a gap, a square one near the top. Through it I could see a second interior wall. Set high in that second wall was a narrow doorway. At one time, it must have connected two second-story rooms, but the rooms were gone, leaving only this headstone-shaped hole as their memorial. The doorway was perfectly aligned with the square gap in the chimney wall, the cleft in the passage wall, and the spot where I stood. If I moved a foot in any direction, I lost sight of it.

I left the passageway at a run and scrambled all over the ruins, looking for a spot where I could get a better view of the floating doorway. It couldn't be seen at all from outside the friary, the exterior walls being too well preserved in that part of the structure. I was able to reach the narrow ground-floor rooms on either side of the wall that held the doorway. In either room I could crane my neck and see the opening, but it was badly foreshortened. Certainly neither room offered as complete a view as the one I'd had in McKinney's passage.

Which was exactly the result I wanted, the result I needed to verify my theory. The end of the passage offered the only clear view of a precise spot in the ruin. McKinney had been drawn to the end of the passage because of that view, because someone had told him that at a certain hour—midnight, probably—the view would include a ghost. And not just any ghost. The spirit of Catriona the fair, not seen in five hundred years.

Examining the floating doorway presented something of a challenge. I tried a little rock scaling, as I'd done on the passage wall under Garvey's supervision, but the interior walls had been built with more care and offered fewer handholds.

After two unsuccessful assaults, I was ready for another approach, and I remembered the farmer who'd been letting his cows in to eat the friary grass. He was still at the gate, urging along some stragglers.

I ran down the hill to him, getting his full attention and then some. Still, I was polite enough to introduce myself and ask his name—Tutty—before I popped my question: "Do you have a ladder I might borrow?"

Tutty did, a fine aluminum one parked next to a stone barn just beyond the gate. He didn't ask why I wanted it;

the fact that I was an American seemed to be a carte blanche explanation for eccentricity. Nevertheless, I babbled something about wanting to check some stone carving. In exchange for that he, Tutty—a man whose skin had been reddened extremely by the same weather that was eroding the friary—offered to help me carry the ladder up the hill. Together we placed it beneath the vestigial doorway. With the farmer securing the ladder's footing, I started up.

I wasn't really looking for physical evidence, though I badly needed some. I wanted to verify that it had really taken two people to work the murder scheme, one to dislodge the stone that had lulled McKinney and one to distract the victim by appearing in the doorway as the ghost of Catriona. Actually, I was secretly hoping that I was wrong, that no one, not even a woman as petite as Breda McKinney, could have found a footing in the old wall, that her husband had been distracted by the promise of a ghost only and not by the appearance of one.

But when I reached the top of the ladder, I found that there was ample footing in the doorway, which was floored with broad, almost-green stones. I also found the physical evidence that I hadn't been expecting to find. The green stones in the base of the doorway, the stones on which the false Catriona had to have stood, had been secured with a grouting of very modern cement, which had barely begun to weather in the three months it had been in place.

I was yanked from my thoughts by the sight of a man hurrying across the gravel space directly beneath the ledge I was studying. It was Tutty, the farmer who was supposed to be holding my ladder. He glanced over his shoulder just before he disappeared around a corner, and his expression suggested that he'd just seen Catriona herself, or perhaps the headless abbot.

I looked down the ladder and saw someone very alive and very large. It was Breda McKinney's one-time beau, Jimmy Kerrigan.

9.

Kerrigan shook the ladder. "Come along down now. We've a visit to make."

I considered scrambling up into the old doorway and pushing the ladder away. But there was no telling when the next load of tourists would happen by. And no way to stop Kerrigan from replacing the ladder and coming up to get me.

So I started down, the ladder rock-steady under the big man's hands.

"That's fine now," he said when I was on the ground. He wasn't gigantic in the full daylight, but he was big enough, his face broad and heavy-jawed but not unhandsome, the eyes I hadn't been able to make out at our first meeting a brownish green.

He took the ladder down and held it easily at his side with one hand. "Don't want anyone getting hurt, do we?" he asked.

I was thinking about making a run for it when he reached out and grabbed my arm, saying, "We're off, then."

Once we were outside the friary, he tossed the ladder onto the ground. I wouldn't have been surprised if he had tied it into a bow first, my fear having granted him such epic qualities. In reality, his grip on my arm was almost gentle. All the same, I didn't see me shrugging it off.

When we reached the gate at the bottom of the grassy

slope, Kerrigan released my arm and put his massive one around my shoulders. We were two pals then, out for a stroll. That disguise would only work on people who didn't come within earshot, since I planned to yell for help to the first passerby we met, in town.

Kerrigan countered that by not taking us through town. We struck off across the field opposite the friary. There were cows in this field, too, but they wisely made way for my guide, who chatted as we walked.

"Didn't take my advice about the west, did you, Mr. Keane? You missed some sights, let me tell you. The Cliffs of Mohr, say. You not being afraid of heights, you could have done some fine scampering on those. And the Connemara Peninsula. They've whole mountains of stone out there, and the ground around them so rough and wild it makes this little valley of ours look like a doily some grandmother needled up."

"If we're going that far," I said, "we should stop for my car."

I felt Kerrigan's booming laugh through my shoulder, which was jammed against his chest.

"We're not going that far. We've a visit to make, as I said. A meeting to attend. You have, that is."

"Who am I meeting? Tim McKinney?"

Neither of us laughed at that or spoke again for a time. I could see by then that we were circling the town, Kerrigan's intention evidently being to approach it from a safer side. Sure enough, shortly after we'd crossed the Newgrange road, we headed up into Slane, into a crooked lane I knew fairly well, the lane that held Breda McKinney's house.

Outside her door, Kerrigan released my shoulders and

seized my arm again. This time there was nothing gentle about his grip.

"Listen," he said. In the filtered light of the lane, his eyes had lost their brownish shading and looked quite green. As green and as hard as the stones of the haunted doorway. "You're going inside to talk with her. I'm staying out here, but don't even think about slipping out the back. I'll be watching through the window. If I see you leave the parlor, I'll be on you faster than the next lie can come to your lips.

"First, though, there's something I want to say. I love Breda. I loved her when she was married to my friend Tim, though it damned my soul to do it. Tim's death should have freed us, freed Breda and me, but it didn't. Breda could only see our sin after that, not our love. She's been punishing herself for that sin ever since. And me with her. You're the latest punishment for me. The only reason you have a tooth left in your head is that I intend to stand my punishment like a man, to say every *Ave* of my penance and so get through to the end of it.

"Now go in there and talk to her. And mind what I said about bolting."

10.

Breda was dressed like a widow today, in a black sweater and slacks. At her neck was a circular silver pin that bore the spiral design I'd seen over and over again at the Celtic tomb in Newgrange. Her black hair was flowing freely again and looked like a nun's veil against her very pale face.

"It's nearly eleven, Owen," she said. We were standing on opposite ends of her hooked rug, facing each other like fighters before the bell. "Time to check out!"

"So to speak."

She let that one pass. "Whatever have you been up to this morning?"

She had to know the answer to that, since she'd known where to send her trained ape to nab me. But I played along. "I've been solving your husband's murder. It was murder, by the way. Tim was lured up to the old friary by the promise of a ghost, so you were right about the murder weapon being something mystical. And it wasn't just any ghost. It was one so rare that it would have established his reputation as a ghost chaser."

"Lured by who?"

I shrugged. "Some drinking buddy." I had a candidate in mind: the man whose grip I could still feel around my left biceps. I could easily picture Kerrigan slipping McKinney the tall tale, explaining that he'd been up to the ruins with some willing girl when Catriona had appeared and scared them both out of the mood. If McKinney had even needed that much convincing.

"And your husband didn't die disappointed. He saw his ghost just before he was killed. That is, he saw his murderer's accomplice, a woman, maybe done up in white, floating in an old doorway twenty feet above the ground."

"You surely don't suspect me of that, Owen? You of all people."

"Me of all people."

"Why? Why would I do it?"

I started to glance toward the window Kerrigan was steaming up and checked myself, afraid that even a stray glance might draw him inside. "To be free of McKinney," I said.

"We've divorce now in Ireland. We don't need to kill our spouses to be free of them. And don't say it was for money. There was no money. Tim's uncle's illness saw to that. This house has always been mine, a legacy from my mother. And don't say it was for the insurance, either, for there wasn't any of that. Though Tim spoke of insurance often over those last few days. The idea of it seemed to be haunting him. I've wondered since if he hadn't had some premonition of his death. But he took none out, I checked."

I decided that she was trying to distract me with all the talk of money and insurance. And I wouldn't be distracted. "How about jealousy for a motive? I've found out that Tim was cheating on you. Suppose you found out three months back? Would that be motive enough?"

"Timmy cheating?" Breda asked, almost hopeful. "Who with?"

"Margaret Mullin."

I thought Breda's laugh would bring Kerrigan charging in. It was that loud and it had that much pain in it.

"Maggie? That simple thing? You must be daft. She and Tim were like cousins. Wasn't Tim's uncle Maggie's godfather and her father's partner? Weren't Tim and Maggie raised together almost? Years back, Uncle Seamus and Mullin tried to push them together, but nothing happened. It would have been better for Tim if something had, if he had fallen in love with Maggie and married her. Then he wouldn't have been cheated out of his share of the pub."

"Your husband's uncle was Mullin's partner?"

"Yes, Seamus Carlin, Tim's mother's brother."

The white-haired man in the old photo in Mullin's house. "How was your husband cheated?"

"He wasn't, really. That's only my anger talking. Tim was supposed to inherit half of the pub. That's what Uncle Seamus always said. But the poor man's last illness left a mountain of bills and no money in the bank. Tim had no choice but to sell his interest in the pub. Mullin gave him more than a fair price and kept Tim on as barman, but it was a cruel blow still. Tim was never the same man afterward. Not to me or anyone else. Our troubles all started then."

"That's when you turned to Kerrigan."

I think I hurt her worse with that than I had with the accusation of murder.

"You of all people," she said again. "My champion. Thinking the worst of me." She covered her face with her hands and started to sway slightly. "What have I done?"

I was asking myself the same question. I'd finally understood why Breda had taken me into her bed. It wasn't just for company or for sex. It wasn't even just as a penance, for herself or for Kerrigan. It was because, on that first night, during our long talk by the fire, I'd described solving a mystery in Africa. She'd set me the task of solving a mystery for her, not by asking me to do it but simply by sending me up to the pub to hear about it. And I'd ended up accusing her, as everyone else in the village had done. Me of all people, her somewhat slow champion.

I gently drew her hands away from her face. "Tell me what your husband said about insurance before he died."

"What? Nothing really. I woke up one night and he was sitting up beside me, muttering the word insurance like it had come to him in a dream. A day or two later, I happened upon him just banging up the phone. He'd only say he'd been talking to an insurance company, but not what they'd been talking about. After he died, I found a list of insurance companies with check marks against some of the names. I called them all, but none had issued him a policy. He must only have been after quotes or something."

"Or something," I repeated.

The front door opened. Through the narrow opening I could see Jimmy Kerrigan and a second man who had one of Kerrigan's arms pinned behind his back. It was Constable Garvey.

"I heard about your little hike with Jimmy here," the policeman said. "One of our shut-ins saw most of it through her window. I thought I'd better come down and see how you were. Will we be discussing charges at all?"

"Yes," I said, "but not against Kerrigan. You'd better get up to the pub and stop Mullin before he takes his daughter away."

11.

As it turned out, Garvey only just made it. Mullin had his daughter packed in the car and ready to go when the constable trotted up. Mullin then tried to drag Maggie back inside the pub, but with Kerrigan as his backup, Garvey had little trouble separating the girl from her father and questioning her. I sat in.

We had our talk in the pub's dining room and photo gallery. It wasn't necessary for the constable to trick Maggie or break her down. Her father had frightened her thoroughly, and she was more than ready to talk.

She told us that Seamus Carlin hadn't died deep in debt, as Tim McKinney and the rest of the village had been told. Carlin had had an insurance policy set aside to pay his last bills and secure his half of the pub for his nephew. But Carlin's executor, Mullin, had hidden the policy away in order to swindle McKinney while pretending to be his benefactor. Somehow McKinney had gotten on the scent of that policy. When Mullin learned that the wronged man was calling insurance companies, he'd worked out a plan to kill him. The pub owner had whispered the ghost story into McKinney's ear. Maggie herself had played Catriona, told by her father beforehand that it was a joke and afterward that it was a joke gone bad.

She'd long suspected the truth about that night, but had been afraid to speak.

Later that day Constable Garvey stopped by as I was stowing my bag in my rental car in the lane outside the Hill of Slane Bed and Breakfast.

"Leaving so soon, Mr. Keane? You solve our mystery for us, secure my promotion to sergeant, and then ride off like that masked fellow on the television?"

"Heigh-ho, Silver," I said, slamming the trunk closed.

"You'll be pleased to hear that Mullin has confessed. Not much point in him holding out after all Maggie told us. It was clever of her dad to pretend to admit to an affair between the girl and McKinney while he was attacking you this morning. Fooled me, I must admit."

"He had to have an excuse for taking her away," I said. "He couldn't trust her any longer. She was too close to cracking."

"Do you suppose he would have hurt Maggie? Silenced her for good, I mean, his own daughter?"

"I don't know."

Garvey sighed. "I don't suppose we ever will know. I took a walk up to the friary and saw that cement work you found in the old doorway. A fine job of masonry. But why did Mullin go to that length? The promise of Catriona alone would have been enough to get Tim in the fatal spot. Mullin didn't have to provide a show."

"The promise would have gotten McKinney there, but would it have distracted him while Mullin was tipping the stone? That had to have made some noise, even if Mullin had had the stone propped up and ready. So Mullin needed a diversion, and to get it, he was willing to risk his daughter's neck. To me, that suggests that she was also at risk today."

Garvey's yellow smile faded out for a moment and then returned. "But I've forgotten to tell you something else I found up there, something you missed: a fat eyebolt stuck in the stone halfway up one side of the doorway. Put there by Mullin to secure a safety line for his daughter. He was looking out for her, you see. So maybe he wouldn't have harmed her after all."

"You're too sentimental to be a policeman," I said.

He laughed. "In New York, maybe. But here . . ."

We looked down toward the valley Kerrigan had compared to a grandmother's doily, to the truncated view of the valley offered by the open end of the lane. At that moment the view included a couple walking hand in hand, a courting couple Garvey might have called the mismatched pair, the giant man and the tiny woman.

"Things seem to have worked out for the best," I said, managing to sound cool and indifferent to my own ear.

But not to Garvey's. "Who's too sentimental for this line of work? Sail home, Mr. Keane."

Tricks

Steve Hockensmith

Steve Hockensmith has covered pop culture and the film industry for *The Hollywood Reporter, The Chicago Tribune, The Fort Worth Star-Telegram, Newsday, Total Movie,* and other publications. In 1999, he began writing mysteries, soon becoming a regular contributor to both *Alfred Hitchcock's Mystery Magazine* and *Ellery Queen's Mystery Magazine.* His first published mystery story, "Erie's Last Day," won the Short Mystery Fiction Society's Derringer Award and appeared in *Best American Mystery Stories 2001.* He is also the creator of two very different heroes: mystery-solving cowboys Big Red and Old Red Amlingmeyer. The Sherlock Holmes-worshipping drovers returned to *Ellery Queen* pages in the February 2005 issue. In addition, he's completed one novel about their adventures (to be published in 2006 by St. Martin's Minotaur) and has begun writing another.

No tricks. That was Larry Erie's goal for Halloween. No toilet paper in his trees. No soap on his car. No rotten eggs splattered against the side of his house.

The year before, Erie had been in a daze. Newly widowed, newly retired, he hadn't even realized it was Halloween until the doorbell rang and he found Batman, Yoda, and a Powerpuff Girl on his front porch. The only "treats" he had on hand were Oreo cookies, so that's what they got. When those ran out, he tried giving away bananas, but most of the kids refused to take them. After a while, Erie just turned off the lights and stopped answering the doorbell.

The next morning, he had to hose down the front of the house, drive to a carwash, and pick long sheets of Charmin from the branches of his elm trees.

So this year, Erie was prepared. He'd asked Andrew Smith, one of the few teenagers he knew, what kind of treats kids really want.

"Everybody loves Snickers," Andrew told him. "And Reese's Peanut Butter Cups. What you don't want to give out is that cheap chewy crap in the orange-and-black wrappers. Or fruit. Man, that'll get you egged before midnight!"

Erie figured Andrew knew what he was talking about. He was a troubled seventeen-year-old his buddy Bass had informally adopted, and Erie had a hunch the kid had thrown more than a few rotten eggs himself over the years. So he followed Andrew's advice, and the day before Halloween he'd bought enough Snickers and Reese's Peanut Butter Cups to feed a small army—which was exactly how Erie thought of trick-or-treaters. They were like little Vikings who invade once a year, sacking and pillaging the villages that don't give in to their demands for candy.

Come Halloween morning, Erie was sitting in his kitchen sipping coffee and munching on a Snickers, figuring there were more than enough to get him through the day unscathed. Then the phone rang.

"Hello?"

"Morning, Larry! Cy Reed here. I was wondering if you were up to anything just now."

"Uhhh . . . no. Not really."

"Good! Why don't you come on over to the zoo then? I've got a little problem that could use the Larry Erie touch."

"Oh. What kind of problem?"

"I'll fill you in when you get here. So I'll see you in—what? Fifteen minutes maybe?"

"Well, I—"

"Alright, twenty then. It's a bit of an emergency, so the sooner the better. And of course I know I can rely on your legendary discretion."

"Oh. Sure. But I—"

"Great! See you soon!"

Click.

Erie hung up, then simply stood there, staring at the phone. After a few seconds, he turned away and poured himself more coffee. Caffeine, that's what he needed. Because he wasn't sure if that phone call had been real or a dream.

The first and last time Erie had spoken to Cy Reed had been six weeks before. A neighborhood girl had asked Erie to track down her dog, and the trail led to a couple of hard-core rednecks who picked up beer money selling roadkill to the local zoo. When they couldn't find enough dead deer and half-flattened skunks, it turned out, they supplemented their haul with people's pets. So Erie had marched into the Hoosier Zoological Garden and Wildlife Refuge, cornered the man in charge, and announced that if he found out any more dogs and cats were being turned into tiger chow, he was going to take the story straight to the *Herald-Times*.

The man in charge was Cy Reed, and his reaction wasn't the one Erie had expected. He didn't deny everything. He didn't throw around words like "slander" and "libel" and "lawsuit." He didn't call for security guards to come drag Erie away. Instead he nodded sadly and said, "Don't worry, Mr. Erie. It won't happen again."

They were in Reed's office, and around them on the walls were pictures of the zoo director with local politicians and celebrities and well-dressed men and women Erie assumed were big-time donors. Reed had been a River City fixture for years, showing up on call-in shows and at street fairs and parades, usually with a parrot on his shoulder or a lion cub in his lap, always shilling for the Hoosier Zoo.

A man like that had to be smooth. He had to know how to tell people what they wanted to hear. Erie fixed him with a hard gaze, unwilling to let his guard down. "Really?"

"Really," Reed said. He was an elderly man, perhaps a full decade older than Erie, and he seemed to shrivel into an empty husk in the blink of an eye. "I'm not as sharp as I used to be. The details around here—they're getting harder to keep track of every day. So I rely on my people. And . . . you know we're a small zoo. We don't have money just lying around. So people look for ways to cut corners. Sometimes they—"

Reed banged the palm of his hand on the desk before him, and suddenly he seemed years younger.

"But those are excuses. Here's what you want to hear. I've been told all about that 'meat' we bought, and it sickened me as much as it sickened you. The appropriate parties have been disciplined, and new rules have been put in place to ensure that nothing like this ever happens again."

Erie had learned a lot during his thirty-three years as a cop, and one of the most useful was how to spot a liar. But as much as he sensed that Reed was a professional BSer, Erie couldn't detect any B.S. in what the man had just said.

"Good," Erie said. "That is what I wanted to hear."

"So we can consider this matter closed?"

Erie knew what that meant. Reed wasn't really asking whether "the matter" would stay closed. He was asking about Erie's mouth.

"Like I said before, as long as I don't hear about anything else like this . . ." Erie shrugged. "Sure. It's closed."

Reed stood up and reached a withered hand across the desk to Erie. Erie took it, and they shook.

"I'm glad we understand each other," Reed said. He stepped around his desk. "You're a private detective, you say."

It didn't sound like a question, so Erie didn't treat it like one. If he had his answer would have been, "Occasionally," which always led to follow-up questions Erie didn't like. He was retired and he had nothing better to do and sometimes things happened, that's all. It always sounded dumb to say it.

Reed pointed at one of the framed photographs on the wall. "So tell me, Mr. Private Eye. Who do you think that is?"

Erie squinted at the picture, then turned to Reed and smiled. "That would be you. With Marlin Perkins."

Reed grinned. "You're good. I'd say that young man up there looks about as much like me as an egg looks like a pile of chicken bones. You know, I worked for ol' Marlin at the Lincoln Park Zoo up in Chicago. A fine man. He told me something once I've never forgotten . . ."

"Ol' Marlin" had said a lot of interesting things, as it turned out. Erie politely listened to Reed spin tales for almost half an hour before a portly, bearded man walked in without knocking and started handing Reed papers to sign.

"Sorry, Larry. Duty calls," Reed had said, and Erie left the zoo actually liking the man.

And now, a month and a half later, he was going back to see Reed again. On his way to the zoo, Erie wondered exactly what kind of problem would require "the Larry Erie touch."

When he walked up to the front gate, a zoo employee was washing something that looked like blood off the turnstiles.

"You Leary?" the woman asked him.

"Uhhh, no. Not quite. Larry Erie."

"Yeah, you're the guy. Overbeck said you could take a look at this if you got here before I was done."

She slapped her sponge into a bucket of pink suds. The water sloshed, sending the smell of ammonia into the air. The woman leaned against the ticket booth nearby, pulled off her rubber gloves, and lit a cigarette.

"Who's Overbeck?"

"Assistant director," she said. "Go on. Have at it."

"What exactly am I having at?"

The woman shrugged and blew out a cloud of smoke. "I don't think I'm supposed to have an opinion," she said.

Erie leaned in close to the metal bars of the turnstiles. There were three sets of three, rising from ankle level to waist level to shoulder level. They were wrapped in a cage of more bars, and the only way for a paying customer to get in or out of the zoo was to step up to the turnstiles, grab one, and move forward, like using a revolving door. Most of the red smears were on one of the middle bars—where someone would take hold and push. The smears looked like they'd been fingerprints before the ammonia began working on them.

"Who told you to wipe this off?"

"Overbeck."

Erie looked at the bars again, scowling. If some kind of crime had been committed, why destroy crucial evidence?

"It's ten-thirty," the woman said, answering the question she could read on his face. "We open in half an hour."

"Ah-ha. Right."

"You done there?"

"Yeah, I guess."

"Then come on in. They're waiting for you in the Monkey House."

Erie moved through the turnstiles by using his foot to push the lowest bar. He didn't ask for directions. He could have found his destination blindfolded thanks to the unmistakable odor that pointed the way like a neon arrow.

The Monkey House was the first big building in the zoo, up a path past a ramshackle souvenir shop. The monkeys and apes were free to go in and out, moving from outdoor chain-link cages to barred indoor habitats as they pleased. As Erie approached the entrance, he spotted a pair of lemurs swinging happily on ropes. Across from them, in another cage, sat a big, gray-bearded chimpanzee. There were other chimps roaming around listlessly behind the fence with him, but he was different. He was watching Erie.

The old chimp was perched on a large rock and had something clutched in the long, curled fingers of his right hand. The ape lifted the hand out toward Erie as he got closer, as if offering him something. Curious, Erie stopped.

"Hello," he said.

The chimp lifted his right arm up over his head, then brought it back down. Was that a wave? Erie smiled.

"He wants you to come closer."

Erie turned to see a fiftyish woman stepping out of the Monkey House. Her salt-and-pepper hair was spiky short, and she had piercing green eyes that glared at him through wire-rimmed glasses. She was wearing a zoo uniform.

"Why?" Erie asked her.

"So he can hit you with the dung he's got in his hand."

Erie took another look at what the chimp was holding, then backed away from the cage.

"Why does he throw dung at people?"

The woman gave him a "Well, *duh*" look. "Because he thinks it's funny," she said. "So you're the detective, huh?"

Erie nodded, aware that he'd already failed to impress the woman with his keen powers of observation and deduction.

"Yeah," he said. "Larry Erie. And you are?"

"Bea Huff. The curator."

She rushed over the words, not offering to shake his hand.

"Come on. You better get a good look at the scene of the crime before it gets hosed down."

She turned and headed into the Monkey House,

pushing through a pair of metal doors with glass window-panes. One of the windows had been shattered, and the shards crackled under Erie's feet as he followed the woman into the building.

Cy Reed was waiting inside with another zoo employee—the bearded man who'd barged into Reed's office six weeks before. The man was nervous energy incarnate, with wide eyes and sweat-soaked underarms, but Reed was all smiles.

"Larry! Thanks for coming on such short notice."

He moved forward using an ornately carved cane—though he didn't seem to have a limp—and shook Erie's hand. Erie was surprised at first by the strength of the old man's grip, but then he remembered who Reed was—the kind of man who'd still be conjuring up charming smiles and hearty handshakes on his deathbed.

"This is Bill Overbeck, my right-hand man."

The bearded man stepped up and gave Erie's hand a shake that was all the more limp and moist in comparison to Reed's.

"And you've already met Bea, I take it."

"I rescued him from Corny," Huff said.

Reed chuckled and shook his head. "That old devil. If only they'd kidnapped *him*."

"There'd be a hell of a lot more blood, that's for sure," Huff said.

Erie held up his hands. "Hold on, guys. Maybe you better tell me what's going on."

Reed nodded. "Right. Of course. Well, you see, Larry, we're a small operation without the budget to—"

Erie prepared himself for a few minutes of spin, but Huff spared him by interrupting her boss.

"One of our animals is missing," she said flatly. "A young capuchin monkey named Maggie. When I came in this morning, she was gone, and the capuchin habitat looked like that."

She pointed toward one of the cages nearby. Erie didn't see anything out of the ordinary at first, just faux rock walls and a jumble of ropes and tire swings. But then a red smear caught his eye, and he moved closer.

There were two doors in the cage—a big one for humans, and a smaller one for the monkeys. The monkey door led outside, to an enclosure identical to the one where Corny sat, luring victims closer like a hairy siren. The human door had two bloody streaks near the knob.

Erie wanted to find out where that door went. He wanted to get a closer look at those streaks of blood. He wanted to get to work.

But he stopped himself.

"Call the police," he said.

Reed smiled grimly and shook his head. Huff glared at Overbeck. Overbeck turned pale and stammered, "We've already . . . we can't . . . no. We decided. No police. Right, Cy?"

"We've already got problems with security, Larry," Reed said. "You've got to build zoos like prisons these days just to keep the real animals out. This place is nearly fifty years old. Any half-wit could break in here with a ladder and a rope."

"Or less," Huff added bitterly.

Reed shot her a long-suffering paternal glance before continuing. "And the truth of the matter is we simply don't have the funds to do anything about it. As you know, Larry, we've barely got enough money to keep the animals fed. We certainly don't have an extra hundred thousand to spend on motion detectors and silent alarms."

"That's too bad. But it still doesn't explain why you're not reporting a serious crime to the police."

"Copycats," Overbeck said.

"Excuse me?"

"Copycats," Overbeck said again, nodding emphatically in agreement with himself.

"Bill's concern—and I happen to share it—is that we would be overrun by vandals, thieves, and thrill-seekers if people realized how vulnerable we are," Reed explained. "Just two months ago we ran off a dozen college kids skinny-dipping in the duck pond. And last spring a couple of drunks broke in because they wanted to ride a zebra. One of them managed to shatter his pelvis, and now *he's* suing *us.* Can you imagine what would happen if it got out that you could actually get in here at night and steal a monkey? Our animals—all of them—would be in grave danger."

Reed was good. Oh yes. Once the man found his footing, he could really shovel it out.

And it was working, too. Erie found that the guilt and sense of responsibility Reed was shifting onto his shoulders actually had some weight.

"So you want me to investigate?"

"Yes," Overbeck said.

"Quietly," Reed added.

Huff fumed wordlessly. It was obvious who'd been overruled that morning.

"I'll do what I can," Erie said. "But if I think there's something more serious than monkeynapping going on, I'll have to go to the police."

"Of course, Larry. Of course," Reed said.

"It's not a 'monkeynapping,'" Huff snapped. "It's theft and it's cruelty and it *is* serious."

"Right. Sorry. No offense."

Huff didn't look appeased.

Erie turned away from her glare and pointed at the monkey cage. "So can I get up in there?"

"Follow me," Overbeck said. He headed for a door with the words ZOO PERSONNEL ONLY stenciled on it. Erie followed. So did Huff.

Overbeck pushed through the door into a small storage room and kitchen beyond, but Erie stopped to examine the knob. The metal around it was scratched and bent.

"Crowbar," Erie said. He looked back at the building's south entrance, the one he'd come in through. "Once they smashed the glass back there, they could reach around and unlock the doors by hand. This one they had to jimmy."

Erie looked at the other side of the door. As he expected, there were smears of blood there. There was blood on the floor, too—a trail of tiny droplets, dried to black. The droplets led to another door. On it was a sign printed from someone's computer.

SECURE DOOR BEHIND YOU! it read. *SMART MONKEYS!!!*

"Whoever our bleeder is, he didn't cut himself on the glass breaking in," Erie said. "There's no blood on the outside of this door, no blood on the outside of the door into the monkey habitat. So he went in okay and came out not so okay."

"It's obvious how the son of a bitch got himself hurt," Huff said. "The capuchins wouldn't let strangers just stroll in there and grab Maggie. They'd put up a fight. We don't need a detective to tell us that."

Erie almost started to explain that he was just trying to

form a mental picture of the night's events, that it wasn't good to jump to any conclusions—even the seemingly obvious ones—until there was physical evidence to back it up. But he didn't. For whatever reason, Huff didn't like him. An explanation wouldn't change that. So he decided to form his mental picture more quietly while she was around.

"Just how big are capuchins anyway?" he asked.

Huff held her hands a little over a foot apart. "Yea big, not counting the tail. An adult male weighs about ten pounds, a female a little less. But don't let the size fool you. They can mess you up if they really want to."

"And they're all outside right now?"

Huff nodded. "Yeah. We closed off the access chute, so they can't get back in till we want 'em to."

Overbeck opened the door to the capuchin habitat. "It's safe, Harry. Come on," he said, his voice quivering with fussy anxiety.

Huff gestured toward the cage. "Yeah, better get a move on, *Harry*," she said to Erie.

She was hostile, but at least she seemed to know that his name was Larry.

Erie ignored her. If he could get away with it, he'd make that his permanent policy. Erie followed Overbeck into the monkey habitat.

Before he could begin searching for relevant details, he had to take a moment and force himself to block out the irrelevant one that immediately slapped him in the face. Even from a distance the zoo's apes and monkeys had a smell that was less than appealing. On the other side of the bars, the stench was downright appalling.

It was a struggle to keep his Snickers bar and coffee down, so he kept his tour of the habitat brief. There were more bloodstains on the floor, including the red outline of a footprint. Someone had stepped in blood, and it left behind the kind of print detectives love. It was so clear Erie recognized the brand (Nike) and could make a good guess on the size (twelve at least, thirteen and a half at most—big).

The footprint was in a back corner of the habitat, where the concrete floor met the fake rock wall. There were more bloodstains concentrated there than anywhere else. Erie crouched down and examined the wall. Caught in its rough yellow surface, about a foot off the ground, was a tuft of fuzzy white fabric about the size of a quarter.

"You're not really going to hose all this down, are you?" he said over his shoulder.

"Well . . . yeah. We are," Overbeck said. "I mean, we don't have any choice. We can't keep the monkeys outside forever. And we certainly can't have them sitting around in blood. It's a . . . a sanitary . . . a health issue."

"A P.R. issue, you mean," Huff snorted.

Erie glanced back at them. Overbeck was hovering nearby, the moist stains under his armpits growing larger. Huff was leaning in the doorway, giving Overbeck the kind of look most people save for insects they find in their food. Erie figured the Hoosier Zoo had some very bumpy days ahead of it if Overbeck and Huff were the only ones waiting in the wings for Reed to retire.

Erie turned back to the white fluff on the wall, debating whether or not he should take it. On the one hand, it wouldn't do him much good: He didn't have a crime lab in his garage. On the other hand, it would be a shame to let a high-pressure hose blast potential evidence down the drain. After a few moments of indecision, he reached out, plucked the material off the wall, and put it in his wallet.

"Okay," Erie said, standing up. "Anything else I need to see?"

"No, that's it." Overbeck looked down at his watch, obviously eager to get the place cleaned up before the general public began strolling in.

"Nobody saw or heard anything out of the ordinary?"

"No. Nothing. I mean . . . other than what you've looked at already." Overbeck was backing toward the door as he spoke, trying to draw Erie out of the habitat. "We just came in this morning and Maggie was gone."

Erie followed reluctantly. A part of him felt like he was betraying something by leaving. He was abandoning a footprint, blood samples, maybe fingerprints, all kinds of evidence that he should have been protecting. But he had no badge to protect it with. So he left it behind.

"Don't you have security guards?" Erie asked as they rejoined Reed. "A night watchman or something?"

"Ha!" Huff scoffed. "We've got a 'something.' "

"Percy Williams is our night keeper," Reed said without looking at Huff. "Unfortunately, he must've been in another part of the zoo when Maggie was stolen."

"Yeah," Huff said. "The part where he keeps his TV and beer."

Overbeck fidgeted and eyed Reed warily, gauging his reaction. He didn't have one. Reed just kept smiling at Erie as if Huff hadn't said a thing.

If they'd been a family, Erie would've told them to go straight into therapy.

"So what kind of person steals a monkey?" he asked.

"I'm afraid you're going to have to tell us that," Reed said.

"You don't have any ideas? I mean—is there a black market for zoo animals?"

"No," said Overbeck.

"Yes," said Huff.

"Not really," Reed said, talking over both of them. "Not for capuchins, not around here. Maybe if we were in Costa Rica . . ."

Reed chuckled. No one else joined in.

"I'm sorry we can't give you more to go on, Larry. But you're a resourceful man. I'm sure if anybody can bring Maggie home, it's you."

Pep talks were all well and good, but Erie preferred leads. He eyed Huff, but she wasn't saying anything more. She was too busy impaling a squirming Overbeck on another nasty glare.

As a former cop, Erie knew all too well that there was nothing less pleasant than stepping into the middle of a family argument. That's just what this felt like, and he hated it. He missed his job sometimes, but not crap like this. Why had he picked up the phone that morning? Why had he gotten out of bed?

"You'll hear from me," he said, and after a handshake and more rah-rah from Reed, he left.

When he was outside, he walked past the lemurs and chimpanzees—keeping a safe distance between himself and the chimps, just in case Corny decided to take a potshot at him—around to the next cage. The weathered, faded information plaque there identified the animals on the other side of the fence as capuchin monkeys. There were seven of them, and Erie recognized them immediately.

They were organ-grinder monkeys. Not that Erie had ever seen a real organ grinder. But he'd seen enough in movies to know they always had the same little sidekick—monkeys with slender bodies and long tails and white faces with large, expressive eyes. Seven sets of those eyes were staring back at him now.

"Wraa!" one of the capuchins screeched as Erie got closer.

"Wraa!" another one answered, and then the rest joined in, all of them screaming and scrambling up into branches—out of reach.

Erie couldn't blame them for being jumpy after what had happened. He imagined the thieves chasing and grabbing at them inside the Monkey House. The animals' shrieking would've been even louder in there, bouncing off all that cement and metal. The perps must've had nerves of steel. Or stomachs of Budweiser.

Erie lingered just long enough to glance at the information plaque. For him, it was more informative for what it didn't say than what it said. There was nothing about capuchin monkeys being rare or endangered. Which meant, Erie assumed, that they weren't particularly valuable.

There could be no argument, however, that they were particularly loud.

"Okay! I'm going! I'm going!" Erie told the monkeys when he was through. They didn't stop screaming until he was almost to the front gate.

The turnstiles at the entrance were gleaming clean when Erie reached them. The woman who'd been wiping them down was in the ticket booth now, reading a paperback novel.

"Excuse me. How are these locked up at night?"

The woman looked up from her book slowly, as if reluctant to leave its reality and reenter the one with the zoo and the guy asking nosy questions.

"What?" she asked.

"These turnstiles. How are they locked?"

"There's a lever around the side there, close to the ground. Push it down all the way and the bars lock up."

"Go ahead, Erie. Try it."

Erie turned to see Huff walking down the path toward him.

"That's the lever there. Step on it."

The lever had a pad on top, like a brake pedal. Erie put his foot on it and pushed, and the lever clicked downwards.

"Now watch."

Huff stepped up to the turnstile, grabbed one of the bars, and gave it a loose shake.

"Locked, right?"

"If you say so."

"I don't."

Huff leaned into the turnstile, pushing against the direction it was designed to rotate. The lever popped up with a loud *clack,* and Huff moved slowly through the barred cage that surrounded the turnstile, pushing herself out of the zoo.

"That's all it takes," she said to Erie through the bars. "Except why bother when there's twenty places you can get in over a wall and twenty other places you can get in under a fence?"

"But this is the way they went last night."

"Obviously."

If Huff had been a little less of a smart-ass, a little less prone to jumping on people's words and stomping them into the dirt, he would've said something, maybe, "Doesn't that suggest anything to you?" But instead he just walked through the turnstile—going in the right direction, unlike Huff—and headed for the parking lot.

"Well, thanks for the extra information. Every little bit helps."

"Wait!"

Erie stopped and turned. Huff was following him.

"Where are you going?" she asked.

"To my car."

The look on her face said, "That's not funny."

"And after that?" she said slowly, as if speaking to someone for whom English was a challenging new language.

"After that I'm beginning my investigation."

When Huff realized that was all she was getting, she closed her eyes and took in a deep breath.

"Look, Erie," she said, her eyes popping back open, "Reed wants me to go with you."

"He *what?*"

It was official now. For the second year in a row, Erie's Halloween was ruined.

"What do you know about monkeys, Erie? What do you know about this monkey? Squat, that's what. I'm the expert, so I'm coming along. Reed's orders."

Erie didn't snap very often, but he snapped now.

"*Excuse me?* What makes you think I take orders from Reed?"

Hull cocked an eyebrow at him. There might have been genuine surprise on her face. Erie couldn't be sure.

"You mean you don't?"

"Why should I? I barely know him."

"You're working for him, aren't you?"

"Well, yeah," Erie said, realizing it for the first time. He hadn't even told Reed his rates. Not that he'd worked out what his rates were yet. This whole private investigator thing was still too damn new. "That doesn't make me his slave."

"So you're refusing to work with me?" There was a challenge in Huff's voice almost as if she *wanted* him to say "Yes."

And he certainly was tempted. But he knew the logical thing to do, even if he didn't particularly want to do it.

"You can come with me," he said. "Because it makes sense, not because Cy Reed ordered it."

"Fine," Huff said, not seeming particularly satisfied by her victory.

They got in Erie's car, left the parking lot, went north on Lamprecht Road and east on Highway 50 toward downtown, all without saying a word. Huff finally broke the silence.

"Look," she said, and Erie wondered if an apology might be forthcoming. It wasn't. "When you hit 41, head north."

"What for?"

"We need to go to Spencer. You can pick up 67 off 41."

"You think Maggie's in Spencer?"

Calling Spencer a dot on the map would be generous. It was more like a speck. Erie had driven through it a hundred times on his way to and from Indianapolis. Spencer was easy to drive through. It was harder to stop there. If you didn't hit the brakes at the city limits, you'd cruise through in a heartbeat. Erie didn't think of it as the kind of town that would be crawling with wildlife—other than rednecks.

"There's an animal dealer up around there named Eyler," Huff said. "Runs his own 'sanctuary' for exotics. He'd just love to get his hands on a young female capuchin. Good breeding stock. The babies are what really bring in the money."

They passed a sign for Highway 41. The turnoff was a mile ahead.

"This Eyler guy—he steals animals?"

"More or less."

"What does that mean?"

"It means it's complicated."

"It doesn't have to be complicated. When I say 'steal' what I mean is 'sneak into a zoo, bust glass, pry open doors, chase monkeys around a cage, let one bite the hell out of him, then wrap it up and haul it out the front gate.' He'd do that?"

They passed another sign for 41. The turnoff was coming up.

"You need to get over."

"Would he do that?"

"You're going to miss the turn!"

Erie missed the turn.

"We're not going to Spencer," he said.

The look on Huff's face made Erie worry that she might be about to bite him.

"I knew it," she snarled.

"We can go later," Erie said quickly, hoping to head off the flood of abuse he saw coming his way. "If this Eyler guy stole Maggie, she's safe. She's merchandise, right? He'll

take care of her. We've got time. But if she was grabbed for
some other reason, she could be in danger."

"Some other reason? Like what?"

Erie made an effort to speak more slowly and softly,
hoping it would rub off on Huff.

"I was a cop for a lot of years. I saw a lot of weird things.
And the weirdest of all? Those were always on Halloween.
Always."

"So what are you saying? Someone stole Maggie so they
could dress her up like a ballerina and take her trick-or-
treating?"

"It wouldn't surprise me."

"Well, I don't buy it."

Huff turned away and slumped back in her seat. Erie
knew the reason she couldn't "buy it." She'd already made
up her mind. The animal dealer did it, she was thinking.
With help.

And maybe she was right. If so, it might actually be good
news. A motive makes a perp predictable. But if the bad
guy's just out for some dumb laughs, anything can
happen.

After a few quiet miles they reached downtown River
City, and Erie zigzagged through the streets to the first
stop of his investigation: St. Mary Mercy Hospital. When he
parked, he told Huff to wait in the car.

"Yeah, right," Huff said as she unbuckled her seat belt
and opened the door.

Erie didn't try to fight it. But as they walked toward the
emergency entrance, he slipped off his windbreaker and
handed it to her.

"Put this on."

Huff scowled back at him as if he'd just taken off his pants, not his jacket. "I'm not cold," she said.

"I'm not trying to keep you warm. I'm trying to keep you anonymous."

Huff looked down at her shirt, with its Hoosier Zoo patch and the plastic tag with her name and title on it.

"Oh," she said.

She put on the jacket.

Erie needed to find a familiar face inside. He got lucky. There were two. He kicked his memory into high gear and came up with names to go with them. Then he glued a smile on his face he was far too irritated to feel.

"Jackie. Lee," he said as he walked up to the admitting nurses. "How you been?"

The two women smiled back.

"Detective Erie! It's been a long time!"

"We heard you retired."

"You heard right."

There was a brief round of chitchat about retirement, the cop who'd taken Erie's slot in Homicide, Jackie and Lee's complaints about supposedly arrogant doctors Erie could barely remember. Huff observed it all silently, ignored, until Jackie turned to her and said, "And who do we have here? Mrs. Erie?"

Erie managed to fake a small laugh and get in his response before Huff could open her mouth. "No, no. This is my friend Bea. I'm helping her out with a private matter. That's what brought me in today actually. I was hoping you could tell me if anyone came in last night with any serious bite wounds."

"Or scratches," Huff added.

"Yeah. Bites or scratches. Anything like that?" Jackie and Lee exchanged a wry glance that either meant they both knew exactly which patient he was looking for or he'd simply supplied them with something juicy to gossip over once he was gone. When they looked back at Erie, Jackie gave him a shrug that told him it was the latter.

"All we had last night was the usual—drunks puttin' their fists through glass and women with black eyes and split lips cuz they walked into a door," she said.

"The big excitement was a guy with a kidney stone," Lee added, chuckling. "He was back there for hours carryin' on, screamin', callin' the doctors every filthy name you can think of."

"Oh yeah," Jackie said. "You shoulda heard what he called Dr. Adad. I've been thinkin' of sayin' the same thing to him for months!"

Everyone laughed, Erie out of politeness more than anything else. He'd struck out, and now he had to extricate himself smoothly before anyone asked. . . .

"So what's this about bites and scratches, Detective Erie?" Lee said. "We got us a werewolf on the prowl?"

"Yeah. Or is it a vampire?" Jackie threw in.

Erie's answer was still nothing more than a half-formed thought, hardly an idea, let alone words, when Huff spoke.

"Neither," she said. "It was my pit bull. He sure as hell sank his teeth into *somebody's* butt last night."

She leaned in closer to the nurses and dropped her voice to a just-between-us-girls whisper.

"Fortunately, I'm pretty sure the butt belonged to my ex."

Jackie and Lee ate it up. Erie took advantage of their laughter to throw out his good-byes and steer Huff toward the door without any further conversation.

"Good save back there," he said once they were in the parking lot.

"So what now?"

"You're a smart lady. Guess."

"Knox Memorial Hospital."

"Very good! You ever moonlight as a detective?"

Huff didn't even crack a smile.

River City's other hospital was twenty-five minutes away. The first ten minutes passed in silence. Erie had plenty he could say, most of it in the form of questions. But he just didn't feel like sticking his head into the lion's mouth. So it was Huff who spoke first, and when she did, Erie knew the words had already been echoing through her brain for hours.

"What if it's her blood?"

Erie glanced over at Huff. Her face had changed. Anguish peeked out from behind the look of cynical disdain she'd been wearing since he met her.

"I don't know," he said. "You tell me."

"Even if she's barely hurt, she could go into shock. Capture trauma. She could be dead already."

She tried to punch out the words, make them hard and clinical. But by the time she reached the word "shock," there was a tremor in her voice, and the last few words barely came out at all.

"Do you think it's her blood?" Erie asked.

Huff sucked in a long breath that seemed to fill the emptiness inside her, inflating her like a balloon.

"Hell no," she snapped, the other Huff, the tough one, back in charge. "She's a capuchin monkey. You think they're cute, just wait till one tries to scratch your eyes out. Anybody who'd try to snatch one out of a group like that's gotta be nuts."

"Really?" Erie said, letting his inflection ask the rest of the question. *If it's so nutty, why would your number-one suspect do it?*

He saw in Huff's eyes that she heard the question. He also saw that she didn't have a good answer—and that it enraged her.

Erie didn't pat himself on the back for poking a hole in her theory. He needed all the theories he could get. If their trip out to the other hospital was a bust, he only had one other idea to fall back on, and he didn't like it.

But a bust it was. Erie and Huff went through the same routine with the nurses at Knox Memorial, with the same result. No bites, no scratches, too many questions. They escaped as quickly as they could.

"You ready for Spencer now?" Huff asked as they walked to the car.

Erie shook his head. "I'm ready for Hart Road."

"What's on Hart Road?"

"My place. I need to make some calls. And if we're gonna drive up to Spencer, I'll need to feed my cats."

"Cats?" The irritation in Huff's eyes seemed to give way to what could have been some small measure of respect. "Plural?"

"Yeah."

"How many?"

"Three."

Huff waved a hand dismissively and looked away. "Is that all."

" 'Is that all?' I've got friends who say it's three too many."

"They don't know what they're talking about. Wanna know how many cats I have?"

"Sure."

"Five."

Erie shrugged. "That's only two more than me."

"Yeah, but then there's the dogs, the rats, the pig, and the parrot on top of that."

"Geez. Do you work in a zoo or live in one?"

"Yeah, yeah, I've heard that one before," Huff said. But for a second there it almost looked like she was capable of smiling.

When they got to Erie's place, Goldie and Mae met them at the door. Huff was a lot friendlier meeting new pets than new people, and she bent down to introduce herself to the cats with ear scratches and tummy rubs.

"Where's number three?"

Erie pointed across the living room. His newest cat, Phoebe, peeked at them from around a corner, her yellow eyes wide and unblinking.

"A shy one, huh?"

"Yeah. I don't blame her. She's been through some rough stuff. She almost ended up an hors d'oeuvre at your zoo, as a matter of fact. Excuse me."

Erie walked into the kitchen and checked his answering machine. There was one new message. He pushed PLAY.

"Hi, this is Bob calling from 21st Century Travel Plus. I'm really sorry I missed you today, because I've got some great news! You've—"

Erie erased the message. He'd heard Bob's "great news" twenty times before. Apparently, Erie had been specially selected—by virtue of having his phone number dialed—to become a member of the 21st Century Travel Plus Luxury Living Timeshare Program. All he needed to do to activate his membership was begin handing over his life savings in simple monthly installments.

One of these days Erie was going to really put his detectiving skills to the test and track Bob down. He hadn't made up his mind what he was going to do when he found him. He was still torn between a pie in the face and a kick in the pants.

Huff stepped into the kitchen, and Erie asked her if she wanted any coffee or water or juice or candy bars before they headed out again. She looked so lost in thought for a moment Erie wasn't even sure she heard the question, but then her eyes refocused on him and she shook her head.

"So," she said, and Erie got the feeling she was as unsure what words would follow as he was. "You said you had some phone calls to make."

"Actually, the first one's yours. I think you should give the zoo a call. Maybe there's been some kind of development."

"Such as what?"

"A ransom demand, or maybe they found Maggie hiding up in a tree. I don't know. That's why I need you to call in."

"Okay," Huff said. "Makes sense."

Erie moved away from the phone, and Huff picked it up and dialed. He had the feeling she'd wanted to check in with the zoo anyway but she felt obligated to run everything he suggested through a B.S. X-ray.

Erie noted that she didn't call Reed or Overbeck. Instead, she chatted with someone she called "Dave." She asked if anything had happened since they'd left and how the remaining capuchins were acting. She also asked what Overbeck had been up to, and Erie noticed that she tried a little too hard to make the question sound like a casual aside. Then she gave "Dave" a gruff good-bye, hung up, and said, "Nothing. What next?"

Now I swallow my pride, Erie thought.

"One other call," he said, reaching out to take the phone. He dialed the number from memory.

"Lieutenant Zirkelbach, please," he told the dispatcher who picked up the call. She didn't recognize his voice, and he was thankful. Erie's friend Bass kept telling him he'd had a "thing" about the River City Police Department ever since he'd applied for a private detective's license.

"It's like you're embarrassed every time you're around 'em," Bass would say.

"I am embarrassed."

"Well, get over it!"

But Erie couldn't. Whenever he took a case, he felt like a kid playing dress-up. He wasn't a cop anymore. Why was he trying to act like one? Who was he trying to fool?

"East Sector, Zirkelbach."

"Mike, it's Larry Erie."

This was the moment Erie dreaded. If he got through the first few seconds, he'd be okay. He just needed Zirkelbach to say something other than, "So how's River City's toughest gumshoe these days?" or, "Hey, Rockford! How are the files comin'?"

"Larry! How ya' been?" Zirkelbach said.

Yet even in those words Erie thought he heard something. A snicker maybe. A roll of the eyes. Or maybe that was just Erie's "thing" about the RCPD playing tricks on him. He did his best to ignore it.

"Oh, you know. This and that. Raking leaves, watching too much TV. The usual old-fart stuff."

"Sounds good to me. Two more years and I'll be out there rakin' leaves with ya. I can't wait."

"Yeah, it's the life all right," Erie said, because it was the kind of thing he was supposed to say, and he had other business to move along to. "So, Mike, I'm just looking into something for a friend. It's no big deal really. But I was wondering—did anything weird go down last night?"

"Weird? Like how do you mean?"

"You know. Out of the ordinary. Noteworthy. Something that would have people talking."

"Nope. Not that I heard."

"How about the other sectors? Same thing?"

"Yeah, same thing. Nothin' weird. Just the usual perps and pervs."

"Okay. One other thing. Do you know if that Mojo kid is still in town?"

"Oh, yeah. We ain't rid of him yet."

"He have any known hangouts?"

"Hold on. DeYoung's right here. I'll ask him."

Erie heard Zirkelbach's thick hand wrap around the receiver.

"Hey, DeYoung!" Zirkelbach called out, his booming voice only slightly muffled over the phone. "Where'd you buttonhole Birdboy last time?"

Erie couldn't hear the response, just Zirkelbach's "Uh-huh."

"Know where he lives?" Zirkelbach asked, his hand still smothering the mouthpiece. "Really? That figures. Larry Erie. I don't know. Yeah. Okay."

Zirkelbach brought the receiver back up to his mouth.

"He works in a coffee shop on Sherman. The Daily Grind. You know it?"

"I know it."

"No known place of residence. The landlords in town talk to each other, y'know. Last time we checked in on him he said he was living in a VW van."

"You're kidding."

"That's what DeYoung says. He says to say 'Hi,' by the way."

"Right back at him."

"So, Larry . . ."

Erie's shoulders tensed, his jaw clenched. Here it came.

"I gotta ask. You callin' up with questions about the East Sector and Dr. Dolittle and all . . . well, I can't help but put two and two and two together. There somethin' else goin' on out at the zoo we should know about?"

Erie eyed Huff. She eyed him back warily, obviously brimming over with questions and distrust.

"Like I said, I'm just looking into something for a friend."

Zirkelbach chuckled. A part of Erie wanted to chuckle right along with him. Another part wanted to ask him what was so damn funny.

"Okay, Larry," Zirkelbach said. "I hope you find whatever you're lookin' for."

"Me, too. Thanks for the help, Mike."

Erie hung up. He wanted a minute to think, scroll back over the conversation, dissect it. But Huff didn't give him the chance.

"What was that all about?" she asked.

"Acquiring information."

Erie walked over to the refrigerator and pulled it open. The shelves inside were brimming with almost every condiment known to man, and almost nothing to put them on. After a little scrounging, Erie found a package of hot dogs buried beneath a loose pile of individually wrapped slices of cheese.

"You sure you don't want something to eat? It's almost one."

"I'll eat after we go to Spencer."

Erie sighed.

"Suit yourself. But it could be a while. It's a long drive, and we've got another stop to make before we hit the road."

Huff cursed so explosively Mae scrambled off the kitchen counter and darted out of the room. Erie put the hot dogs back in the fridge, his appetite suddenly gone.

"Let's just go," he said.

He tried to explain once they were in the car.

"Have you ever heard of Animal Freedom Now?"

"No." She drew the word out as she said it, the inflection meant to tell him, "Why should I have? I don't believe a word you say."

"It's an animal-rights group. Or at least that's what it's supposed to be. As far as we can tell, it's really just one guy."

"We?"

She'd caught him there. Not we. *They.*

"The police," Erie said. "Last March, somebody *liberated* a bunch of chickens from a farm outside town. There was a message left behind—a crackpot letter from Animal Freedom Now. It spooked certain people, and the case got a lot of attention."

"Then how come I never heard of it?"

"*Internal* attention. The RCPD, the county sheriff, and the state police were all in on the investigation. It got cracked on a lucky breakthrough. A noise complaint."

"Let me guess. Crowing."

"Pecking and scratching, actually. The guy took more than fifty chickens, but he didn't know what to do with them. So he just kept them in his apartment. By the time the police showed up, the place was covered wall to wall in—"

"I work with animals. I know."

"Yeah. Well, all the chickens were recovered, and nobody wanted to give this Animal Freedom kid any publicity because that's all he was really after in the first place. He calls himself Major Mojo, and he figured he needed some ink to attract recruits. I think he was actually looking forward to a trial. So certain interested parties talked the farmer into dropping charges, and—"

"And the whole thing was kept quiet."

It wasn't just a statement of fact. It was some kind of accusation. Erie couldn't quite figure out what he was being accused of.

"That's right," he said. "Now every time anybody so much as crank-calls a farmer, an officer has a few words with Major Mojo. I don't think he's been up to much since then beyond handing out flyers in front of McDonald's, but who knows? Maybe he thought up another way to make a name for himself."

"You said you think this kid works alone?"

Erie nodded.

Huff shook her head.

"There's no way in hell anybody could grab Maggie without help, not with seven other capuchins there, too," she said. "No way."

"Maybe there's a Sergeant Mojo now, too."

Erie knew it was a lame joke, but it was the only

response he had in him. Because Huff was right. And if Major Mojo turned out to be a wild-goose chase, Erie was going to have a mutiny on his hands.

The Daily Grind was one block from the Midwest's most awkwardly named campus: Indiana University–Purdue University River City. The locals shortened that to IUPURC, but even that was a mouthful.

Before they even parked, Erie knew he'd find Major Mojo in the coffee shop. The VW van out front told him that. Erie stopped to get a better look at the van before they went inside. It was covered with flaking orange paint and enough bumper stickers to wallpaper a small house. I DON'T EAT MY FRIENDS, one of the stickers read. Another was a picture of a little cartoon boy relieving himself on a pair of golden arches.

Erie tried to move quickly, glancing down to check all the door handles as he circled the van. They looked grimy, but free of blood. He'd told Huff to wait on the curb, but she stayed a step behind him, peering in through the windows.

"You're being conspicuous," he said under his breath.

"Oh really?"

One of the windows was cranked down a few inches, and Huff pushed her nose up against it and gave the air inside a long whiff.

"Oh man," she said, grimacing.

"What?" Erie's heart beat a little faster. "Does it smell like Maggie?"

"No. It smells like doobie. A lotta doobie."

Erie almost asked her how she knew what "doobie" smelled like, but he thought better of it.

"Come on," he said instead. "Let's go inside before—"

"How can I help you today, officers?"

When Erie turned toward the voice, he found himself facing Fidel Castro circa 1959. He was a young man wearing combat fatigues, big black boots, and a thick beard that threatened to grow over his smiling face like kudzu.

"Do you want a signed confession? Or were you hoping to beat it out of me?" Major Mojo asked.

"We're not cops," Erie said, but Huff was already talking over his words, drowning them out.

"What do you have to confess?"

Major Mojo shrugged happily. "What you got? It don't matter. You're gonna hassle me anyway, right?"

"We're not cops," Erie repeated.

Major Mojo winked at him. "Hey, I understand. It's Halloween, right? You wanna say you're not cops, that's fine by me. So what are you then? Tourists?"

"Look, we're just—"

"Where were you last night?" Huff asked.

Erie moaned and rolled his eyes. If he ever took another case—if—he would have an unbreakable rule: Clients never, ever take part in an investigation.

"I was just hangin' with some friends, y'know—startin' a bonfire with Old Glory, plottin' acts of sedition. The usual," Major Mojo said.

He thought they were cops, and he loved it. He was dressed like Fidel Castro, but Erie could see who he really wanted to be: Abbie Hoffman.

That was the angle Erie had to play. The kid's self-image. He was the heroic freedom fighter, they were stooges of The Man. All right. Erie would make him prove it. He opened his mouth . . . and Huff beat him again.

"You say you like animals?" she asked.

Major Mojo nodded. "Love 'em all, big and small."

"And you want to help them?"

"That's what I'm all about."

"Then here's your big chance."

She stepped toward him quickly, moving until she was almost standing on his toes, and for the first time Erie could see the fear behind Major Mojo's bluster. His smile drooped, he took a step backwards, his hand came up as if to ward off a blow.

"There's an animal out there somewhere," Huff said, her voice dropping low but the intensity ratcheted up high. "She's scared, alone. Maybe hurt, maybe dying. And every second I waste here on your B.S. is a second I'm not out looking for her. So stop playing games and answer me *right now*. Where were you last night?"

Major Mojo looked slightly dazed, but Erie could tell it wasn't just that he was overwhelmed by Huff—or the effects of too much "doobie." He was thinking. The pause that followed was over so quickly most people wouldn't even notice it. But a cop would.

"I worked here till eight, then I went to my girlfriend's place," Major Mojo said. "We watched a movie and went to bed. That's it. That's all. Really."

"I believe him," Huff announced without hesitating. "Let's go." Then she walked away, heading for Erie's car up the block.

Erie watched her go in stunned silence. So much for the quiet investigation Reed had asked for. Another outburst like that and they'd wind up on the evening news.

When Erie turned to look at Major Mojo again, he saw that the distant, confused look was still on the young man's face. There was no trace of the grin with which he'd greeted them.

Erie waited for him to ask, "What's she talking about?" or, "Where are you people from?" But he didn't. Which meant Erie had more questions for him.

Now wasn't the time and place, though. Huff had seen to that. Their conversation had turned a few heads on the sidewalk, and everyone inside the coffee shop was staring at them. It was time to go.

"Thanks," Erie said before shuffling reluctantly after Huff.

She was already in the passenger seat when Erie got to his car, her seat belt buckled. She was ready to travel. Erie wasn't.

"Look," he said as he slid in behind the steering wheel.

"Just drive." Huff's words were clipped and tight, as if she had to fight to keep them from spiraling up into a scream.

"Look," Erie said again. "I think that kid knows something."

"Oh, please. Just cuz he's a little fringy doesn't make him the bad guy."

"It's not just that. I've got a feeling—"

"You've got a feeling? I've had a feeling from the very beginning! But no. We had to—"

Erie shook his head. "I know what you're thinking and it just doesn't hold together. Spencer's a waste of time."

Erie saw the spark in her eyes before the explosion came. He'd given her what she'd been waiting for. A trigger. An excuse to blow up. And she did it.

She started with some generic cursing, then grew more

specific, telling Erie exactly what he was and what he could go do to himself. Then she told him why.

He wasn't even trying to find Maggie, she told him. He was just trying to sweep her under the rug.

Erie hated losing his temper, hated himself on those rare occasions when he raised his voice. But he'd heard enough.

"Look, lady, I don't know anything about your petty squabbles at the zoo. But I do know they've got you so twisted around you can't see facts when they're staring you in the face. Whoever stole Maggie, they're amateurs, and that means odds are they're right here in town."

"What facts am I not facing, Erie? Cuz you're right—I don't see 'em. All I see is a detective who's bending over backwards not to follow up his best lead."

"You want to see my best lead? Here's my best lead. In fact, it's the only damn evidence I've got."

Erie pulled out his wallet and showed her the piece of fabric he'd tucked away there earlier.

"I found this in the monkey habitat this morning. Do you know what it is?"

Huff gave her shoulders an angry, jerking shrug. "Some lint you just pulled out of your pocket?"

"I think it's a piece of a blanket. Do you get what that means? These guys didn't bring a net or tranquilizer darts or whatever. They showed up to catch a monkey with a *blanket*. Whoever they are, they're not just amateurs—they're idiots."

"Or maybe that's what it's supposed to look like."

"What? A trick?"

"Sure."

"Well, if that's what it was, they took it pretty far. The

zoo's got a back entrance, right? It must. There's no way you guys bring animals in and out through the front gate."

"Yeah. So?"

"So if these guys were pros, if they had help, why would they go to all the trouble of getting an angry monkey out through those turnstiles?"

"We don't know they did."

"The blood—"

"That doesn't prove a thing. It could have been planted."

Erie almost fired off a salvo about her pigheaded stubbornness, but he stopped himself. She was right. The blood, the fuzz, everything he'd seen at the zoo—it could be an elaborate ruse.

It could be . . . but it wasn't. That's what his gut told him. He'd spent three decades staring people in the eye while they lied to him. He'd listened to a thousand bogus accusations and ten thousand phony alibis. People had tried to con him from the day he put on his uniform to the day he handed in his badge. And this didn't feel like a con. It felt like a stupid, stupid joke.

But why should he trust his instincts? They can trick you, too. Huff was proof of that. She was jabbering away at him, throwing around the words "Overbeck" and "Eyler," getting angrier as it grew more obvious that Erie was only half-listening.

At least her instincts gave her ready-made bad guys. Erie's left him with a whole city of suspects. You never heard a cop say, "Somebody's pulled a dumb-ass prank on the East Side—round up the usual suspects."

Wait.

Erie had heard cops say that. There'd even been a few times he'd said it himself.

"Of course," he mumbled, shaking his head, wondering why he hadn't thought of it before.

Then again, he couldn't judge himself too harshly. He might have made the connection hours ago if he'd been working alone.

"Let me guess," Huff said. "You've got just *one more place* we've got to check before we go to Spencer."

"Yes," Erie said.

Huff coughed out a bitter, scoffing laugh. "Erie, you have truly lost your mind if you think I'm gonna buy whatever load of crap you're about to unload."

Her words, her scorn, they didn't bother Erie at all, and he spoke with such renewed confidence that Huff actually listened.

"This morning Reed said your night watchman recently chased off some college kids who'd been skinny-dipping somewhere in the zoo."

"Yeah. So?"

"He didn't catch them?"

"No, they got away."

"So how did he know they were college kids?"

"He said they were frat boys and their girlfriends."

"But how did he know they were frat boys?"

"One of them had a sweatshirt with, you know, Greek letters."

Erie shook his head. "IUPURC doesn't have any fraternities."

A scowl twisted Huff's face, but it was different than the scowls Erie had seen there already. It wasn't bitter or angry. Just confused.

"Let me show you something," Erie said.

He started the car. Less than two minutes later, he was shutting it off again. They were on a quiet side street just a few blocks from the coffee shop. One side of the street was lined with the kind of low-rent apartment complexes favored by college kids living off campus. Facing them was a row of houses that, judging by the gleaming Jeeps and SUVs parked out front, catered to students with a little more money. Over the doorway to one of the homes hung three twinkling horseshoes—the Greek letter omega done up in white Christmas lights.

"They call themselves The Omega Men," Erie said. "Or at least they did last I heard. They've lived in that house for more than twenty years. Not the same ones, of course. Different guys coming and going. Just like a frat, which is exactly what they'd be if the school were a little bigger and they could get picked up as a chapter of one of the national fraternities."

Spider-Man strolled by the car, and both Erie and Huff did a double take. Walking with him were a hobbit and an adolescent girl who was either dressed as a streetwalker or Britney Spears. They were chattering loudly and swinging plastic buckets shaped like pumpkins.

"They're getting an early start."

"Erie, why are we here?"

It wasn't just another jab. She was actually prepared to listen—if he said the right things.

Erie began counting off with his fingers.

"One, if your night watchman's right, they've probably been in the zoo before. That explains how they knew their way around in there at night. Two, there's a twenty-four-hour student clinic on campus, which is why whoever got hurt wouldn't have gone to a hospital. Three, these guys have a reputation for crazy stunts and wild parties. The RCPD has to send a car out here at least once a month, and I could tell you stories about homecoming that would curl your hair. And four, there's what they call their head-quarters there."

"What's that?"

"Animal House."

Huff stared at the house for a moment, then looked back at Erie.

"Okay," she said, and from the way she said it, Erie could tell she believed him. Which wasn't the same thing as believing he was right. She just believed he wasn't lying. "If Maggie's not in there, we go to Spencer, right?"

"You'll get no argument from me. If they don't have her, I'm just your chauffeur from here on in, because I'll be all out of ideas."

As they marched up the walk to the front door, they passed Spidey and his friends, who were grumbling about the "candy" they'd just been given: fried eggs.

"Funny guys," Huff said, not amused.

"Unzip the jacket," Erie told her.

They were almost to the porch.

"What? Why?"

"I want to see what they think of your costume. Now *please* let me do the talking this time."

He reached out and rang the bell, and while he and Huff waited for someone to answer, Erie put on his own cos-tume. It was nothing more than a mask, one he carried with him at all times, buried deep. His cop face. Stern, stiff, dry, unforgiving.

When a brawny Omega Man came to the door with a pan of fried eggs in one hand and a spatula in the other, Erie got the reaction he was looking for. First a bad-boy grin, the kid assuming they were neighborhood parents furious about the "treats" he was giving out. Then a closer look at Erie's face and Huff's zoo uniform, and the grin lost its balance, tipping over into a lopsided grimace.

The kid had something to hide, Erie was sure of that. But finding out if that something included a stolen monkey could be tricky. He and Huff had no legal authority to conduct a search. If the wannabe frat boy wanted to stonewall them, he could. Erie hoped he'd panic.

But he didn't. The kid recovered quickly. His grin righted itself, and he snaked a foot around the door and pulled it tight to his side, blocking their view into the house.

"Aren't you two a little old to be trick-or-treating?" the kid asked.

"You know why we're here," Erie said.

"You came for the Grand Slam breakfast?"

"You boys are in a lot of trouble."

"What? Because of this?" The kid waved the pan in their direction. "Hey, eggs are delicious *and* nutritious. A hell of a lot more healthy than candy bars. You ought to be thanking us."

He was smooth, Erie had to give him that. A political-science major probably. Pre-law. He had the bland, doughy good looks of a state politician. He'd go far, if Huff didn't kill him first. The air around them was practically crackling with her seething rage.

"We don't want to call the police," Erie said. "But we will

if we have to. It'll be a lot better for everybody if it doesn't come to that."

The kid furrowed his brow in mock confusion and laughed. "Man, what are you smoking? You are making no sense."

"If you deal with us, this'll all be over in minutes. But the cops . . ." Erie shook his head and shrugged. "We'll have to press charges. We won't have a choice."

"Okay, man," the kid said, still forcing out a string of unconvincing chuckles. "Whatever."

Erie saw what was coming next. He could read it in the college boy's eyes. Close the door. Get rid of the evidence. Get rid of it fast and without pity.

"Happy Halloween," the kid said as he started to push the door shut.

It had been a long, long time since Erie had stuck his foot in a closing door. You have to do it just right or you end up with a shattered ankle or crushed toes or a thigh the color of grape jelly. Fortunately, with his hands full, the kid couldn't slam the door hard, and Erie's foot stayed on the end of his leg.

"Don't be stupid," Erie said.

He was pressed up against the door, bringing his face just inches from the kid's.

"Back off, man! Back off or I'm calling the cops!"

"Do it," Erie bluffed. "Please."

"Get out of here!"

The kid poked at him with the spatula, wiping dried bits of egg on his face. The last drop of patience in Erie's body evaporated.

"Hey!" someone shouted.

"Stop him!"

It took both Erie and the kid a moment to realize all the shouting wasn't about them. Something else was going on inside the house, something involving yelling and running and scuffling and finally a series of piercing, inhuman shrieks. The kid looked over his shoulder to see what he could see. Erie looked over his own shoulder to see if Huff was still there.

She was.

"Go!" she said.

Erie went, giving the door a hard shove just as the kid turned back toward him again. The edge caught him across the face, flattening his nose, and he and his frying pan went down in a messy, clattering pile. Erie stepped over him, pushing words like *trespassing* and *assault* out of his mind as best he could as he headed for the stairs. The screams seemed to be coming from the second floor. Huff pushed past him, taking three steps at a time.

A guy dressed as Tarzan met them at the top of the stairs. He actually looked relieved to see them.

"You from the zoo?"

"Yes," Huff said.

"Some guy got in the house and now he's in my room with the monkey and I think it's killing him!"

"Which room?" Huff asked, but a fresh round of screams told her exactly where to go.

She and Erie pushed past more young men in the hallway, most in costume. Erie noticed that one of them, a hulking redhead dressed as Frankenstein's monster, had real stitches over his forehead and across his chin. Fresh ones. Erie glanced down at the young man's feet. Size twelve, at least. The shrieks were coming from a closed door just beyond him.

"Hey," the redhead said as Huff and Erie approached, "I don't think you wanna go in there."

Huff stepped around him and opened the door. The Omega Men ran for cover.

Huff didn't open the door all the way, but it was enough. A familiar odor assaulted Erie's nostrils, and a disgusted, involuntary "Ewwww" slipped past his lips. His eyes watering, he peered over Huff's shoulder, looking for the source of the smell in the room beyond.

It was a bedroom, and it looked as if it had been picked up by a giant, shaken like a snow globe, and put back in place upside down. Lamps and chairs had been over-turned, posters torn off the walls, beer and wine bottles shattered, clothes and magazines and notebooks strewn about the floor, brown clumps splattered here and there over just about everything.

A tattered blanket lay crumpled in a corner next to a length of stained rope. Hunched nearby was a panting, wild-eyed monkey.

"Wraaa!" Maggie yelled as she scrambled on top of a stereo speaker, knocking over the bong that had been perched there. "Wraaa!"

"Is somebody there?" asked a trembly, muffled voice. "You gotta help me. Please. I'm trapped."

"Where are you?" Erie asked.

"Down here. In the corner."

Protruding from under one of the beds was a pair of combat boots and fatigue-covered ankles.

"Major Mojo?"

There was a pause, then a pitiful, "Yes?"

Erie wasn't sure what would happen next. Would they have to get tranquilizer darts from the zoo? Chase Maggie around with a blanket? Given the wounds he'd seen on Frankenstein, he wasn't anxious to play monkey in the middle himself.

Huff answered his question by simply stepping into the room and saying, "Hi, sweetie."

Maggie jumped off the speaker and charged at them. Erie brought up his hands, sure that within seconds he was going to be pulling a clawing, screaming monkey off his face.

Instead, he watched as Maggie leapt onto Huff, climbed into her arms, and huddled there.

"It's okay, baby," Huff said, her voice taking on a soothing, nurturing quality Erie hadn't heard all day. "Calm down. Everything's fine."

Maggie wrapped her long arms around Huff's neck, looking suddenly like a very skinny, very fuzzy child.

"You two get out," Huff said, still using the low, sing-songy tone even though she was talking to Erie and Major Mojo. "I need a few minutes to make sure she's totally calm before I try to move her. And keep those morons out of the hallway. I don't want them scaring her on the way out."

Erie walked over and nudged the bottom of Major Mojo's boot with his foot.

"Come on. Let's go."

The young activist slithered backwards out of his hiding place and rolled over to look up at Erie, revealing a large purple-blue bruise across the left side of his face. He looked a little embarrassed to be seen cowering under a bed, but by the time he and Erie were out in the hallway he'd managed to straighten up his spine and put a haughty gleam in his eyes.

"You want to tell me what you were trying to do in there?" Erie asked him.

"No."

Frankenstein's monster poked his head out a nearby doorway. "So you're taking it back to the zoo?"

Erie nodded. "That's right."

"Thank God."

The Omega Men began stepping out into the hallway again, looking both sheepish and relieved. When they saw Major Mojo, though, their expressions turned sour.

"Okay, so you're from the zoo," one of them said to Erie. "But what the hell is he doing here?"

"Good question." Erie turned to Major Mojo. "Why don't you answer that for us while I escort you out of the house."

Major Mojo got it right away. He'd just lost a fight with an eight-pound monkey. He wouldn't do any better against a dozen two-hundred-pound college students.

"Yeah, sure, fine," he said.

"The rest of you follow us. We need the hallway clear if we're going to get your other guest out of here." Erie held out his hand toward the stairs. "All right, Major. Walk and talk."

That's just what he did.

"I've got my sources," Major Mojo said, sounding offi-cious, as if the uniform he had on was more than a costume. "Everybody around here knows I'm Mr. Help-the-Animals. So I had three different people come into the Grind today to tell me these guys had a stolen monkey. So I planned an action for tonight. But then—"

"An *action?*"

"Yeah. An operation."

"Oh, right," Erie said. "You mean you were going to steal the monkey back yourself."

"Liberate, man. I was gonna *liberate* the monkey. Later tonight. But then you guys showed up and, you know, I had to speed things up."

"Why not just help us?"

"I thought about it. But hey, zoos are prisons, man. And this one we've got here is like . . . like . . . What's a really bad prison?"

"Alcatraz?"

"Yeah. Like Alcatraz. It's the worst."

"So what were you going to do with Maggie?"

"With who?"

"Maggie. The monkey."

"It's a she? Wow." He rubbed the side of his face ruefully. "Well, I hadn't planned things out that far. I thought I'd just liberate her and then take it from there."

"Only she didn't want to be liberated."

"No way, man. She wanted to take my damn head off."

They were outside now, on the back porch.

"All right," Erie said "I guess that's that."

"So I'm free to go?"

Erie nodded. "Consider yourself liberated."

"Oh. Okay."

Major Mojo walked away slowly. He seemed disappointed to be getting off so easy. Some police brutality might have cheered him up, but Erie didn't feel like obliging.

The gaggle of Omega Men had dutifully followed Erie

and Major Mojo to the back of the house. They peeked at Erie through the screen door, their anxious expressions asking, "What about us?"

"Okay, guys," Erie said to them as he stepped back inside. "If you want this story to have a happy ending for yourselves, you're going to tell me everything."

There wasn't much to tell, really. The Omega Men were having a Halloween party that night, and they wanted to make it "something special." After all, as residents of Animal House, they had a reputation to live up to. They already knew how easy it was to break into the zoo, so why not borrow one of the animals—just for Halloween? They settled on a monkey because "monkeys are funny."

"When you see 'em on TV they're just like little people. You know, they're just goofy and cute," said the kid Erie had dealt with downstairs, who was pressing a red-stained paper towel to his nose. "But they're not."

Frankenstein's monster pointed at his stitches. "That one we caught was one of the smallest ones in there, and she still managed to do this to me."

An Omega Man dressed as Abe Lincoln showed Erie a black eye. "I got this from her tail."

"Yeah," Tarzan said. "And there was this big one that got hold of my hair—"

There were footsteps on the stairs, and the room fell silent.

"You guys stay here," Erie said. He pushed through the crowd in the kitchen to the foyer. Huff was waiting for him with Maggie still snuggled in her arms.

"Let's go," Huff said.

Erie walked her to the car, both of them trying to move

fast but not too fast. Fortunately, the block was tem-
porarily free of costumed kids, and they managed to get to
Erie's Corolla without being spotted.

Once Huff and Maggie were in the car, Erie started
around for the driver's side. But he stopped himself as he
rounded the trunk. There was one more bit of business to
attend to. He went back to Animal House.

It was like trick-or-treating in reverse. The Omega Men
were inside, all of them done up in ridiculous costumes,
peering at the stranger outside their door who had the
power to hand them something nice or something nasty.

Erie knew they had nothing to be nervous about. Reed
would want everything kept quiet. Which meant no criminal charges.

Which meant they would get away with it.

Erie could tell them that, give them a little speech about
how they'd be fine as long as they kept their mouths shut.
He pictured their relieved smiles, heard how they'd tell the
story around the keg that night, and he said to himself, *No*.
He took a moment to think up the most bone-chilling,
spine-tingling, hair-raising words he could.

"You'll be hearing from our attorneys," he said. And he left.

"What was that all about?" Huff asked him when he slid
into the driver's seat.

Erie told her, and she laughed in a way that said she'd
laugh a lot harder if she didn't have a stressed-out monkey
in her arms.

"To the zoo?" Erie asked.

She nodded. "To the zoo."

On the way, he filled her in on Major Mojo and the
Omega Men. She shook her head once or twice, frowned a

bit, but now that Maggie was in her arms, she seemed almost unflappably relaxed.

"You two seem close," Erie said when he'd wrapped up his report.

Huff grinned. "Oh yeah. When she was barely a year old, she caught pneumonia. Almost died. I nursed her back to health by hand. She pretty much lived with me for three months. Monkeys don't forget something like that."

"Neither do people."

Huff stared at Erie a moment, her expression turning quizzical. "Let me ask you something," she said. "Back at your house, you made a crack about one of your cats. What did that mean?"

"What crack?"

"Something about one of them almost ending up an hors d'oeuvre at the zoo."

"Oh. She was one of the animals I rescued," Erie explained. Huff didn't nod or say "I see" or make any indication she knew what the hell he was talking about. "From the people who were selling roadkill to the zoo." The blank look stayed on her face. "The ones who were stealing people's pets."

"Stealing people's pets?" Huff's face twisted in a way that said she was fighting to hold back a string of curses. "You'd better tell it from the beginning," she said.

So he did. As he told Huff the story, her expression changed from barely controlled rage to horror and finally, as he described the ultimatum he'd given Reed, embarrassment.

"You didn't know any of this?" he asked when he was done.

"Just bits and pieces. I knew Overbeck was buying

roadkill on the sly. And I heard that got us into some kind of hot water, and a private detective got us out of it."

"What?"

Erie finally understood Huff's hostility. As far as she'd known, he was just a cheap fixer, someone who hushed up scandals for a living.

"I'm really sorry," Huff said, reading his mind. "I know I've been a real bitch today."

Erie didn't contradict her.

"I thought you were someone else, you know what I mean?" Huff continued. "I was so convinced you were hooked in with . . . I don't know . . . something skanky that I . . . well, I made up an excuse to tag along."

"Wait a second. Reed didn't tell you to come with me?"

Huff shook her head, looking chagrined. "It was my idea. I wanted to keep an eye on you. See if you were really going to look for Maggie or just jerk me around."

"Geez," Erie said with a sigh. "Well, you got me, I'll give you that. I didn't see that one coming."

"Really, I'm sorry. If it hadn't been for the rumors I'd heard, I would've known you were a good guy."

"Oh yeah? How?"

"Well, come on. Three cats? You had to be okay."

Huff was smiling at him again. And Maggie was looking at him, too, the look on her small, round face tentative but not fearful.

It had been a very strange, distressing day, but Erie just didn't have any talent for holding grudges. He smiled back.

By the time he dropped Huff off at the zoo's rear entrance, she'd promised to make it all up to him by taking him out for dinner sometime. He wasn't sure how he felt about that—he could tell she was a lady with edges even on a good day—but he said yes all the same. It seemed like the safest thing to do.

It was growing dusky dark by the time Erie left the zoo, and he quickly realized two things: He hadn't eaten a thing since that morning's Snickers, and he'd earned a better dinner than cheese sliccs and hot dogs. So he stopped off for a pizza and a bottle of wine on the way home.

He was feeling pretty good as he turned onto Hart Road. His old instincts had come through for him. The badge was gone, but the cop remained.

The satisfied look on his face didn't last long, though. Up ahead, long strands of white waved like ghostly tentacles from the branches of his elm trees.

His house had been egged, too.

A Tale of One City

Anne Perry

Anne Perry's two most popular series are novels set in Victorian England. In one series, Inspector Thomas Pitt works through official channels, while his wife, Charlotte, uses her highborn status to help solve crimes. In the second series, private detective William Monk and nurse Hester Latterly work together. Both teams employ female investigators who are well ahead of their time, both in their sleuthing and their interest in the motives behind human behavior. In addition, Perry exposes the rigidity and hypocritical pomposity of Victorian society with detail and wry humor. These days she's added a third and widely hailed series set in World War I. Her most recent novel is *Long Spoon Lane*.

Sydney Carton sat alone at a table near the door of the Café Procope, staring at the dregs of the red wine in his glass. He did his best to ignore the voices shouting, laughing, swearing around him in the suffocating heat. It was the seventh of July, 1793, and Paris was a city oppressed by hunger and fear. In January the Convention had sent the strangely dignified figure of Louis XVI to the guillotine. Predictably, by February, France was not only at war with Austria and Belgium, but with England as well.

In the Place de la Revolution the scarlet-stained blade rose and fell every day, and tumbrels full of all manner of people, men and women, old and young, rich and poor, rattled over the cobbles on their last journey. The streets smelled of refuse piled high and rotting in the heat. Fear was in the air, sharp like sweat, and people along the Rue St. Honoré complained because the streets stank of blood. You could not drive cattle down them anymore because the stench terrified them and they stampeded out of control, mowing down passersby and crashing into house and shop windows.

All that Carton cared about was Dr. Manette's daughter Lucie, whose husband was locked up in the prison of La Force, with no hope of escape. Carton would have done anything he could to ease her distress, but he was utterly helpless.

The café door was wide open to let in a little air, and he did not notice anyone coming or going until a small man with tousled hair and a cheeky, lopsided face sank into the chair opposite him, having ordered wine from Citizen Procope as he passed.

"At least there's still wine, even if there's no bread," he said with a grunt. "Do you know what they're charging for a loaf now?" he demanded Carton's attention. "Three sous! Twelve sous for four pounds! That's more than a carpenter earns in a day, and twice a week's rent. And the laundresses down at the river are creating hell because there's no soap! Never mind a Committee of Public Safety! What's the point of being safe if the sides of your belly are sticking together?"

"I'd keep a still tongue in your head, if I were you, Jean-Jacques," Carton replied dryly. "If you criticize the good citizens of the Committee, your belly'll think your throat has been cut, and likely it'll be right!"

Jean-Jacques's wine came; he thanked Citizen Procope and handed him five sous. He sniffed the bottle and pulled a face. "Not bad," he observed. "Want some?"

Carton never refused wine. "Thank you." He held out his glass.

Jean-Jacques filled it generously. "You know my sister?"

"Amelie?"

"No, no! Amelie's a good woman, she never does anything except what she's told. Marie-Claire." He drank half of his glass. "I wish I had some decent cheese to go with this."

Carton liked Jean-Jacques. There was a good humor about him, an optimism, misplaced as it was, that lifted the spirits. He was pleasant company.

"What about Marie-Claire?" he asked, to be civil. He did not care in the slightest. To tell the truth there was very little he did care about. He had no belief in himself, nor any in justice or the goodness of life. Experience in London as a lawyer had proved his skill, but it had not always led to victory, acquittal of the innocent, or punishment of the guilty.

Jean-Jacques leaned forward over the table, his round

eyes bright, his face alive with suppressed excitement.
"She has a plan," he said softly. "To get a whole crateful of
cheeses, and not just any cheeses, but perfectly exquisite,
ripe Camembert! And a side of bacon!"

In spite of himself, Carton's imagination was caught.
Even the bare words conjured up the fragrance of rich, del-
icate flavor, food that satisfied, that filled the nose and lay
on the tongue, instead of the rough bread and stew with
barely any meat in it that had become the common fare.
Even though these days one was glad enough to have more
than a spoonful or two of that. "What sort of a plan?" he
said dubiously. Marie-Claire was an erratic creature,
younger than Jean-Jacques, probably not more then
twenty-two or three, small like him, with wide brown eyes
and wild hair that curled just as hectically as his, only on
her it was pretty. She had been one of the women who had
marched on the Palace at Versailles demanding food and
justice in the early days of the Revolution when the King
was still alive—fruitlessly, of course. The King had listened
to everybody, and then done whatever he was told by the
last person to speak to him, which was always some min-
ister who did not listen at all.

Jean-Jacques was still smiling. His teeth were crooked,
but they were very white. "There is a particularly large and
greedy fellow called Philippe Duclos on the local committee," he replied. "The man with the cheeses, whose
name I don't know, has hidden them so well no one knows
where they are, except that they are somewhere in his
house, of course. Marie-Claire is going to use Philippe to
put his men there, so that the good citizen can no longer
get to his cheese in secret." He smiled even more widely.

"Only he is, of course, going to warn Citizen 'Cheese' beforehand, so he will have the chance to move them. Then . . ." He clapped his hands together sharply and made a fist of the right one. "We have them!" he said with triumph. "Half for Philippe, half for Marie-Claire. She will eat some, and sell some, which I will buy." He opened his hands wide in a generous, expansive gesture, and his irregular face was alight with pleasure. "In two days time we shall dine on fresh bread, I have some decent wine, not this rubbish, and ripe Camembert! How is that, my friend?"

"Unlikely," Carton replied ruefully, but he did smile back.

"You are a misery!" Jean-Jacques chided, shaking his head. "Are all Englishmen like you? It must be your climate: it rains every day and you come to expect it. "

"It doesn't rain in London any more than it rains in Paris," Carton answered him. "It's me." It was a confession of truth. His general cynicism stretched beyond his own lack of worth to include everyone else.

"Cheese," Jean-Jacques said simply. "And more wine. That must make you feel better!" He reached for the bottle and poured more for both of them. Carton accepted with a moment of real gratitude, not so much for the wine as for the friendship. He thought the plan was doomed to failure, but it would be pointless to say so.

Carton deliberately put the cheese out of his mind. Even in Paris torn apart by the violence of revolution and sweating with fear, it was necessary to earn a living. He could seldom practice his usual profession of law, but he had a superb gift of words, even in French, which was not his own language, and Paris was awash with newspapers, pamphlets, and other publications. There was the highly popular, scurrilous *Père Duchesne* edited by the foul-mouthed ex-priest Hébert, which slandered just about everyone, but most particularly the Citizeness Capet, as Queen Marie Antoinette was now known. The latest suggestion was that she had an unnatural relationship with her own son, who in the normal course of events would now have become Louis XVII.

And of course there was *L'Ami du Peuple*, edited by that extraordinary man Jean-Paul Marat, who liked to be known as "The Rage of the People." Someone had had the audacity, and the lunacy, to haul him up before the Revolutionary Tribunal in April. He had stormed in, filthy and in rags as usual, carrying the stench of his disease with him. The whole body of them had quailed before him, terrified, and he had been carried out shoulder-high in triumph. There was now no stopping him. The Paris Commune was his creature, to a man.

Carton always took good care to avoid him. Even though Marat lived here in the Cordeliers District, as did most of the revolutionary leaders, it was possible to stay out of his way. Instead Carton wrote for small, relatively innocuous publications, and earned enough to get by.

So it was that two days later, on July 9, he sat in the Café Procope again, near the door in the clinging, airless heat. He was eating a bowl of stew with rough bread—more than some could afford—when Marie-Claire came in. Even before she turned toward him, he could see the fury in her. Her thin little body was rigid under its cotton blouse and long, ragged blue skirt, and her arms were as stiff as sticks. She looked left and right, searching, then turned far enough to see Carton and immediately came over to him. Her face was white and her eyes blazing.

"Have you seen Jean-Jacques?" she demanded without any of the usual greeting.

"Not today," he replied, clearing a little space on the table so she would have room for a plate. "But it's early. Have some stew while there still is some. It's not bad."

Her lip curled. "What is it? Onions and water?" She sat down hard, putting her elbows on the table and both hands over her face. "I've lost my cheeses! That son of a whore took them all! It was my idea, my plan!" She looked up at him, her face burning with indignation. "He didn't even know about them, Fleuriot, until I told him!"

Carton was disappointed. He realized he had been looking forward to the richness and the flavor of cheese. It seemed like a long time since he had eaten anything that was a pleasure, not merely a necessity, although he was aware how many had not even that. The crowds pouring out of the areas of factories, abattoirs, and tanneries, such as the Faubourg St. Antoine, with their acid-burned, copper-colored faces, hollow-eyed, dressed in rags and alight with hatred, were witness enough of that. They were the people who worshipped Marat and gave him his unstoppable power.

Citizen Procope came by, and Carton requested a bowl of soup and bread for Marie-Claire. She thanked him for it, and for a moment the rage melted out of her eyes.

"Forget the cheese," he advised regretfully. "There's nothing you can do anyway. It's gone now."

Her face hardened again. "The pig! Slit his throat, and he'd make a carcass of bacon to feed us for a year! He won't have got rid of all that food, he'll have it stored some-where. The Committee could find it, because they'd take his house apart, if they had to."

Carton's stomach tightened. "Don't do it!" he said urgently. "Don't say anything at all! It'll only come back on you. You've lost them—accept it." He leaned forward across the table, stretching out his hand to grasp her thin wrist. "Don't draw attention to yourself!"

She glared back at him. "You'd let that pig get away with it? Never!" Her teeth were clenched, the muscles tight on her slender jaw. "I'll make him sweat as if the blade were already coming down on his neck. You see!"

Citizen Procope brought her soup and Carton paid for it.

She took the bowl in both hands, as if it might escape her. "You see!" she repeated, then picked up the spoon and began to eat.

The next morning Carton was again sitting at his usual table at the café with a cup of coffee that tasted like burnt toast, and possibly bore a close relationship. At the next table three men were laughing uproariously at the latest joke in *Père Duchesne,* and adding more and more vulgar endings to the tale, when Jean-Jacques came storming in through the open door, his hair tangled, his shirt sticking to his body with sweat. His face was white and he swiveled immediately toward Carton's table and staggered over, knocking into chairs.

Carton was alarmed. "What is it?" he asked, half rising to his feet.

Jean-Jacques was gasping for breath, choking as he struggled to get the words out. "They've arrested her!

Marie-Claire! They've taken her to the prison! You've got to help me! They'll . . ." He could not bring himself to say it, but it hung in the air between them.

Carton found his own voice husky. "What have they charged her with?" It was all unreal, like a fluid fear turned suddenly solid. He knew when Marie-Claire had spoken of it that it was a bad idea to seek revenge, but this was different, it was no longer thought but fact, shivering, sick and real.

"Hoarding food!" Jean-Jacques said, his voice rising toward hysteria, as if he might burst into mad laughter any moment. "She doesn't even have the damn cheeses—or the bacon! Philippe has!"

"I don't suppose that makes any difference." Carton sank back into his chair and gestured for Jean-Jacques to sit down also. It was always better to be inconspicuous. They did not want anyone looking at them, or remembering.

"That's enough to send her to the guillotine!" Jean-Jacques obeyed, the tears running down his face. "We've got to get her out of there! You're a lawyer—come and tell them that she wasn't even there! It's Philippe, because she reported him! You've got to hurry. If someone stands up for her, we can make them realize it's him. They'll catch him with the cheeses, and that'll be proof."

Carton shook his head. "It won't be so easy." In spite of the heat there was a coldness settling inside him. "Philippe will have thought of that . . ."

Jean-Jacques half rose to his feet, leaning forward over the table. "We've got to do something! We've got to help! She didn't take them. There has to be a way to prove it!"

Carton rubbed his hand wearily across his brow,

pushing his hair back. "It isn't about taking them," he tried
to explain. "It's about reporting Philippe. The cheeses are
gone. He can't afford to be blamed, so he's blaming her. If
they can't find them, who's to say which one is guilty?"

Jean-Jacques straightened up with a jolt. "Exactly! No
one at all! Come on! We've got to hurry. For that matter,
who's to say there ever were any? Citizen Fleuriot can't
admit to having lost them without admitting to having had
them in the first place! It's perfect. Hurry!"

Carton stood up and went after the rapid and highly agi-
tated figure of Jean-Jacques. There was a kind of logic to
it. The only trouble was that logic counted for very little in
Paris these days.

Outside, the street was hot and the sour smells of rubbish and effluent assaulted the nose. The air itself tasted of
fear. A wagon rumbled by, half empty, a few casks in the
back. An old newspaper stirred a little in the gutter and settled again. There was a group of Revolutionary Guard at the
corner, laughing at something, muskets slung idly over
their shoulders, red, white, and blue cockades in their hats.

Jean-Jacques was almost at a run, and Carton had to
increase his pace to keep up with him. They had not far to
go; there were district headquarters and prisons all over
the place. Carton's mind was racing, trying to think what
to say that would help Marie-Claire now, and not simply
make it worse. He would have to offer some explanation as
to why Philippe was blaming her. And it would have to be
a story that left no guilt with him! If only Jean-Jacques
would slow down and allow more time to think!

They passed a woman on the corner selling coffee, and
a group of laundresses arguing. There were people in

queues for bread. Of course they were far too late! Or perhaps it was for the candle shop next door, or soap, or any of a dozen other things one could not buy since spring.

Then they were at the prison. A huge man with a red bandana around his head stood outside the doorway, barring their entrance. Jean-Jacques did not even hesitate. "I have business with Citizen Duclos," he said confidently. "Evidence in a case." He waved his arm in Carton's direction. "Citizen Carton is a lawyer. . . ."

"We have no need of lawyers!" the man with the bandanna spat. "Justice gets no argument here."

"Never say that, Citizen," Jean-Jacques warned, glancing over his shoulder as if he feared being overheard. "Citizen Robespierre is a lawyer!"

The man with the bandanna rubbed the sweat off his face and looked nervously at Carton.

Carton cursed Jean-Jacques under his breath. "We have our uses," he said aloud.

"Go in, Citizen." The man ushered them past.

Jean-Jacques obeyed with alacrity, Carton with great reluctance. The place seemed to close in on him as if the walls were human misery frozen solid. Their footsteps had no echo, and yet there were sounds all around them, snatches of voices, cries, someone weeping, the clang of a door slamming shut. He had been here only minutes, and he was already longing to leave, his body trembling, his stomach knotted tight. He thought of Charles Darnay locked in the prison of La Force nearly a year now, not knowing if he would ever leave, and Lucie outside, every day trying to see him, imagining his suffering, helpless to affect it at all.

Jean-Jacques had reached the official in charge and was speaking to him. He was a lean, ferret-faced man with a scar on his shaven head, and most of his teeth missing. What hunger and injustice there had been in his life one could not even guess. He gestured to Carton to come forward.

Carton obliged, his hands slick with sweat, his shirt sticking to him. How had he ever allowed himself to get caught up in this? It was insanity! He stood in front of the man with the scar and forced himself to speak.

"Citizen, I have certain information you may not have been given regarding a matter of hoarding food. Cheeses to be exact."

"We know all about the cheeses, and the bacon," the man replied. "We have the hoarder in custody. She will be dealt with. Go about your business, Citizen, and leave us to do ours."

Jean-Jacques was fidgeting, wringing his hands, moving his weight from one foot to the other. It was hopeless, but Carton was terrified he would say something, and so involve both of them. It did not need much to make people suspicious.

"Ah!" Carton burst out. "Then you have recovered the cheeses! I was afraid you would not!" He saw the man's expression flicker. "Which would mean you had not caught the principals in the act."

Jean-Jacques froze.

The man scowled at Carton. "What do you know about it?" he demanded.

Carton's brain raced like a two-wheeled carriage cornering badly. "I think you are a just man and will need evidence," he lied. "And if goods are in the wrong hands, then the matter is not closed until that is put right."

The man leaned toward him. He smelled of stale wine and sweat. "Where are these cheeses, Citizen? And how is it you know?" His eyes were narrowed, his lip a little pulled back from his gapped teeth.

Carton felt his body go cold in the stifling heat. Panic washed over him, and he wanted to turn on his heel and run out of this dreadful place. Memories of past prison massacres swarmed in his mind like rats, the priests hacked to death in the Carmes in September of ninety-two, and the women and children in the Salpetriére. God knew what since then.

"We know where they were taken from, Citizen, and when!" Jean-Jacques broke in. "If we put our heads together, find out who knew of them, and where they were, we can deduce!"

The man scowled at him, but his eyes lost their anger, and interest replaced it. "Wait here," he ordered. "I'll go and find out." And before Carton could protest, he turned and strode away, leaving them under the watchful eyes of two other guards.

The minutes dragged by. There was a scream somewhere in the distance, then dense, pulsing silence. Footsteps on stone. A door banged. Someone laughed. Silence again. Jean-Jacques started to fidget. Carton's fists were so tightly clenched, his nails cut the flesh of his hands.

Then there were more screams, high and shrill, a man shouting, and two shots rang out, clattering feet, and then again silence.

Jean-Jacques stared at Carton, his eyes wide with terror.

Carton's chest was so tight he was dizzy. The stone walls swam in his vision. Sweat broke out on his body and went cold when his wet shirt touched him.

There were footsteps returning, rapid and heavy. The man with the scar reappeared, his face bleak. He looked at Carton, not Jean-Jacques. "You are wrong, Citizen lawyer," he said abruptly. "The woman must have been guilty. Maybe she gave the cheeses to a lover or something."

"No!" Jean-Jacques took a step forward, his voice high. "That's a lie!"

Carton grabbed his arm as the man with the scar put his hand to the knife at his belt. Jean-Jacques pulled away so hard he lost his balance and fell against Carton's side, stumbling.

The man with the scar relaxed his hand. "It's true," he said, staring at Jean-Jacques. "She attacked Citizen Duclos, then tried to escape. The innocent have nothing to fear."

Jean-Jacques gave a shrill, desperate cry. It was impossible to tell if it was laughter or pain, or both.

Carton's lips and throat were dry. "Did you get them back?" He had known this would be hopeless, whatever the truth of it. He should never have come. "Maybe she was just . . ." He stopped. There was no air to breathe.

The man with the scar shrugged. "It doesn't matter now, Citizen. She was shot running away. Your job is finished." He smiled, showing his gapped teeth again. "I guess you won't get paid!"

Jean-Jacques let out a howl of grief and fury like an animal, the sound so raw even the man with the scar froze, and both the other guards turned toward him, mouths gaping.

"Murderers!" Jean-Jacques screamed. "Duclos stole the cheeses, and you let him murder her to hide it!" He snatched his arm away from Carton's grip and lunged toward the man with the scar, reaching for his knife, both their hands closing on the hilt at the same time. "Her blood is on your soul!" He had forgotten that in Revolutionary France there was no God, so presumably men had no souls, either.

The other guards came to life and moved in.

Suddenly Carton found his nerve. He put his arms around Jean-Jacques and lifted him physically off the ground, kicking and shouting. His heels struck Carton's shins and the pain nearly made him let go. He staggered backward, taking Jean-Jacques with him, and fell against the farther wall. "I'm sorry!" he gasped to the man with the scar, now holding the knife with the blade toward them. "She was his sister. It was his responsibility to look after her." That was a stretching of the truth. "You understand? He doesn't mean it." He held Jean-Jacques hard enough to squash the air out of his lungs. He could feel him gasping and choking as he tried to breathe. "We're leaving," he added. "Maybe we didn't really know what happened."

Jean-Jacques's heels landed so hard on his shins that this time he let go of him and he fell to the ground. The guards were still uncertain.

Philippe Duclos could appear at any moment, and Carton and Jean-Jacques could both finish up imprisoned here. Ignoring his throbbing leg, Carton bent and picked up Jean-Jacques by the scruff of his neck, yanked him to his feet, and gave him a cuff on the ear hard enough to make his head sing and—please heaven—rob him of speech for long enough to get him outside!

"Thank you, Citizen," he called to the man with the scar, and half dragged Jean-Jacques, half carried him to the entrance and the blessed freedom of the street.

He crossed over, turned right, then left down the first narrow alley he came to before he finally let go of Jean-Jacques. "I'm sorry," he said at last. "But you can't help."

Jean-Jacques shook himself. "Let me go back and get her." His voice was thick with sobs. "Let me bury her!"

Carton seized his shoulder again. "No! They'll take you, too!"

"I haven't done anything!" Jean-Jacques protested furiously. "For what? For coming for my sister's corpse? What are you, stone? Ice? You English clod!"

"I am alive," Carton responded. "And I mean to stay alive. And yes, coming for her corpse would be quite enough for them to blame you, and if you used a quarter of the brain you've got, you'd know that."

Jean-Jacques seemed to shrink within himself.

Carton was twisted inside with pity. He refused to think of Marie-Claire's bright face, her vitality, the dreams and the anger that had made her so vivid.

"Come on, friend," he said gently. "There's nothing we can do, except survive. She'd want you to do that. Come and have some wine, and we'll find a little bread, and perhaps someone will have onions, or even a piece of sausage."

Jean-Jacques lifted up his head a little. "I suppose so." He sighed. "Yes—survive. You are right, she would want that."

"Of course she would," Carton said more heartily. "Come on."

They started to walk again, crossing the river and turning south for no particular reason, except that neither of them was yet ready to sit still. Finally they came to a wine shop with the door open. The smell of the spilled wine inside was inviting, and there was room to sit down.

The proprietress was a handsome woman with a fine head of black hair, long and thick like a mane. She stared at them, waiting for them to speak.

"Wine?" Carton asked. "Start with two bottles. We have sorrows to drown, Citizeness. And bread, if you have it?"

"You would feed your sorrows as well?" she asked without a smile.

"Citizeness . . ." Carton began.

"Defarge," she replied, as if he had asked her name. "I'll bring you bread. Where's your money?"

Carton put a handful of coins on the table.

She returned with a plate of bread, half an onion, and two bottles. Half an hour later she brought another bottle, and half an hour after that, a fourth. Carton kept on drinking—his body was used to it—but Jean-Jacques slumped against the wall and seemed to be asleep.

Citizeness Defarge remained, and in the early evening brought more bread, but by then Carton was not hungry.

Jean-Jacques opened his eyes and sat up.

"Bread?" Carton offered.

"No." Jean-Jacques waved it away. "I have worked out a plan."

Carton's head was fuzzy. "To do what?"

"Be revenged on Philippe Duclos, of course! What else?" Jean-Jacques looked at him as if he were a fool.

Carton was too eased with wine to be alarmed. "Don't,"

he said simply. "Whatever it is, it won't work. You'll only get into more trouble."

Jean-Jacques looked at him with big, grief-filled eyes. "Yes, it will," he said with a catch in his voice. "I'll make it work . . . for Marie-Claire." He stood up with an effort, swayed for a moment, struggling for his balance. "Thank you, Carton," he added formally, starting to bow, and then changing his mind. "You are a good friend." And without adding any more, he walked unsteadily to the door and disappeared outside.

Carton sat alone, miserable and guilty. If he had really been a good friend, he would have prevented Marie-Claire from setting out on such a mad plan in the first place. He had spent his whole life believing in nothing, achieving pointless victories in small cases in London, and now here writing pieces that did not change the Revolution a jot. It carried on from one insane venture to another regardless. The Paris Commune, largely ruled by Marat, whatever anyone said, made hunger and violence worse with every passing week. France was at war on every side: Spain, Austria, Belgium, and England. Since the hideous massacres last September when the gutters quite literally ran with human blood, Paris was a city of madmen. Charles Darnay was a prisoner in La Force, and Lucie grieved for him ceaselessly, every day going to wait outside the walls, carrying their child, in the hope that he might glimpse them and be comforted.

And here was Carton sitting drunk in Defarge's wine shop, sorry for himself, and ashamed that Jean-Jacques called him a friend, because he had no right to that name.

* * *

Two days later, July 12, Carton was back in the Café Procope, taking his usual midday bowl of soup when two soldiers of the Revolutionary Guard came in, red, white, and
blue cockades on their hats, muskets over their shoulders.
They spoke for a moment with the proprietor, then walked
over to Carton.

"Citizen Carton," the first one said. It was not a question
but a statement. "You must come with us. There is a
matter of theft with which we have been informed that you
can help us. On your feet."

Carton was stunned. He opened his mouth to protest,
and realized even as he did so that it was totally pointless.
It was his turn. Sooner or later some monstrous injustice
happened to everyone. He had been informed on and there
was no use fighting against it. He obeyed, and walked out
between the guards, wondering what idiotic mistake had
occurred to involve him. It could be something as simple
as the wrong name, a letter different, a misspelling. He had
heard of that happening.

But when he got as far as the Section Committee prison
where Marie-Claire had been shot, and walked along the
same stone corridor, with the same smell of sweat and fear
in the air, he knew there was no such easy error.

"Ah—Citizen lawyer," the man with the scar said, smiling.
"We know who you are, you see?" He nodded to the soldiers.
"You can go. You have done well, but we have our own
guards here." He gestured toward three burly men with
gaping shirts and red bandannas around their heads or
necks. In the oppressive heat their faces and chests were
slick with sweat. Two had pistols, one a knife. The soldiers left.

"Now, Citizen Carton," the man with the scar began, taking his seat behind a wooden table set up as if it were a judge's bench. Carton was left standing. "This matter of the cheeses that were stolen. It seems you know more about that than you said before. Now would be a good time to tell the truth—all of it. A good time for you, that is."

Carton tried to clear his brain. What he said now might determine his freedom, even his life. Men killed for less than cheese these days.

"You don't have them?" He affected immense surprise.

The man's face darkened with anger and suspicion that he was being mocked.

Carton stared back at him with wide innocence. He really had no idea where the cheeses were, and he had even more urgent reasons for wishing that he did.

"No, we don't," the man admitted in a growl.

"That is very serious," Carton said sympathetically. "Citizen . . . ?"

"Sabot," the man grunted.

"Citizen Sabot." Carton nodded courteously. "We must do everything we can to find them. They are evidence. And apart from that, it is a crime to waste good food. There is certainly a deserving person somewhere to whom they should go." The place seemed even more airless than before, as if everything that came here, human or not, remained. The smell of fear was in the nose and throat, suffocating the breath.

Along the corridor to the left, out of sight, someone shouted, there was laughter, a wail. Then the silence surged back like a returning wave.

Carton found his voice shaking when he spoke again.

"Citizen Sabot, you have been very fair to me. I will do everything I can to learn what happened to the cheeses and bring you the information." He saw the distrust naked in Sabot's face, the sneer already forming on his lips. "You are a man of great influence," he went on truthfully, however much he might despise himself for it. "Apart from justice, it would be wise of me to assist you all that I can."

Sabot was mollified. "Yes, it would," he agreed. "I'll give you two days. Today and tomorrow."

"I'll report to you in two days," Carton hedged. "I might need longer to track them down. We are dealing with clever people here. If it were not so, your own men would have found them already, surely?"

Sabot considered for a moment. Half a dozen revolutionary guards marched by with heavy tread. Someone sang a snatch of the Marseillaise, that song the rabble had adopted when they burst out of the gaols of Marseilles and the other sea ports of the Mediterranean, and marched all the way to Paris, killing and looting everything in their path. Carton found himself shaking uncontrollably, memory nauseating him.

"Tomorrow night," Sabot conceded. "But if you find them and eat them yourself, I'll have your head."

Carton gulped and steadied himself. "Naturally," he agreed. He almost added something else, then while he still retained some balance, he turned and left, trying not to run.

Back in the room he rented, Carton sank down into his bed, his mind racing to make sense of what had happened, and his own wild promise to Sabot to find the cheeses. He had been granted barely two days. Where could he even begin?

With Marie-Claire's original plan. She had intended to have Philippe tell Fleuriot that he was going to post guards, so he had moved the cheeses and the bacon to a more accessible place. Only he had done it earlier than the time agreed with Marie-Claire. Presumably his plan had worked. Fleuriot had moved the cheeses, and Philippe had caught him in the act, and confiscated them. Fleuriot had said nothing, because he should not have had the cheeses in the first place. So much was clear.

Marie-Claire had heard of it and attempted to accuse Philippe, but either she had not been listened to at all, or if she had, she had not been believed, and Philippe had silenced her before she could prove anything. According to Sabot, no one had found the cheeses, so Philippe must still have them.

Maybe Carton should begin with Fleuriot. He at least would know when the cheeses had been taken, which—if it led to Philippe's movements that day—might indicate where he could have hidden them. Carton got up and went out. This was all an infuriating waste of time. He should be working. His money was getting low. If it were not his own neck at risk, he would not do it. All the proof of innocence in the world would not save poor Marie-Claire now. And it would hardly help Jean-Jacques, either. No one cared because half the charges made were built on settling old scores anyway, or on profit of one sort or another. Those who had liked Marie-Claire would still like her just as much.

He walked along the street briskly, head down, avoiding people's eyes. There was a warm wind rising, and it smelled as if rain were coming. Old newspapers blew along the pavement, flapping like wounded birds. Two laundresses were arguing. It looked like the same ones as before.

He went the long way around to the Rue St. Honoré, in order to avoid passing the house where Marat lived and printed his papers. He had enough trouble without an encounter with the "Rage of the People." A couple of questions elicited the information as to exactly which house Fleuriot lived in, next to the carpenter Duplay. But Fleuriot was an angry and frightened man. The loss of a few cheeses was nothing compared with the threatened loss of his head. He stood in the doorway, his spectacles balanced on his forehead, and stared fixedly at Carton.

"I don't know what you're talking about, Citizen. There are always Revolutionary Guard about the place. How is one day different from another?"

"Not Revolutionary Guard," Carton corrected patiently. "These would be from the local Committee, not in uniform, apart from the red bandanna."

"Red bandanna!" Fleuriot threw his hands up in the air. "What does that mean? Nothing! Anyone can wear a red rag. They could be from the Faubourg St. Antoine, for all I know. I mind my own business, Citizen, and you'd be best advised to mind yours! Good day." And without giving Carton a chance to say anything more, he retreated inside his house and slammed the door, leaving Carton alone in the yard just as it began to rain.

He spent the rest of the afternoon and early evening getting thoroughly wet and learning very little of use. He asked all the neighbors whose apartments fronted onto the courtyard, and he even asked the apothecary in the house to the left, and the carpenter in the yard to the right. But Philippe was powerful and his temper vicious. If anyone knew anything about exactly when he came with his man, they were affecting ignorance. According to most of them, the place had been totally deserted on that particular late afternoon. One was queuing for candles, another for soap. One woman was visiting her sick sister, a girl was selling pamphlets, a youth was delivering a piece of furniture, another was too drunk to have known if his own mother had walked past him, and she had been dead for years. That at least was probably honest.

Carton went home wet to the skin and thoroughly discouraged. He had two slices of bread, half a piece of sausage, and a bottle of wine. He took off his wet clothes and sat in his nightshirt, thinking. Tomorrow was July 13. If he did not report the day after, Sabot would come for him. He would be angry because he had failed twice, and been taken for a fool. And what was worse, by then Philippe himself would almost certainly be aware of Carton's interest in the matter. He must succeed. The alternative would be disaster. He must find out more about Philippe himself, where he lived, what other places he might have access to, who were his friends. Even better would be to know who were his enemies!

He finally went to sleep determined to start very early in the morning. He needed to succeed, and quickly, for his own survival, but he would also like to be revenged for Marie-Claire. She had not deserved this, and in spite of his better judgment, he had liked her. It would be good to do something to warrant the friendship Jean-Jacques believed of him.

In the morning he got up early and went out straight away. He bought a cup of coffee from a street vendor, drank it and handed back the mug to her, then walked on past the usual patient queues of women hoping for bread, or vegetables, or whatever it was. He passed the sellers of pamphlets and the tradesmen still trying to keep up some semblance of normality at what they did: millinery, barrel-making, engraving, hairdressing, or whatever it was, and retraced his steps to the local committee head-quarters. It was a considerable risk asking questions about Philippe Duclos, especially since he was already known and Philippe would be on his guard. He knew he had taken the cheeses and would see threat even where there was none. But Carton had to report to Sabot by midnight tonight, and so far he had accomplished nothing. It was not impossible that in his fear of Philippe, Fleuriot had already warned him that Carton was asking questions.

Affecting innocence and concern, Carton asked one of the guards where he might find Citizen Duclos, since he had a personal message for him.

The man grunted. "Citizen Duclos is a busy man! Why should I keep watch on him? Who knows where he is?"

Carton bit back his instinctive answer and smiled politely. "You are very observant," he replied between his teeth. "I am sure you know who comes and goes, as a matter of habit."

The man grunted again, but the love of flattery was in his eyes, and Carton had asked for nothing but a little harmless information. "He is not in yet," he replied. "Come back in an hour or two."

"The message is urgent," Carton elaborated. "I would not wish to disturb him, but I could wait for him in the street near his lodgings, and as soon as he comes out, I could speak with him."

The man shrugged. "If you wake him, you'll pay for it!" he warned.

"Naturally. I am sure his work for liberty keeps him up till strange hours, as I imagine yours does, too."

"All hours!" the man agreed. "Haven't seen my bed long enough for a year or more!"

"History will remember you," Carton said ambiguously. "Where should I wait for Citizen Duclos?"

"Rue Mazarine," the man replied. "South side, near the apothecary's shop."

"Thank you." Carton nodded to him and hurried away before he could become embroiled in any further conversation.

He found the apothecary's shop and stood outside it, apparently loitering like many others, occasioning no undue attention. People came and went, most of them grumbling about one thing or another. The pavement steamed from the night's rain and already it was hot.

Twenty minutes later a large man came out, bleary-eyed, unshaven, a red bandanna around his neck. There was a wine stain on the front of his shirt, and he belched as he passed Carton, barely noticing him.

Carton waited until he had gone around the corner out of sight, and for another ten minutes after that, then he went under the archway into the courtyard and knocked on the first door.

A woman opened it, her sleeves rolled up and a broom in her hand. He asked her for Philippe Duclos and was directed to the door opposite. Here he was fortunate at last. It was opened by a child of about eleven. She was curious and friendly. She told him Philippe lodged with her family and he had one room. Carton asked if Philippe were to be given a gift of wine, did he have a place where he could keep it?

"He could put it in the cellar," she replied. "But if it is a good wine, then one of the other lodgers might drink it. It would not be safe." Was there not somewhere better, more private? No, unfortunately there was no such place. Might he have a friend? She giggled. The thought amused her. She could not imagine him trusting a friend, he was not that kind of man. He did not even trust her mother, who cooked and cleaned for him. He was always counting his shirts! As if anybody would want them.

Carton thanked her and left, puzzled. Again he was at a dead end. He went back to the neighbors of Fleuriot to see if he could find anyone, even a child or a servant, who might have seen Philippe's men moving the cheeses, or if not cheese, then at least the bacon. One cannot carry out a side of bacon in one's pocket!

He spoke to a dozen people, busy and idle, resident and passerby, but no one had seen people carrying goods that day, or since, with the exception of shopping going in. Even laundry had been done at the well in the center of the yard, and the presence of the women would have been sufficient to deter anyone from carrying anything past with as distinctive a shape as a side of bacon, or odor as a ripe cheese.

He saw only one rat, fat and sleek, running from the well across the stones and disappearing into a hole in the wall. Then he remembered that there was a timber yard next door, belonging to the carpenter Duplay. Shouldn't there be plenty of rats around?

What if no one had seen Philippe move the cheeses because he hadn't? They were still here—the safest place for them! Fleuriot would guard them with his life, but if Sabot should find them, then Fleuriot would take the blame, and Philippe would affect total innocence. He would say he knew nothing of them at all, and Marie-Claire, the only person who knew he had, was dead and could say nothing. It made perfect sense. And above all it was safe! Philippe simply took a cheese whenever he wanted, and Fleuriot was too frightened of him to do anything about it. Certainly he would not dare eat one or sell one himself.

Carton walked away quickly and went back to the Café Procope and ordered himself a slice of bread and sausage and a bottle of wine. He sat at his usual table. Every time the door swung open, he looked up, half expecting to see Jean-Jacques, and felt an unreasonable surge of disappointment each time it was not. He had nothing in particular to say to him, apart from to forget his plan for revenge, whatever it was, but he missed his company, and he hurt for his grief. Perhaps he even would have liked to talk of Marie-Claire and share some of the pain within himself.

If the cheeses were still in Fleuriot's house, then it would take a number of men, with the authority of the Commune itself behind them, to search. The local authority was no good, that was Philippe himself. How could Carton get past that? He stared into his glass and knew there was only one answer—the one he had been avoiding for the last half year—ask Marat! Marat was the Commune.

There must be another way. He poured out the last of the wine and drank it slowly. It was sour, but it still hit his stomach with a certain warmth. So far he had avoided even passing the house in the Rue des Medicines where Marat lived. He had rather that Marat had never even heard of him. Now he was about to ruin it all by actually walking into the house and asking a favor! Never mind drunk, he must be mad! He upended the glass and drained the last mouthful. Well, if he were going to commit suicide, better get on with it rather than sit here feeling worse and worse, living it over in his imagination until he was actually sick.

He went outside and walked quickly, as if he had a purpose he was intent upon. Get it done. The fear of it was just as bad as the actuality. At least get this achieved.

He was there before he expected. He must have been walking too rapidly. There was an archway on the corner leading into a cobbled yard with a well in the center, just like any of a thousand others. At one side a flight of steps led up to an entrance, and even from where he stood Carton could see bales of paper piled up just inside the open doorway, boxes beyond, and printed newspapers ready to deliver. There was no excuse for hesitation. It was obviously Marat's house. He took a deep breath, let it out slowly, then walked across and up the steps. No one accosted him until he was inside and peering around, looking for someone to ask. A plain, rather ordinary woman approached him, her face mild, as if she expected a friend.

"Citizeness," he said huskily. "I am sorry to interrupt your business, but I have a favor to ask which only Citizen Marat could grant me. Who may I approach in order to speak with him?"

"I am Simonne Evrard," she replied with a certain quiet confidence. "I will ask Citizen Marat if he can see you. Who are you, and what is it you wish?"

Carton remembered with a jolt that Marat had some kind of common-law wife—Marat of all people! This was her, a soft-spoken woman with red hands and an apron tied around her waist. "Sydney Carton, Citizeness," he replied. "It is to do with a man hoarding food instead of making it available to all citizens, as it should be. Unfortunately he has a position in the local committee, so I cannot go to them."

"I see." She nodded. "I shall tell him. Please wait here."

She was gone for several minutes. He stood shifting his weight from foot to foot, trying to control the fear rising inside him. It even occurred to him to change his mind and leave. There was still time.

And then there wasn't. She was back again, beckoning him toward her and pointing to the doorway of another room. Like one in a dream he obeyed, his heart pounding in his chest.

Inside the room was unlike anything he could conceivably have expected. It was small, a sort of aqueous green, and the steam in it clung to his skin and choked his nose and his throat. The smell was ghastly, a mixture of vinegar and rotting human flesh. In the center was a tin bath shaped like a boot, concealing the lower portion of the occupant's body. A board was placed across it on which rested a pen, inkwell, and paper. Even through the heavy steam Carton could see Marat quite clearly. His toadlike face with its bulging eyes and slack mouth was almost bloodless with the exhaustion of pain. There was a wet towel wrapped around his head. His naked shoulders, arms, and upper chest were smooth and hairless.

"What is it, Citizen Carton?" he asked. His voice was rough and had a slight accent. Carton remembered he was not French at all, but half Swiss and half Sardinian. The stench caught in his throat and he thought he was going to gag.

"Would you rather speak in English?" Marat asked—in English. He was a doctor by profession and had held a practice in Pimlico in London for some time.

"No, thank you, Citizen," Carton declined, then instantly wondered if it was wise. "Perhaps you would indulge me should my French falter?"

"What is it you want?" Marat repeated. His expression was hard to read because of the ravages of disease upon his face. He was in his fifties, a generation older than most of the other Revolutionary leaders, and a lifetime of hate had exhausted him.

"I believe a certain Citizen Duclos has discovered a quantity of exceptionally good food, cheeses and bacon to be exact, in the keeping of a Citizen Fleuriot, and has blackmailed him into concealing that food from the common good." Carton was speaking too quickly and he knew it, but he could not control himself enough to slow down. "Citizen Duclos is in a position of power in the local committee, so I cannot turn to them to search and find it."

Marat blinked. "So you want me to have men from the Commune search?"

"Yes, please."

Marat grunted and eased his position a little, wincing as the ulcerated flesh touched the sides of the bath. "I'll consider it," he said with a gasp. "Why do you care? Is it your cheese?"

"No, Citizen. But it is unjust. And it could be mine next time."

Marat stared at him. Carton felt the steam settle on his skin and trickle down his face and body. His clothes were sticking to him. The pulse throbbed in his head and his throat. Marat did not believe him. He knew it.

"A friend of mine was blamed for it, and shot," he added. Was he insane to tell Marat this? Too late now. "I want revenge."

Marat nodded slowly. "Come back this evening. I'll have men for you," he assured. "I understand hate."

"Thank you," Carton said hoarsely, then instantly despised himself for it. He did not want to have anything in common with this man, this embodiment of insane rage who had sworn to drown Paris in seas of blood. He half bowed, and backed out of that dreadful room into the hallway again.

He returned to his rooms and fell asleep for a while. He woke with a headache like a tight band around his temples. He washed in cold water, changed his clothes, and went out to buy a cup of coffee. He would have to think about something more for publication soon, as he would run out of money.

It was half past seven in the evening. He had not long before he would have to report to Sabot.

He was almost back to Marat's house when he heard shouting in the street and a woman screaming. He hastened his step and was at the entrance archway when a Revolutionary Guardsman pushed past him.

"What is it?" Carton asked, alarm growing inside him.

"Marat's been killed!" a young man cried out. "Murdered! Stabbed to death in his bath. A mad woman from Calvados. Marat's dead!"

There were more footsteps running, shouts and screams, armed men clattering by, howls of grief, rage, and terror.

Dead! Carton stood still, leaning a little against the wall in the street. In spite of all his will to stop it, in his mind he could see the ghastly figure of Marat in that aqueous room, the steam, the shriveled skin, the stench, the pain in his face. He imagined the body lifeless, and blood pouring into the vinegar and water. And with a wave of pity he thought of the quiet woman who for some inconceivable reason had loved him.

He must get out of here! Maybe he would be lucky and the widow would not even remember his name, let alone why he had come. He straightened up and stumbled away, tripping on the cobbles as he heard the shouts behind him, more men coming. Someone let off a musket shot, and then another.

All his instincts impelled him to run, but he must not. It would look as if he were escaping. A couple of women accosted him, asking what was wrong. "I don't know," he lied. "Some kind of trouble. But stay away from it." And without waiting, he left them.

When he finally got inside his own rooms and locked the door, he realized the full impact of what had happened. Marat, the head of the Commune, the most powerful man in Paris, had been murdered by some woman from the countryside. The revenge for it would be unimaginable. But of more immediate concern to Carton, he did not have

Marat's men to search Fleuriot's house for the cheeses. And Sabot would expect an answer tonight or Carton himself would pay the price for it. He would have to do something about it himself, and immediately.

He dashed a little water over his face, dried it, put his jacket back on, and went outside again. The one idea in his mind was desperate, but then so would the result be if he did nothing.

Rats were the key. If he could not get Marat's men to search Fleuriot's house, than he would have to get someone else to do it. The carpenter Duplay, with his wood yard next door, was at least a chance. He could think of nothing better.

He walked quickly toward the Rue St. Honoré, hoping not to give himself time to think of all the things that could go wrong. He had no choice. He kept telling himself that— no choice! It was a drumbeat in his head as he strode along the cobbles, crossed to avoid a cart unloading barrels, and came to the archway at the entrance to the carpenter's house. He knocked before he had time to hesitate.

It was opened within two minutes by a young woman. She was small and very neat, rather like a child, except that her face was quite mature, as if she were at least in her middle twenties. She inquired politely what she could do to help him.

"I believe the Citizen who lives here is a carpenter," he said, after thanking her for her courtesy.

"Yes, Citizen. He is excellent. Did you wish to purchase something, or have something made, perhaps?" she asked.

"Thank you, but I am concerned for his stock of wood, possibly even his finished work," he replied. "I have reason to believe that food is being stored in the house next door—cheese, to be precise—and there are a large number of rats collecting. . . ." He stopped, seeing the distaste in her face, as if he had spoken of something obscene. "I'm sorry," he apologized. "Perhaps I should not have mentioned it to you, but I feel that the Citizen . . ."

There was a click of high heels on the wooden stairway and Carton looked beyond the young woman to see a man whose resemblance to her was marked enough for him to assume that they were related. He was about thirty, small and intensely neat, as she was, almost feline in his manner, with a greenish pallor to his complexion, and myopic green eyes that he blinked repeatedly as he stared at Carton. He was dressed perfectly in the manner of the Ançien Regime, as if he were to present himself at the court of Louis XVI, complete with green striped nankeen jacket, exquisitely cut, a waistcoat and cravat, breeches and stockings. It was his high heels Carton had heard. His hair was meticulously powdered and tied back. He fluttered his very small, nail-bitten hands when he spoke.

"It is all right, Charlotte, I shall deal with the matter."

"Yes, Maximilien," she said obediently, and excused herself.

"Did you say 'rats,' Citizen?" the man asked, his voice soft, accented with a curious sibilance.

With a shock like ice water on his bare flesh, Carton realized what he had done. Of all the carpenters in Paris, he had knocked on the door of the one in whose house lodged Citizen Robespierre, and apparently his sister. He stood frozen to the spot, staring at the little man still on the bottom stair, as far away from him as he could be without being absurd. Carton remembered someone saying that Robespierre was so personally fastidious as to dislike anyone close to him, let alone touching him. He had constant indigestion for which he sucked oranges, and anything as gross as a bodily appetite or function offended him beyond belief.

"I am sorry to mention such a matter," Carton apologized again. He found himself thinking of Jean-Jacques and his grief, and how alive Marie-Claire had been, how full of laughter, anger, and dreams. "But I believe Citizen Fleuriot next door is hoarding cheese, and it is unfair that he rob the good citizens of food by doing so, but it is also a considerable danger to his immediate neighbors, because of the vermin it attracts."

Robespierre was staring at him with his strange, short-sighted eyes.

Carton gulped. "I have not the power to do anything about it myself," he went on. "But I can at least warn others. I imagine Citizen Duplay has a great deal of valuable wood which could be damaged." He bowed very slightly. "Thank you for your courtesy, Citizen. I hope I have not distressed the Citizeness."

"You did your duty," Robespierre replied with satisfaction. "The 'Purity of the People'"—he spoke as if it were some kind of divine entity—"requires sacrifice. We must rid France of vermin of every kind. I shall myself go to see this Citizen Fleuriot. Come with me."

Carton drew in his breath, and choked. Robespierre waited while he suffered a fit of coughing, then when Carton was able to compose himself, he repeated his command. "Come with me."

Carton followed the diminutive figure in the green jacket, heels clicking on the cobbles, white powdered head gleaming in the last of the daylight, until they reached Fleuriot's door. Robespierre stepped aside for Carton to knock. The door opened and Fleuriot himself stood in the entrance, face tight with annoyance.

Carton moved aside and Fleuriot saw Robespierre. A curious thing happened. There could not be two such men in all France, let alone in this district of Paris. Fleuriot's recognition was instant. He turned a bilious shade of yellowish-green and swayed so wildly that had he not caught hold of the door lintel he would have fallen over.

"I have been told that you have some cheeses," Robespierre said in his soft, insistent voice. "A great many, in fact." He blinked. "Of course I do not know if that is true, but lying would make you an enemy to the people. . . ."

Fleuriot made a strange, half-strangled sound in his throat.

Carton closed his eyes and opened them again. His mouth was as dry as the dust on the stones. "It's possible Citizen Fleuriot does not own the cheeses?" he said, his voice catching. He coughed as Robespierre swiveled around to stare at him, peering forward as if it were difficult to see. Carton cleared his throat again. "Perhaps he is frightened of someone else, Citizen?"

"Yes!" Fleuriot said in a high-pitched squeak, as if he were being strangled. "The good citizen is right!" It was painfully clear that he was terrified. His face was ghastly, the sweat stood out on his lip and brow, and he wrung his hands as if he would break them, easing his weight from foot to foot. But the fear that touched his soul was of Robespierre, not of Philippe Duclos. He gulped for air. "The

cheeses are not mine! They belong to Citizen Duclos, of the
local committee. I am keeping them for him! He has threatened to have my head if I don't. . . ." His voice wavered off
and he looked as if he were going to faint.

Robespierre stepped back. Such physical signs of terror
repelled him. The Purity of the People was a concept, an
ideal to be aspired to, and the means to achieve it was
obviously fear, but he did not want ever to think of the
reality of it, much less be forced to witness it. "Philippe
Duclos?" he asked.

"Yes . . . C-Citizen . . . R-Robespierre," Fleuriot stammered.

"Then Citizen Carton here will help you carry the
cheeses out, and we will give them to the people, where
they belong," Robespierre ordered. "And Citizen Duclos will
answer with his head." He did not even glance at Carton
but stood waiting for an obedience he took for granted.

Carton felt oddly safe as he followed Fleuriot inside.
Robespierre was a tiny man with no physical strength at
all—Philippe could have broken him with one blow—but it
was not even imaginable that he would. Robespierre's
presence in the yard was more powerful than an army of
soldiers would have been. Carton would not even have
taken a cheese for Sabot without his permission.

When the food was all removed, the yard was completely
dark, but Robespierre was easily discernible by the gleam
of his powdered hair. Carton approached him with his
heart hammering.

"Citizen Robespierre?"

Robespierre turned, peering at him in the shadows.
"Yes, what is it? You have done well."

"Citizen Sabot of the local committee is a good man." His

voice shook, and he despised himself for his words. "I would like him to have an opportunity to be rewarded for his service to the people by receiving one of the cheeses."

Robespierre stood motionless for several seconds. He drew in his breath with a slight hiss. "Indeed."

"He works long hours." Carton felt the blood thundering in his head. "I must report to him tonight, to show my honesty in this matter, or . . ." He faltered and fell silent.

"He does his duty," Robespierre replied.

Carton's heart sank.

"But you may be rewarded," Robespierre added. "You may have one of the cheeses."

Carton was giddy with relief. "Thank you, Citizen." He hated the gratitude in his voice, and he could do nothing about it. "You are . . ." he said the one word he knew Robespierre longed to hear ". . . incorruptible."

He took the cheese and went to the local committee prison. Sabot was waiting for him. He saw the cheese even before Carton spoke.

Carton placed it on the table before him, hating to let go of it, and knowing it was the only way to save his life.

"I found them," he said. "Citizen Robespierre will arrest the hoarder. You would be well advised to take this home, tonight—now! And say nothing."

Sabot nodded with profound understanding and a good deal of respect. He picked up the cheese, caressing it with his fingers. "I will leave now," he agreed. "I will walk along the street with you, Citizen."

Philippe protested, of course, but it availed him nothing. Fleuriot would never have dared retract his testimony, and apart from that, there was a sweetness in having his revenge on Philippe for having stolen his hoard and then terrifying him into guarding it for him, adding insult to injury.

Reluctantly, Sabot was allowed his one cheese in reward. It was all over very swiftly. Robespierre was not yet a member of the Committee of Public Safety, but it was only a matter of time. His star was ascending. Already someone had whispered of him as "The Sea-Green Incorruptible." Philippe Duclos was found guilty and sentenced to the guillotine.

Robespierre never personally witnessed such a disgusting act as an execution. The only time he ever saw the machine of death at all was at the end of the High Terror still a year in the future, when he mounted the bloodspattered steps himself.

Carton had not intended to go, but memory of Marie-Claire was suddenly very sharp in his mind. He could see her bright face under its tumbled hair, hear her voice with its laughter and its enthusiasm, as if she had gone out the door only minutes ago. Half against his will, despising himself for it, he nevertheless was waiting in the Place de la Revolution, watching with revulsion Citizeness Defarge and her friends who sat with their knitting needles clicking beside the guillotine when the tumbrels came rattling in with their cargo of the condemned.

As usual they were all manner of people, but not many of them wore the red bandanna of the Citizens' power, and Philippe was easy to see.

Carton felt a joggle at his elbow, and turning for an instant, he thought it was Marie-Claire. It was the same wide brown eyes, the tangle of hair, but it was Jean-Jacques, his face still haggard with grief. He looked at Carton and his cheeks were wet.

Carton put out his hand to touch him gently. "I'm glad you didn't try your plan," he said with intense gratitude. He liked this odd little man profoundly. It was stupid to have such a hostage to fate, but he could not help it. Afterward they would go and drink together in quiet remembrance and companionship. "It would never have worked," he added.

Jean-Jacques smiled through his tears. "Yeah, it did," he answered.

Permissions